THE LIBRARY GIRLS OF THE EAST END

PATRICIA MCBRIDE

Boldwood

First published in Great Britain in 2023 by Boldwood Books Ltd.

Cover Design by Colin Thomas

Cover Photography: Heritage Image Partnership Ltd, Alamy and Nathaniel Noir,

A CIP catalogue record for this book is available from the British Library.

Paperback ISBN 978-1-78513-991-8

Large Print ISBN 978-1-78513-987-1

Hardback ISBN 978-1-78513-986-4

Ebook ISBN 978-1-78513-984-0

Kindle ISBN 978-1-78513-985-7

Audio CD ISBN 978-1-78513-992-5

MP3 CD ISBN 978-1-78513-989-5

Digital audio download ISBN 978 1 78513 983 3

Boldwood Books Ltd
23 Bowerdean Street
London SW6 3TN
www.boldwoodbooks.com

1

THE NEW JOB

England, summer 1940

Lady Carmichael looked at her daughter in dismay. 'You're not serious! The East End of London? Why on earth would you want to work there? All sorts of unsavoury people live there. Poor people, immigrants, criminals, Jews.' She frowned. 'And where is this Silvertown? I've never heard of it. Is it the principal London centre for making jewellery?'

'No, Mother. It's part of the East End, between Canning Town and the Thames.'

Her mother's eyes widened. 'Really, Cordelia, that sounds just dreadful. I think you are making a massive mistake. An area like that will be full of people who'd never use a library. You'll be completely wasting your time. You could do far more good here in the village.'

Cordelia sighed as she gazed out of the window towards the sweeping drive. Her mother was a wonderful woman who did a great deal for charity, but she selected her projects carefully. She avoided actually meeting the poor and needy as that wouldn't appeal to her at all. It was more her style to be in charge of a few chosen women in the village, telling them what to do to help the local underprivileged.

Though her advice was often sound, Cordelia couldn't help but feel that her mother could be more compassionate towards the poor in the village. After all, they had lives and aspirations of their own. Yet, as lady of the manor, her mother's word was law and her friends and people in the village rarely challenged her ideas.

But now wasn't the time to remind her of all that. Cordelia had to choose her words delicately. Not that her mother could make her alter her mind about the job she'd just accepted. She'd long ago decided she wouldn't be her mother's carbon copy. Her mother enjoyed her life, but it would bore Cordelia to death. She could have found positions in several other libraries, but wanted to work somewhere where she could make a difference and help the local people. She was young to have a head librarian position and knew it was because so many men were away at war. That, and the fact that the library was relatively small. Nonetheless, she was determined to make a go of it.

She'd visited Silvertown Library when she had her interview, and it was badly in need of a new broom. She worried that the two women who would work for her, Jane and Mavis, wouldn't like the changes she planned. They were well established and used to doing things the way Mr Bartlett, the previous manager, had dictated. She'd have to tread carefully and remember they had a wealth of knowledge she still had to learn.

'Mummy, you do a lot. You've always got some charity event or other on the go.'

Her mother smoothed her already perfect ash-grey hair. 'That's different, Cordelia, and you know it. People there have all sorts of terrible things, fleas, TB, and goodness knows what. What if you catch something?'

Jasper, Cordelia's brother, who'd been quietly sipping a whisky, butted in. 'Mater, she's going to be in charge of a small library, not nursing consumptives in a sanatorium. Delia will share the flat in the West End with me. War or not, we'll have a high old time.'

'That's the only good thing I can see. She can keep you in order and tame some of your more worrying ways. Goodness knows someone needs to. I have paid off your gambling debts for the last time, Jasper. Don't waste your time asking me again. It's time you took responsibility for your actions.' Lady Carmichael sighed and twisted her wedding and engagement ring with its massive solitaire diamond. 'I dread to think what your father would say if he found out, so don't ask him to help you. I've covered up for you until now, but no more. And why do you insist on calling Cordelia Delia? Cordelia is such a lovely name, and you're not children any more.'

Jasper stood and reached for his grey cashmere coat, admired himself in the gilt mirror over the fireplace and blew his image a kiss. He was good-looking and knew it. His blonde hair and striking blue eyes had caught many a girl's attention. 'I've always called her Delia, Mater, you know that. Somehow it suits a bookworm, although I like bluestocking better.'

Her mother ignored him and directed her comments at her daughter, shaking her head. 'It's bad enough that you went to that university, Cordelia. Three years away from your family and you never even got a degree! I don't know what to say to my friends about it when they ask to see the graduation photos. And, in any case, you should look for a suitable husband now. After all, you are twenty-three. You'll soon be too old to find a fitting match. You don't want to be left on the shelf.'

Cordelia swallowed her irritation and looked at her watch. 'You know the University of Cambridge doesn't give women degrees. Just tell your friends that. Perhaps you could start a campaign to get the university to behave differently.' As always happened when she spent time with her mother, Cordelia needed to escape from the stifling attitudes, however well meant. 'Anyway, I want to say hello to Cook before I get my train. I'll pack, then pop in to say goodbye before I leave.'

A maid, Stella, came in with a tea tray laden with tiny triangular ham sandwiches and cupcakes as well as tea, milk and sugar in silver pots.

'Will that be all, madam?' Stella asked.

'Yes, thank you. You can go now.' Her mother turned to her. 'Will you have some tea?'

But Cordelia's need to escape was greater than her need for a drink. 'No, thanks, Mother. I'll be off now.'

Her mother leaned over so Cordelia could kiss her cheek and she then patted her arm absent-mindedly by way of dismissal.

'Oh, by the way, Cordelia. Tomorrow I am leaving for Scotland for a week or two. I expect you'll remember your Great-Aunt Bess from our holidays on the Isle of Skye when you were a child. You and Jasper had such fun running around the beach. She's had some bad news so I am going to comfort her.' She turned away and picked up the teapot, signalling it was time for Cordelia to leave.

Glad to escape, Cordelia went upstairs to pack her case, wondering how she could be expected to keep Jasper in order. She was his big sister, but only by two years. Even as a child she'd tried to stop him doing crazy things, rarely with success. There was that time he climbed a tree and couldn't get down. Worse, he stole from Cook's purse. Cordelia had raided her piggy bank to replace the money before Cook noticed. Then, when he was sixteen, she'd found him with gypsy girls in the woods by the river. She'd dragged him home and told their father what he'd been up to. Their father had beaten him and grounded him for a month. Jasper had sulked about the house the first week, calling her a traitor and saying he'd just been kissing the girls. The second week he'd gone out every night and returned at dawn unabashed. He somehow charmed his way out of trouble every time.

Despite his ability to get into mischief, they'd been close until about two years earlier when he'd changed almost overnight. Heavy drinking, unsavoury companions and gambling now dominated his life. It was as if he was a different person. Her stomach twisted with worry as it did whenever she thought about Jasper's errant ways. He'd almost become a stranger and she missed their old easy friendship. They used to bicker and fight, but it was all in good fun, now they had little to say to each other.

Her case packed and sighing at the memories of those good times, Cordelia went down to the kitchen to see the family cook, Mrs Taylor.

The cook's kind face lit up when she saw her, and wiping her hands on her pinny, she rushed over and wrapped her in a warm embrace. The heat from her familiar face was like the sun breaking through cloud, warming Cordelia's heart. Mrs Taylor's red cheeks radiated her usual good health and her eyes twinkled with liveliness. She smelt of cinnamon and baked biscuits.

'I'm sorry your visit's been so short, Cordelia. We've hardly had time to catch up.' She turned to stir something on the stove. 'I heard you got that job in the library, not that your mother is at all pleased.'

Mrs Taylor had been a lifelong confidante of Cordelia's, listening to her tales of troubles at school, fights with Jasper and her exasperation at the role her parents expected her to play as a girl. Cook was always willing to listen without judgement and give sound advice if asked.

Cordelia leaned over the table and snatched one of Mrs Taylor's delicious rock cakes.

'Mmm,' she said, taking a bite. 'No one cooks as well as you.' She sat down and wiped the crumbs from her top. 'After the interview, I went to see your brother Derek like you suggested. Did you know he's moved?' She reached into her pocket, took out a piece of paper, and handed it to her. 'This is his new address. It's only a couple of doors along.'

Mrs Taylor frowned. 'Why on earth did he move? He's been there for ages.'

'It's a sad story. He's friendly with a Jewish man he's known for a year, a barber who cuts his hair. When this friend called to see your brother, the landlord saw him and threw your brother out.'

'You mean he's a Jew hater? A blackshirt?' Cook's face had gone pale.

Cordelia nodded. 'He must be. There's a fair bit of unrest around there. You'd think people would be more sympathetic. After all, a lot of the Jewish immigrants have come because of what that awful man Hitler is doing to them.'

Mrs Taylor shook her head. 'It's shameful, that's what it is. I'll never understand people like that as long as I live.' She folded up the tea towel she'd been using. 'How did you get on with my Derek?'

Cordelia remembered the tiny front room he had shown her into. It was obviously only used for visitors and special occasions.

'Very well. He's a lovely man, and he says he'll volunteer in the library. He only works part-time now, so he'll be able to fit it in. But the poverty in that area is just unbelievable, I was shocked when I looked around. Do you know some people still don't have electricity? In 1940! You'd think we were still in Victorian times. I hope I can find ways to help people through the library.'

Mrs Taylor put the kettle on. 'A lot of the people live in dreadful rented property with no running water, a shared kitchen with the whole tenement and don't get me started about the toilets! But knowing you, you'll find a way to help. I've heard the government is building new council houses out of London. Maybe Derek will get one.'

She stopped when someone tapped at the back door.

'It's only me, Mrs T, my angel, my sunshine,' an elderly man in a brown cotton coat said, putting his head round the door. 'Come to deliver this week's meat order to my favourite customer.'

Mrs Taylor nodded and handed him a paper bag containing two rock cakes.

'Here, I got these ready for you. You're always hungry. Put the meat in the cold room, please.'

When he'd gone, she turned back to Cordelia. 'If you hadn't been here, he'd have proposed again.' She grinned. 'He does it every time. Like I'd want to get married again. No, thank you. I'm not washing an old man's socks and pants. He even got down on one knee once. You could have heard his knees cracking from the end of the garden!' She chuckled. 'Still, I suppose it's good for my ego. Anyway, I hope you've got time for a cuppa before you go.' Cordelia nodded and Mrs Taylor continued to chat. 'One thing you need to know about the people in the East End. A lot of them had to leave school real early to bring in money for the family or look after their younger brothers and sisters. Some of them can't even read and write properly. But they're just smart as you and that brother of yours. Just never had the chance to use their brains in a way that gives them a step up in life.'

Cordelia reached for another rock cake, but Mrs Taylor slapped her hand.

'You wait for the tea, young lady!' she said, reaching for the brown teapot with its knitted red, white and blue wool cosy.

As they waited for the tea to brew, Cordelia leaned over and squeezed Mrs Taylor's hand affectionately.

'I don't know what I'd have done without you when I was a child,' she said. 'Coming in here to see you was always my safe place, where I was allowed to be myself.'

Mrs Taylor poured the tea. 'Seems to me, and I may be speaking out of turn, that posh people, monied people, worry about keeping up appearances much more than the rest of us. And goodness knows that's not saying much. Still, you've ploughed your own furrow in the end, and I can see it's made you happy. That's the main thing. Still, the right man comes along and you might think again. Are you over that bloke you almost got engaged to? I remember it broke your heart.'

Cordelia grimaced. 'I think my heart is well and truly mended, but it'll be a long time before I trust anyone else with it, so don't get your best wedding guest outfit ready yet,' she said. 'I'm in no hurry. I promise if the right man comes along, you'll be the first to know! But it won't be any time soon.' Having eaten another rock cake, she finished her tea. 'I'd better get going or I'll miss my train.'

She hugged Mrs Taylor again.

'Now for my exciting challenge. See you next time I'm home.'

2

FAMILY TROUBLE

10 July 1940

Mavis grimaced as she left home on her way to work. Old Kempson, the rent collector, was knocking on her neighbour's door hard enough to break it down.

'I know you're in there!' he shouted, his bowler hat almost falling to the ground. 'Come on, time to pay up!'

Mavis tapped him on the shoulder. 'No good knocking there. Mary's just 'ad another nipper. She ain't got no money for the rent.'

Kempson glared at her. 'Nipper or no nipper, she has to pay her rent, same as everyone else.' His jacket was shiny with wear and his shoes were so old the soles were probably padded with cardboard. Mavis often wondered if he managed to pay his own rent. The miserable git of a landlord obviously didn't pay him much. Not that it made her feel sorry for him.

'Leave 'er alone! She can't pay the bloomin' rent and that's that.'

His shoulders sagged. 'Okay, but she'll have to pay double next week.'

Mavis took a step towards him, swinging her large handbag, and he took a nervous step back. 'If she ain't got the rent this week, she ain't going to 'ave double next week, is she, you stupid man?'

She reached into her purse and handed him half a crown.

''Ere, take that off 'er bill. Maybe she can pay a bit more next week.'

He put the coin in his leather satchel and strode on to the next house without another word.

Closing her bag, Mavis glanced at Mary's window. The edge of the snowy-white net curtains moved a couple of inches and Mary's pale, exhausted face appeared. She smiled her thanks. Mavis winked at her and hurried towards the library. No bus today. She'd have to walk now she'd given that half-crown to the rent man. And she'd have to live on bread and dripping for a couple of days. It wouldn't be the first time.

As she walked on, she passed old Mrs Hoffman on the corner, selling her little round doughnuts straight from the pan. The woman's smiley, plump face was framed by a grey felt hat she'd worn for years. She was bending over the steaming vat of oil as she slid a fresh batch of dough into the bubbling fat. A strong smell of cinnamon and sugar rose from the pan, making Mavis's stomach rumble. She often bought one on her way to work, but she'd have to wait a few days. They were only a ha'penny, but she couldn't spare it.

'*Shabbat shalom*,' she called with a wave. She didn't know exactly what it meant, but had heard her Jewish neighbours greet each other with the words often.

Mrs Hoffman held out her big metal spoon. 'Here, *bubbeleh*, I saw what you did. Have this one on the house.' She put a doughnut in a square of newspaper and pressed it into Mavis's hand. Mavis took it gratefully, biting into it and closing her eyes with pleasure as she savoured the sweet treat.

Mavis looked at her watch and walked more quickly. Wouldn't do to be late on the first day with the new boss. She didn't like change and old Mr Bartlett had suited her just fine. He was her idea of a perfect library manager with his stiff back, black suit, bowler hat and precise way of speaking. Pernickety, and quick to find fault, but you always knew where you were with him. Every day the same. Life in her neighbourhood offered more than enough excitement, thank you very much.

She'd never admit it, but this new one, Miss Carmichael, made her feel inferior with her fancy clothes and way of speaking, like she was royalty or something. She was in for a shock when she got to know what was what.

Mavis went to cross the road and was almost pushed aside by a lad in a black cap with a bucket and shovel running to collect droppings from the coalman's horse that had just passed by.

Yes, Miss C – as Mavis already thought of her – would need a peg on her nose when old Bert came in to read the newspapers, stinking to high heaven. Then there was the old Jewish man, beard halfway down his chest. He sat there every day, scratching away on a notepad. She called him the Professor, but she had no idea what his background was. His accent was so thick, she had trouble understanding anything he said.

Her thoughts returned to Ken, her son, who was on leave and eating her out of house and home. She sighed with relief, remembering he was due back in barracks the next day. She rubbed her forearm where the sleeve of her jumper concealed a deep bruise he'd given her the night before when she'd refused to give him all her money. He'd searched high and low in their three rooms, upturning furniture and making it look like burglars had ransacked the place. But she was smarter than him, and the money she'd scrimped and saved was safe and well hidden. For now.

Although the bruise on her arm was covered, she still felt its immediate ache, could hear the slap of his hand as he struck her. She remembered the sickly-sweet smell of the alcohol on his breath. Ken wasn't especially tall or well built, but he was strong nevertheless and had a vein-pounding temper. His face had been a vision of frustration and anger as he hit her, wanting his own way as usual. If he hadn't been her son, she'd have reported him to the police – not that they'd have done anything. As far as they were concerned, violence within four walls was none of their business.

'I know you've got money somewhere, you bitch!' he'd hissed, his nostrils flaring as he swept her precious little ornament of a girl onto the floor. It smashed into a dozen pieces. It was a cheap fairing, a little painted shepherdess, but she was fond of it because it reminded her of happier days when she went to the fair with her friends. She'd won it by getting hoops over a piece of wood. They'd all jumped up and down with excitement as if she'd won the football pools. Now it was beyond repair.

Shoving her aside so hard she'd have fallen to the floor if a chair hadn't been in the way, Ken had stormed out of the front door, slamming it so hard it rattled. She turned the kitchen chair the right way up and collapsed onto it, breathless, her heart beating fast. At least he seemed to have forgotten about wanting to know about his dad, thank goodness.

Mavis was still up when Ken arrived home. He didn't even notice her as he pushed his way out of the back door to the outside lavvy, then, trousers still half undone, collapsed on his bed.

So, when she got up, the first day with the new boss ahead, she had tiptoed around, making herself some tea and toast as quietly as she could. Even though Ken was leaving, she didn't want to wake him. Experience told her he was unbearable when he had a hangover, and would look for a fight over the smallest thing. She quietly tidied the kitchen. She'd leave the front doorstep unscrubbed for once in case she woke him, although she knew that would be noted by some of the nastier women in the street. They thought anyone who didn't scrub their step first thing was a filthy slut. She'd sighed. So be it. With her coat on, she put a cup of tea on the floor near the bed, shook Ken's shoulder and rushed out of the house before he properly came to.

It began to rain, not heavily but enough to soak her. She pulled her hat lower on her head and put up her umbrella. Immediately, the traffic sounded different, louder. Now petrol was rationed there were more horses and carts on the streets, more people using bicycles or, like her, buses.

She hurried past factories, market stalls, butchers, bakers and all the other places that were the heart of the East End, greeting half a dozen people as she usually did. She loved it all, the sounds of the barrow boys calling out their wares, the smells of cooking from a dozen different nationalities, the variety of languages and the day-to-day challenges of living in a poor, crowded area. She hoped never to move. The lack of air attacks so far, following the end of what the newspapers called the phoney war, gave her hope that her home was safe.

A clock nearby struck the half past, and she hurried faster. She'd just make it.

3

A HARSH MOTHER

'I don't know why you want to work in that stupid library, my girl!' Jane's mother said as she took her hands out of the washing tub and wiped little Helen's nose. 'Why can't you work on the sewing machines like all the other girls round here? We've always been in the rag trade in our family. You'd never be outta work.'

Jane hugged her little girl, breathing in her girlish scent, stroking her smooth young skin and hating having to leave her. Leave her with the woman whose harsh mothering she'd experienced all her life.

'I'll see you later, sweetheart,' she whispered, kissing her again. Putting on her coat, she turned to her mother. 'The library is a good job, Mum, and people will always want books.'

She grabbed her bag and tried to leave the house as quickly as possible. She couldn't bear the look on her mother's face, disapproving and disparaging. It was a horribly familiar expression.

Her mother snorted. 'Huh, shows what you know. Us East Enders don't 'ave time for book reading. Oh, no...'

Jane edged closer towards the door, knowing her mother was going to start one of her rants.

'Oh, no... we spend all our time just keeping the 'ouse clean and trying to find enough money for the rent and food...'

Gritting her teeth, Jane leaned forward and kissed her mother on the cheek. 'There's a new boss starting today, Mum. Miss Carmichael.'

Her mother's jaw dropped. 'A woman? In charge of the library? Are they mad? That's a man's job or my name's not Hilda Richards.'

Jane opened the front door, letting in cold air, noxious from all the factories in the tight-knit streets. 'I'll see you both later,' she said, and stepped outside. The air might be tainted, but at least she was away from her mother's vicious tongue.

''Ello, *bubbeleh*,' called Mrs Cohen from next door. 'I 'eard your mum going on at you again. Wasn't earwigging on purpose, mind. I reckon the walls between your 'ouse and mine are only 'eld up with wallpaper.'

'It'd be easier arguing with a lump of rock,' Jane replied with a shrug. 'Still, she has her good points. Remind me what they are if you spot them!'

'Any word from your man, yet?' Mrs Cohen asked. 'Terrible 'im being called up an' that, when we'd 'ardly known there was a war on. Coulda been 'ere 'elping you bring up your little 'un.'

Jane's heart tightened at the thought of her husband. When they married, they were thrilled to get a home, even if it was only two rooms. Their few months together had been everything she'd dreamed of. George was kind and thoughtful, even helping around the place sometimes. They'd had precious little money, but enjoyed the occasional visit to the pictures or a walk by the Thames. Each time she looked into his lovely blue eyes or felt his strong arms around her, she felt safe and loved. Feelings she'd never had at home with her mother. But the war put paid to their contented life all too soon. When George was called up, she'd had to move in with her mum to manage. Every night she prayed he would be safe and there would be a way out of her situation.

She took off her wedding ring and put it in her purse. Married women weren't allowed to work in the library. It was a secret she fought hard to keep. They allowed widows like Mavis, though, something that seemed illogical to Jane.

Waving goodbye to her kind neighbour, Jane hurried up the street towards the bus stop.

She hadn't gone more than a few yards before cheeky Wally Walker from number 37 ran past her, shouting to his mate to wait for him. But he wasn't looking where he was going, tripped over his own feet and went flying.

'Wally!' Jane called, bending over to help him up.

Not that he wanted help, not from a girl.

'Let me look,' she said, getting out her hankie and wiping his grazed knee. 'It's not too bad. Go home and give it a wash or it might go septic.'

He brushed away her hand and ran off. She grinned, knowing he had no intention of following her advice.

She stood at the bus stop, aware that the girls working in the clothing sweatshops would already have been at work for more than half an hour. She could hear the machines humming away from where she stood. Most of her school friends went into the rag trade at fourteen. There'd been hell to pay when she told her ma she wanted to stay on.

'Stay on! Stay on? No, you won't, my girl. I've set you up to see Mr Jones at Barton's fabrics. You'll start on Monday.'

Trembling, Jane had stood her ground, yet didn't quite dare look her mother in the eyes.

'No. I'm not going there. Mrs Smith says I'm bright and can do better than factory work.'

Her mother looked as if she'd have a stroke, her eyes bulging and her breath fast and heavy.

'You'll do as I say or leave this house and don't bother coming back.'

With that, she slammed down the iron she was holding and turned away.

Jane had waited for her to say more, but, her back rigid, her mother carried on with the ironing. Fighting back tears, Jane had gone upstairs and put her few belongings into two old pillowcases. She didn't tell her mum that Mrs Smith had offered her a tiny box room and food in return for babysitting and housework when she wasn't at school. Her heart heavy, she'd taken her bags and left after saying, 'I'll let you know where I am, Mum.' She got no reply.

She walked to Mrs Smith's that day feeling a sense of relief as she approached the cosy house. It was the only place where she felt truly welcomed. The warm summer breeze flowed through her hair as she knocked on the front door. The house wasn't much bigger than her mum's, but Mrs Smith had it all to herself and didn't have to share the outside lavvy.

Jane stayed on at school for another two years and passed her school certificate. She'd always be grateful to that kind teacher who saw something in her that her mother never saw.

She'd put a note through her mum's door telling her the good news about passing the exams. They hadn't spoken in all that time, but her mum sent a note back congratulating her, and that was the beginning of them talking again. Not that their conversations were easy, even then.

Still, why couldn't her mother be pleased she'd done well at school and got a decent job? She didn't earn much, but it was more than factory work. Once she moved back in with her mum when George went to war, she handed over most of her wages each week. It was never enough to satisfy her mother, though.

She sighed and wondered if she should take the chance to evacuate to the country with her little girl. But then she'd have to give up her good job and, despite what her mother might say, she'd struggle without her.

As she sat on the bus, she looked out at the familiar run-down houses. Most of them had two or more families living in them. Some of the tenements were in a dreadful state, crumbling, unsanitary and full of vermin.

Her mum's house was full. They had three rooms, and a young couple lived in the small attic rooms. They shared an outside lavvy with three other houses. The smell was something rotten, especially in the summer.

Two women came and sat behind her.

'Look at all this stuff they've done,' one said, looking out of the window. 'White lamp posts and things. And don't talk to me about the blackouts! I'm sick of them little ARP Hitlers always telling me off.'

The other one joined in. 'Still, if this war ever does get properly started, I suppose we'll be changing our tune and grateful. Hope it never does, though. Mind you, if bombs don't get us, the blackout will. My neighbour walked into a lamp post a couple of nights ago and knocked himself out!'

Jane dragged her thoughts away from the women and shook herself out of her gloomy mood. This Miss Carmichael, her new boss, must have known what she was coming to, and despite being taken aback by her voice and expensive clothes when she met her after her interview, Jane thought she seemed nice and friendly.

'So, you're Jane,' she'd said, and shook her hand as if she was an equal. 'I'm looking forward to working with you.'

Jane started at that. Old Mr Bartlett never thought he worked *with* her. She worked *for* him, as far as he was concerned. If he saw her outside work, he barely acknowledged it. Sometimes she wondered if he even recognised her.

Nothing had changed in the library for years and years, and Jane hoped Miss Carmichael would bring it up to date. Not that her co-worker would agree. Mavis liked things to stay as they were. Jane was fond of her. They were good friends, but she was a little cautious of Mavis's sharp tongue.

'We've got enough to deal with, what with another war. Be careful what you wish for!' she'd said when Jane told her how nice the library in Boots the Chemist was.

'Library!' the conductor shouted, bringing her back to the moment. She stepped off the bus, wondering what the day would bring.

4

A NEW START

Cordelia stood outside the library, which was much grander than anything nearby. It stood on the junction of two roads and was two storeys high with a large cupola on top. She knew it also had a basement, although she hadn't been shown inside.

She took a deep breath, wondering what the future would bring for her here. Her stomach rolled as she considered what she'd taken on. Her friends who'd also trained as librarians thought she'd lost her mind taking on such an enormous challenge. Silvertown Library couldn't be more different from the library at Girton College, Cambridge. There, everything was revered. Books were treated with respect, girls walked quietly to avoid disturbing others, learning was paramount. All was hushed and learned.

But everything around her on the junction of Barking Road and Silvertown Road was noisy business – cars, trams, horse and carts, and hundreds of people hurrying to get to wherever they were going. The air was full of so many smells, it was hard to distinguish them all: smoke from the chimneys, horse dung, cooking, factory fumes and others Cordelia couldn't identify.

Moving the bundle of newspapers she'd bought on her way over, she reached for the key the interviewers had given her when she accepted the job, and mounted the two steps to the double front door. To her surprise, it was already unlocked.

Worried that anyone could have wandered in, Cordelia stepped into the library cautiously. The bundle of newspapers clumsily shifted in her arms, the pages rustling in the sudden stillness. She felt a chill of apprehension as she looked around the empty entrance hall.

'Is anyone there?' she called out softly.

The silence that followed seemed to echo in the air. Cordelia held her breath as she listened for any sign of life. But the only sound she heard was the slight creaking of the floorboards beneath her feet.

She took a deep breath and decided to explore further. As she wandered down the aisles of books, she couldn't shake off the feeling that someone or something was watching her. She felt a strange presence in the air, a feeling she couldn't put her finger on.

Suddenly, she heard a noise coming from the back room. A loud thud, as if something was being thrown or dropped. Cordelia jumped and her heart began to race. Her grip on the newspapers tightened.

Then she heard footsteps clipping importantly along from deeper inside the building. The sound was marked by a slight echo, bouncing off the library's walls, amplifying its significance. And there, dressed in a brown tweed suit and a hat with a bird feather, was Mrs Montague-Smythe, a local councillor.

'Oh, there you are!' she said, frowning. 'I thought you were never coming. I was inspecting the place while I waited.'

Cordelia's heart sank, but she had already decided to start as she meant to go on with this councillor. She'd got the measure of her at her interview.

'I'm an hour early, Mrs Montague-Smythe.' She smiled sweetly. 'Perhaps your watch is wrong.'

Mrs Montague-Smythe grunted. 'Well, at least you're here now. You'd better come through so I can show you around.'

Cordelia followed her to the main lending room.

'That's very kind of you, but the temporary manager already showed me around last week. And he left me detailed instructions on how to run the library. He was very thorough.'

Seemingly at a loss for how to assert her authority, Mrs Montague-Smythe rubbed her fingers along one of the library shelves.

'Dust!' she exclaimed. 'You'll need to have a word with the cleaner. We must uphold standards, you know. Public libraries are a breeding ground for germs. We don't want to be responsible for our readers getting polio – or worse.'

'I understand that Janet, the cleaner, was poorly last week, but she's due back today.'

With the amount of traffic and dust coming through the doors, Cordelia secretly thought it would take an army of cleaners to keep the place pristine.

They were interrupted by the back door opening as both Mavis and Jane came in. When they saw Mrs Montague-Smythe and Cordelia, they hesitated, unsure of what they should do.

Cordelia took a step forward. 'Do come in, and I see you're nice and early. You know Mrs Montague-Smythe, I think.'

They both nodded, but said nothing.

'She was very kindly welcoming me on my first morning.' Cordelia turned to the councillor. 'I very much appreciate your kind thought, especially when you're such a busy person. I've already heard all about your good works for the area.'

Mrs Montague-Smythe, wrong-footed again, could think of nothing to say, her mouth flapping emptily. 'Well... I...'

Cordelia turned and stepped towards the door. 'You must be very busy, so I won't keep you any longer. We need to get ready to open up for the day.'

The councillor, mesmerised, began to walk towards the door, then stopped. She turned to Mavis and Jane.

'I expect you two to show your new manager here the ropes. She has a lot to learn.'

The three of them silently watched her as she continued to walk towards the front door. The skirt of her suit was a bit tight across her backside, Cordelia noticed.

It seemed that her new colleague also spotted this.

'Two ferrets in a sack!' Mavis muttered, looking at the retreating rear.

Cordelia pretended not to have heard and struggled to look serious. She tried to be professional and keep a straight face. She really did, but a chortle exploded from her lips like a cork from a bottle.

They all laughed so much, they were doubled over. Luckily, Mrs Montague-Smythe had just left and was out of earshot.

* * *

'Okay,' Cordelia said after she'd wiped her eyes. 'Who usually opens up?'

'Mr Bartlett, well, he did,' Jane said apologetically. 'But since he died, God rest his soul, we've had a variety of different managers.'

'Yeah, and every single one thought the library should be run in a different way. Enough to drive you nuts.' Mavis raised her eyes to the sky as she spoke.

'Right, well, I'll carry on Mr Bartlett's way and open the doors. Except when it's my day off, of course.'

Cordelia headed towards the door, wondering what all the noise outside was. She soon found out when she opened it. Three tramps almost pushed her against the wall, rushing in from the wind. The smell of one of them, she couldn't tell which, trailed behind him like ghostly ectoplasm. She followed them into the main lending room. None looked for a book, or returned one. Two of the men sat on the floor, leaned against a wall, and promptly fell asleep. The other went to a rectangular table.

It's a far cry from Boots the Chemist library, she thought. Subscription only meant patrons were comfortably off. Being mostly middle-aged or older women, they could browse the books and sit in comfortable armchairs for as long as they liked. The ones who paid for the higher service were treated like royalty, their every need catered for, as Cordelia witnessed every time she went there. 'Do you have any books you'd like us to get for your next visit, Lady Cordelia?' the girl would ask. They kept a list of all the higher-paying patrons, along with books they'd read and ones they might like.

A shout wrestled her attention from these comforting memories.

'Where's the papers? There's always papers 'ere first thing!' the man at the table shouted. 'What sort of a library is this? No papers!'

Jane quickly picked up the batch of papers Cordelia had put on the counter and ran over to him.

'Here you are, Bert. We're a bit behind today, I'm afraid. New boss. Miss Carmichael.'

Cordelia was close behind her and apologised for the delay in getting the papers out. Bert merely grunted.

There was no time to dawdle. The door opened again and in walked a mother with two children, one in a pram that had seen better days. The other one was a little girl aged about four. She had blonde curls, rosy cheeks and carried a well-loved teddy bear.

'Got any books for kids?' the woman asked. 'Can't afford none meself.'

Mavis handed her the book catalogue. 'Choose what you want from here and I'll fetch it for you.'

The little girl sneezed and wiped her nose on her sleeve. Her mother told her off and gave her a handkerchief to use instead.

'What! I can't look at the books first? How'm I supposed to choose when I only see the title? That's daft, that is.'

Mavis's jaw set. 'Them's the rules. You're not allowed to get the books yourself.'

Cordelia stepped in, unsure how to handle the situation and not wanting to step on Mavis's toes.

'Do you have a library card?' she asked the mother.

'Card? What do I want a card for?' the woman asked, rocking the pram to settle the baby.

Cordelia turned to Mavis. 'Will you explain the system to this lady, please, Mrs Kent? I'll find a book if you're happy to trust me. Do you want one to read to your daughter?'

The woman looked relieved. 'Yes, she can't read herself yet, can she? She's only four.'

'You're a smart mother, Mrs...'

'Gregory. I'm Doris Gregory and this one...' She patted her daughter's head. 'This is Hetty. Hetty's a good girl, ain't ya?'

Hetty nodded and clutched her mother's hand tight. 'I'm a good girl and I'm five, not four!' she announced proudly.

'Go and have a look round while I talk to the lady,' Doris said.

Hetty wandered off towards the newspaper table, and they soon heard her outraged words. 'Mister, you smell bad! Doesn't your mummy make you wash?'

'Oh dear,' Doris said, flinching. 'You can count on kids to tell the truth, can't you? Anyway, I want to teach her to read. It's shocking all the schools have closed.'

Mavis nodded in agreement as she began to prepare new library cards for them.

'Terrible, it is. My friend sent 'er little boy off to the country, evacuated, but got 'im back yesterday. No point 'im being away when we wouldn't know there was a war on, is there? But to close all the schools! What was the government thinking of?'

Bert stood up and shouted at them. 'Schools can't teach little girls to be polite. Oh, no. Time you did that, Mother!'

He promptly sat down again and put his head back in the newspaper. His Woodbine, down to a stub, had stayed attached to his bottom lip throughout his outburst.

Doris hurried over and took Hetty back to the desk.

'Look, Hetty, the nice lady has given you your very own library card.' Hetty wriggled, keen to get back to exploring, but the moment was saved by Cordelia returning.

'This is quite a new book,' she said. It was *The Family from One End Street* by Eve Garnett. She knew it was about a poor but happy family, so thought it might be just the thing.

The baby started grizzling and Doris rocked the pram some more. 'Better get going before he screams the place down.'

She waited until the book was stamped and pulled Hetty towards the door.

Mavis looked at Cordelia. 'You didn't think you'd come 'ere for a quiet life, did you? What do we call you, anyway?'

Jane had joined them and waited for the answer.

'How about we use Christian names when no one's around, but our titles when there are readers about? So I'll be Miss Carmichael or Cordelia.'

Little did they know she really had a title. She planned to keep that secret as long as possible.

The returned books were stacking up on the trolley. It normally stood behind the wooden reception desk, under the picture of King George VI.

'Do you have a routine for who does what throughout the day?' she asked.

'Mr Bartlett tells us what to do,' Jane said in her timid way.

'Like we can't work that out for ourselves!' Mavis said, bitterness in her voice. 'I like a routine, me, but I don't need telling to do the bleedin' obvious!'

The sharpness in her tone took Cordelia aback. 'Well, in some libraries the staff take jobs in turns, an hour each. An hour on the desk, an hour fetching books, an hour returning books to the shelf. Does that sound like something you'd be interested in?'

Mavis folded her arms. 'And are you going to be on this rota, then?'

'I'll be on it, but not as much as you two. Sometimes I'll have office work to do.'

Jane lifted a hand as if asking permission to speak. 'Mr Bartlett only came out of the office to tell us what to do—'

'Or to tell us off...' Mavis interrupted.

'Help! Help me!' The pitiful cry came from the hallway.

Cordelia jumped up and ran towards a woman who was lying on the floor, surprised at the slow response from the other two.

A middle-aged woman dressed entirely in brown was moaning that she was dying, her handbag beside her. Her hat was on sideways and she was clutching her leg.

'Help me! Help me! I need help!' she repeated again and again. She looked at Cordelia pleadingly.

Cordelia bent down beside her, noticing she smelled of lavender and mothballs.

'Are you okay? Have you broken anything?' she asked.

To her amazement, Jane took the lead, pulling the woman up by one arm.

'Come on, Flossie, enough of your pretending. Go on, get on your way, we don't have time for you today.'

Flossie stood up, shook herself free of Jane's hand and glared at them all. Then she put her hat straight, picked up her bag and strode out without a word.

Cordelia looked at the others, astounded at what she'd just seen.

'That's old Floppy Flossie,' Mavis said. 'She ain't fallen over, she just lies down when no one's looking and cries for 'elp. You'll see 'er trying that trick all over the place. I even saw 'er on the floor in Rathbone Market once. Snowing it was, too. Just wants some attention, mad as a box of frogs.'

After that start, Cordelia wondered if she'd ever get used to the East Enders.

As the day passed by, she met many more interesting people. There was the man who came in wearing a shabby morning jacket, a battered top hat and a monocle; a woman who sat in the corner reading Tarot cards for hours; an eccentric artist who scoured art books for inspiration; and an older woman who wore a purple velvet floor-length cape and carried a beaded evening bag with half the beads missing.

But towards the end of the day, a very different person walked up to the desk when she was on duty. Little did she know how significant he would be in her future.

5

A NIGHT OUT

'I tell you, Rosalind, this doctor who came into the library today was the spitting image of David Niven, but with blonde hair and blue eyes.'

Cordelia had been trying to banish her thoughts of Robert Fernsby since he'd visited the library, but the way he'd awakened a desire within her, despite being entirely businesslike, had left her mind in turmoil.

Rosalind leaned back, adjusting her coat round her shoulders.

'He sounds dreamy, just the ticket,' she said, putting another Chesterfield cigarette into her long black holder and lighting it. 'Has he asked you out? By the way, aren't you a little underdressed for this bar, sweetie?'

Cordelia slapped her hand. 'I've come straight from work. I don't think turning up to an East End library dressed up to the nines would make me fit in.' She looked around the bar. The lighting was discreet and the whole place was a total contrast to the library she'd spent the day in. Huge Art Déco mirrors lined the wall behind the bar where bottles were reflected and sparkled in the light. Uniformed waiters hurried here and there to meet the needs of the customers, all of whom were also vastly different to the people she'd met in the East End. There was no Floppy Flossie or angry Bert disturbing the peace. Looking around, she wondered if she'd find her out-of-work life dull in the future. But Rosalind could always be counted on to liven things up.

Blowing a smoke ring, Rosalind called over to a waiter. 'Two Manhattans, please.' She turned back to Cordelia. 'So what did this hunk want? Can I meet him? Is he good for a night out?'

Cordelia slapped her wrist. 'Stop it! Be serious for a minute.'

'I *was* being serious. If he's as gorgeous as you say, I want to meet him. Pronto!'

'He's a doctor. And he's looking for a room to use half a day a week for free. As a GP.'

Rosalind tapped the ash off her cigarette and frowned. 'Why on earth would he want to do that? Is he some sort of do-gooder?'

The waiter came with the drinks, unobtrusively removing the used glasses and emptying Rosalind's ashtray.

Cordelia took a sip of her Manhattan. 'Yes, he's trying to do good. No shame in that, is there? You've no idea of the poverty in the East End. There are kids with no shoes all year round and most of them haven't got two pennies to rub together. They only call a doctor when it's desperate. They can't afford it otherwise. This man, Robert Fernsby, will have an endless queue wanting help.'

Rosalind reached for her bag and took out a pound note and handed it to Cordelia. 'Here, buy someone some shoes.'

Cordelia sighed, her shoulders sagging in resignation. She was getting used to this sort of thing; the condescending attitude of people like her friend, who knew nothing of the harsh realities of life in the poorer parts of the city. As kind as Rosalind's gesture was, a pound was a mere drop in the ocean in the needs of the people she would see every day. People suffering poor diet, poor housing and often poor life expectancy.

No matter how much she wanted to, Cordelia knew she couldn't change Rosalind's mind on how much help was needed. She might be able to in future, though, so she decided not to give up. She'd keep the pound – give it to Mavis and Jane and let them choose how best to use it.

She smiled despite herself, feeling a little bit of warmth spread through her. Perhaps Rosalind's gift wasn't so insignificant after all.

'Cooeee, over here!' Rosalind called out, distracting her from her thoughts.

Cordelia looked towards the door to see two men she didn't recognise.

But they wore RAF officers' uniforms, had expensive haircuts and would fit in with her 'set'. Or what used to be her set, at least. Once upon a time, seeing men like them would have interested her. Now, though, she could guess what they would be like – glib, superficial.

'I met them in a bar in the West End last night,' Rosalind whispered. 'Got very friendly with one of them, if you know what I mean.'

'Rosalind, you've got to be careful...'

Rosalind held up her hand. 'If I had a pound for every time you've said that to me, I could buy shoes for all of those poor kids you're going on about.' She took another drag of her cigarette. 'You may think I'm, well, a bit of a girl, but I never let them go all the way. I'm not stupid.' She glanced around. 'Anyway, shhh, they're here now.'

The two men kissed them on the cheek and sat down, calling to the waiter for more drinks.

'Aren't you going to introduce us, then?' one asked, looking at Cordelia.

'Of course, this is my friend, Cordelia Carmichael. Cordelia, these two handsome chaps are Martin and Thomas.'

'Not much point learning our names, though. We're off to battle tomorrow. So we plan to have a terrific last night.'

When the drinks came, Rosalind held out her hand to the men.

'Cordelia is working in a library in the East End. A lot of kids around there don't have any shoes. Imagine, no shoes in the middle of winter! I suggest you give her two pounds each to buy some. Come on now! You'll only spend it on whisky otherwise.'

'But...' Martin began.

'No buts, hand it over!'

She kept her hand out until she'd collected four pounds from her unwilling victims, then she passed them to Cordelia.

'Actually, I have an announcement to make,' she continued, then paused for dramatic effect. 'You may think I'm just a brainless socialite, but I'm going to be a... you'll never guess...'

'A bar lady!' one of the men guessed.

'A WRVS lady in sensible tweeds handing out tea!'

'A lady of the night!'

Rosalind held up her hand. 'Stop it, you horrible pair. I'm going to do something really useful. I'm going to be a bus driver.'

Cordelia's jaw dropped. 'But you've driven nothing bigger than that little sports car you whizz about in.'

'That's where you're wrong, sweetie. While you were filling your head with goodness knows what at Cambridge, I was helping on the farm.'

Martin's eyes widened. 'What, getting your hands dirty? Not with those nails.'

She patted his arm. 'Don't be silly, darling. We have people for that. No, I was driving the tractor, not just on the farm but up and down country lanes, too. I was rather good at it. And it's time I helped the war effort like you three. I start my training next Monday.'

Thomas lifted his glass. 'Good for you. Just let me know what route you're on so I can avoid it.' He laughed. 'Let's drink to all of us. May we have a fine old time and stay alive until peace returns at Christmas.'

They sipped their Manhattans in silence for a while, then Cordelia asked, 'Do you really think it'll be over that soon?'

They spent another half hour talking about the war, then Rosalind clapped her hands.

'Enough of this. It's too depressing. Let's go to a club and forget all about it.'

'Jolly good idea,' Thomas said. 'I know just the place.'

Cordelia thought about all she had to do. 'Not for me. I'm sorry to let you all down but I'm going to head home. I've got a lot to do before work tomorrow and I'm tired out.'

Martin put his arm round her shoulders. 'Come on, Delia, it'll be a gas. We'll cut a rug until we drop.'

They tried everything to get her to change her mind, but she was adamant.

As she walked through the darkened streets of the West End with her shielded torch, she noticed it wasn't just the sights here that were different. The smells differed from the East End too. No scents from the river, just from the perfume of women she passed or the aromas of cooking from the nearby restaurants. There were cooking smells in the East End, of course, but they were spicier and mostly she couldn't identify them.

The evening was mild and the sky clear. The moon shone brightly, its halo gently cradling it. Although they had experienced few bombings so far, it was the type of night already being called a bombers' moon. The moon reflected brightly on the Thames, making the route easy for bombers to follow to their targets. She shivered at the thought, hoping the war would indeed be over by Christmas and they would experience no more horrors.

As she sat on the bus, she reflected on the evening. She wondered if she knew who she was any more. If she'd ever known. She had never fitted in with her parents, whose views were a million miles from her own. Not that she saw them much. At boarding school, she seemed to have different interests from the other girls, preferring to have her nose in a book to talking about film stars and make-up. The University of Cambridge was where she fitted best. The hushed rarified air, surrounded by others who were bluestockings like herself. So why, she wondered, had she decided to work in the East End? She certainly didn't fit in there and probably never would, but that didn't mean she couldn't really help people.

Then she remembered how often she'd listened to Mrs Taylor as she cooked for the family. *She* had grown up in the East End and was full of stories of its fascinating people. At the time, it had seemed to the young Cordelia like they were characters from a storybook. Mrs Taylor had always said everyone in the East End was poor, but that they stuck together, especially families. They helped each other out and most areas had an unofficial 'aunty'. The aunties would lay out dead bodies, deliver babies, write letters and give support in many other informal ways. They weren't usually paid, although sometimes they might be given some eggs or a cabbage from the allotment.

Cordelia compared her upbringing, the opposite of the close-knit community Mrs Taylor talked about. Her childhood had been comfortable and her parents were kind when she saw them, in a distant sort of way. But no one would say they were a cosy, loving family. She often wished she had grown up in the sort of environment Mrs Taylor talked about. She instinctively knew she'd be more at home there.

She sighed and told herself to stop being down and to look forward to all her plans for the library's future.

She got off the bus and got her key out of her bag, wondering how Jasper would be when she got in. Would he be the charming, chatty young brother she'd grown up with, or the argumentative drunk he so often was?

6

AN UNEXPECTED DELIVERY

Mavis was relishing a peaceful evening at home. The people upstairs were rowing again, but she'd learned to block that out. Ken had gone back to barracks, and she hoped it would be a good long while until he got leave again. She'd checked her little savings nest and was relieved to see he hadn't found it.

She thought back through her day at work with the new boss. Maybe this Miss Carmichael, Cordelia, would be okay, but it was too soon to tell. She wasn't planning to put up with any nonsense, like too many changes for the sake of it. New brooms were fond of doing that, and not always for the best, in her experience.

She settled in her little armchair, picked up her knitting and turned on the radio to listen to a new programme, *It's That Man Again*. Tommy Handley always made her laugh.

But her planned evening wasn't to be. A frantic knocking on her front door almost made her jump out of her chair. The door opened before she had time to get to it.

'Mavis, come quick, it's Jeannie. The baby's on the way, and she says it won't be long now.' The speaker was a paper-thin man in so much of a hurry he'd run down the street with no jacket on and with his braces hanging round his hips.

'It's a couple of weeks early, Jack,' Mavis said, fetching the bag she used when helping to deliver babies. 'Is she sure it's coming? Not a false alarm?'

Jack was almost hopping up and down with anxiety. 'It's 'er sixth, so she oughta know by now.'

Mavis followed him out, closing the door behind her. With luck, the baby would come quickly so she could get back home and get some sleep. It wouldn't do to be half asleep at work the next day with the new boss. In the dim light, she was almost run over by a lad being pushed by his mate on a home-made cart.

'Outta the way, missus!' he called.

'Cheeky blighter!' she shouted after him. 'You should be in bed by now!'

But he was gone, whizzing down the street, steering round potholes and horse droppings with enviable expertise.

Jack tugged at her arm. 'Come on, it's comin' real quick, this one.'

'Where are the others?' The last thing Mavis wanted was an audience of the other five kids.

'Gone to me sister's.'

He pushed open his front door. As she walked in, she could hear Jeannie groaning.

'Right,' she said, taking off her coat and hat. 'You know the drill. Get some water on to boil.' She fished some scissors out of her bag. 'Boil these for a few minutes then wrap them in a clean towel. Bring me them when they're done. And find as many newspapers as you can, we'll need them. And while you're at it, tie a knot in your chopper. You've got too many kids already. You're wearing 'er out, you selfish git.'

She hurried to the couple's tiny bedroom, relieved the landlord had recently had electricity installed. There was a narrow dining chair on either side of the bed and a small chest of drawers. The faded wallpaper had once boasted bright pink roses. Now it showed damp in the corners. A picture of Christ hung above the bed.

Jeannie was lying on a double bed which was already covered in newspapers. Her skin was ashen and her hair stuck to her sweat-soaked forehead. Next to her was her youngest sister, Kate. She was sitting twisting her hands.

'I've never seen one born before,' she whispered as Mavis walked in. ''Er waters went 'alf an hour ago, she said you'd want to know that. I don't know what to do.'

'I'll tell you when you've gotta do something.' Mavis turned to Jeannie. 'Right, my girl, let's see 'ow far you've got. Come on, spread them legs. You know 'ow. You've done it often enough for that man of yours.'

Another contraction made Jeannie groan, and she clutched her sister's hand so tight it went white.

''Elp me, Mavis, it's coming... ahhh...'

While she was having the contraction, Mavis examined her.

'Push 'ardest when it's most painful,' she ordered. 'You can't shirk from the pain. It's gotta be done.'

The door opened a crack and, without showing his face, Jack slid a pile of newspapers through before hastily retreating. On top was the clean towel with the sterilised scissors.

Mavis picked them up, groaning as her knees complained.

'Right, there's going to be even more mess any minute. Let's change the newspapers.'

With Kate's help, they pushed Jeannie from one side of her bottom to the other, pulling out soiled newspapers and laying down fresh ones. Jeannie groaned and cursed them the whole time.

'Oy, you, Kate, come 'ere,' Mavis said when that task was done. 'Now, 'old one of 'er legs up, I'll 'old the other. The nipper'll be 'ere any minute. Don't you go fainting on me. I've got no time to see to you and all. Jeannie, I can just see the 'ead. You're nearly done, girl. Doing well. Next pain, give it all you've got, you know 'ow.'

Jeannie's head flopped on the pillow, exhausted. 'I can't...'

'Yes, you can. Come on, one last big push and the 'ead'll be through. Then you'll soon 'ave another baby in your arms and forget all the pain.'

Mavis and Kate both pushed Jeannie's legs hard, forcing her knees to bend wide. Mavis noticed that Kate tried not to look at her sister's private parts, but the coming birth drew her attention against her will.

'Let it be a boy,' Jeannie gasped through her pain. 'The old man wants a boy. Five girls are enough.'

'Well, you'll soon know, and you'll love it either way. You're a good mum, Jeannie. I've always said that.'

Two more big pushes and the baby, wet and slippery, slid from its warm home. Mavis clamped the cord in two places, cut it, wiped down the baby with a damp cloth, then wrapped her in the clean towel. Jeannie was already holding out her arms for the latest addition to her family.

When Mavis passed over the baby, Jeannie unwrapped her and inspected her. 'Another girl then. Still, she's got all her fingers and toes.'

Clutching the baby to her breast, she leaned back on the pillow with a happy sigh.

'Ay, Jack,' Kate shouted. 'You've only gone and got another girl! You're doing something wrong!'

Mavis silenced her. 'Don't let him in until we get the afterbirth done.' She turned to Jeannie. 'Now, Jeannie, one more pain, push 'ard and we'll 'ave the afterbirth out. Then you can 'ave a rest. You did good.'

But the next push produced nothing, nor did another one.

'We give it thirty minutes, then we get the doc,' Mavis said, trying to hide her fear. An afterbirth not coming out could lead to heavy bleeding, even the mother dying.

Just as she checked her watch, the air-raid alarm sounded.

'Oh, blooming 'eck, that bloody man Hitler.' She opened the door and shouted to Jack. 'You got an Anderson shelter?'

'Next door's got one.'

Mavis bit her thumbnail. She couldn't move Jeannie while she was waiting for the afterbirth to come. That might cause a lot of bleeding.

Jeannie's eyes were wide with fear and she clutched her baby tighter.

'Why are we waiting? I can walk, we can go next door.'

'Still waiting for you to let go of that afterbirth, sweet'eart. Shouldn't be long.'

Outside, they heard people running to shelters, either their own or the Underground. The air-raid warden shouted encouragement, telling them to hurry up.

Mavis looked again at Jeannie, hoping to see signs of the afterbirth, but what she saw instead made her face pale and her hands go clammy. Blood was trickling onto the newspaper. Not a torrent, but more than she wanted to see.

She looked up. 'Right, Kate. Go outside and tell that ARP bloke we need an ambulance, and we need it now! No arguments, just do it!'

Kate's eyes widened in fear and her bottom lip trembled, but she ran out of the room without a word.

'What's wrong?' Jeannie asked. 'Why do we need an ambulance?'

Was it Mavis's imagination, or was she looking paler than usual? Hard to tell when just minutes before she'd been a beetroot colour from all the exertion of pushing a baby out.

'Your afterbirth 'asn't come out, so we need to go to the 'ospital. Just being careful. No need to worry, just 'ug that little one. She's a beauty, looks just like you.'

She was being careful for herself as well as Jeannie. She had no training as a midwife, but her mother knew plenty about it, and she'd helped her deliver babies from when she was about five years old. Then, when her mum got too old, she took over. Her mum had been the 'auntie' for the local streets and somehow she'd inherited the role. She'd lost count of how many babies she'd seen safely into the world and she'd never lost a mother or baby.

Was she going to get in trouble when they got to the hospital? She couldn't contemplate letting Jeannie go without her. The doctors must know that loads of poor people used laywomen like herself when they couldn't afford a qualified midwife or doctor. Working in the library had given Mavis plenty of opportunity to read up on childbirth so she knew that what was happening to Jeannie was called a retained placenta, but when she spoke to her she used language she'd be familiar with. She also knew the dangers, even though she'd never seen it before. That's why she wanted the ambulance urgently. Every minute counted.

It arrived just as the all-clear sounded and life came back to the normally busy streets. A small crowd gathered round as the ambulance men carried Jeannie and the baby in on a stretcher. Several called out to her.

'See you soon, Jeannie.'

'What did you have?'

'Is the baby okay?'

Everyone knew everyone in these streets.

Mavis and Jack got in the back, their nerves frayed.

If they use their siren, I'll know they think it's serious, Mavis thought, hoping her worries were unfounded. But within seconds, the siren was blaring as it rushed them to St Mary's. They pulled up outside the Accident Department, and the men hurried in with Jeannie and the baby. Mavis and Jack ran behind, breathless with fear.

'She'll be okay, won't she?' Jack asked.

She was at a loss to know how to answer. Instead, she just nodded to a doctor who was coming towards them. 'He'll tell us what's what,' she said.

With eyes only for her patients, it took her several minutes to recognise the doctor who was quickly and competently taking charge of the situation. The department was full of hospital noises, shoes on lino, trolleys being pushed, hushed voices, equipment humming. The smell of disinfectant battled with the gentler scent of soaps. They headed to a curtained-off area, accompanied by a nurse wearing a royal-blue dress under a starched apron. She smiled at them and squeezed Jack's hand.

'Try not to worry. You're in the right place,' she whispered.

Jeannie handed the baby to Mavis as they wheeled her into a cubicle.

'I'll be back in a minute to tell you what we're going to do,' the doctor said without looking at them.

They sat on hard chairs in the unfriendly corridor, minds full of dread. Jack leaned over and looked at the baby for the first time.

'Is she okay?' he asked, his voice trembling.

'She's perfect. You'll be able to open your own garment factory with all these girls.' Mavis's attempt at a joke raised only a smile, which didn't meet his eyes.

'We'll have to think of a name for her. We were so sure it would be a boy this time, we didn't choose a girl's name.' The baby began to fret, and Jack took her from Mavis and put her over his shoulder, patting her back. 'There, there, little one, your mummy will be fine. You'll see her soon.'

They saw a second doctor hurry into the cubicle and caught odd words from their hushed conversation. *Urgent, immediate, surgery.*

Although Mavis expected this, she still felt terror for Jeannie and her six daughters, who might be without a mother before the day was finished.

A few minutes later, the first doctor came out and spoke to them.

'We're taking Mrs Gilbert for an immediate operation. It's a small one and usually very successful, although I don't want to make any promises at this stage.' He stopped and looked at the baby. 'So, this is the new one? She's beautiful. You must be very proud, Dad.'

Only then did he seem to look properly at Mavis, and recognition lit in his eyes.

'Oh, we've met before, haven't we? Just this morning in the library. I'm Dr Fernsby. I can't chat now but I'll come back and speak after the operation. Do give my very best wishes to Miss Carmichael. I enjoyed talking to her. I'm looking forward to seeing more of you all.'

Although it was less than ninety minutes until he returned, it seemed like hours. Jack was so tense, he was striding up and down the corridor, all the while talking to his new daughter. It was as if he hoped to outpace bad news.

When they heard the doctor striding towards them, Jack almost ran towards him.

'Is she okay? Will she live?'

Dr Fernsby smiled. 'She is absolutely fine. The operation went very well. She's still sleepy from the anaesthetic and won't be allowed to have visitors until tomorrow, but she'll probably be able to go home the next day. You can head for home now yourselves.' He turned to Mavis. 'I just want to assure you, you did nothing wrong, and it was correct that you called an ambulance when you did. You may have saved her life.'

He hurried off.

Mavis calculated she might get two hours' sleep if she could catch a bus soon.

'Are you coming?' she asked Jack, who was still holding his new daughter.

He shook his head. 'I reckon I'll stay here for a while. Find someone who can give me a bottle of milk before this one screams the place down. Then I'll try to sweet-talk someone into letting me see the missus before visiting time.'

Mavis smiled and kissed the sleeping baby.

'I'm so glad it's all turned out well. And remember to get her diphtheria vaccination at the clinic before she's a year old.'

Wearied, she walked to the bus stop, her feet dragging. She hoped this experience would never be repeated, and was relieved Dr Fernsby hadn't told her she had made any mistakes.

7

SETTLING IN

As the bus rattled along the West End streets as Cordelia travelled to work, she reflected on her first week managing the library and wondered what the coming week would bring. The bus passed several theatres, their doors firmly closed at this early hour. A few shops were open, along with some cafés, but most of the shops were shut as their customers weren't early risers. Despite the strips of paper criss-crossing the windows, they still gave an air of luxury.

It seemed that at every stop there was a decline in wealth. Gone were the signs of monied people – the expensive clothes in shop windows, the furniture and electrical goods for sale – replaced by crumbling brick buildings with flaking paintwork. Queues of worn-out women, faces poverty-scoured, snaked out of shops that sold meagre rations of whatever food was available.

Cordelia wondered how working women like Mavis and Jane got enough food to feed their families. Some, like Jane, would have a relative to help, but those living alone like Mavis must have to queue, feet weary after a long day's work. Then they'd have to cook and clean before falling into bed, exhausted. Cordelia was both relieved and embarrassed because she and Jasper had a woman, Margaret, who shopped and cleaned for them three times a week.

Her mind was drawn from these thoughts, when at a stop an elderly woman slipped as she got off the bus. Her skirt was in disarray and, still groaning from the fall, she tugged it down to cover her pink knee-length knickers. Her shopping had scattered around her as she lay on the floor. Cordelia went to stand up, but two passers-by beat her to it, helping the old lady and rescuing her potatoes and carrots. She looked shaken and although she appeared to turn down offers of more help, she still hadn't moved by the time the bus continued on its way.

Cordelia brought her thoughts back to the past week. She'd learned so much about how the library worked, helped by Jane and Mavis, who seemed surprised to be asked about anything. She felt she knew her way round the everyday systems and had met some of the regular readers. But she still had a lot to learn from the others about how to deal with some of the more eccentric library visitors. Several times she'd watched them in awe as they dealt with exactly the type of people her mother had warned her about. Each time it left her feeling sadness for the plight of those people, even Floppy Flossie. She 'fell over' most days somewhere in the library, ever hopeful of attention.

The conductor's cry of 'Silvertown Library!' made Cordelia jump to her feet, having totally forgotten where she was.

As she walked the short distance to the library, she realised she could now identify some of the smells she encountered. The East End had always been a magnet for poor immigrants and the cooking smells from their various traditional cuisines drifted through the air, making her mouth water. Then there was the sour smell of the Thames, polluted and full of industrial waste, and the sounds of the cranes and lorries moving consignments from the ships that had just landed.

She let herself in the back door to avoid Bert and others who were waiting on the library front steps, always seemingly there, no matter how early she was. She had an hour before Jane and Mavis arrived, so she'd start by tackling the pile of paperwork in the office. But first she put the newspapers she'd bought on her way in onto the readers' table. She'd learned her lesson.

Last week, Cordelia had announced to Mavis and Jane that they would open half an hour later every Monday so they could have a staff meeting, though, aware of Mavis's attitude, she didn't call it that. Instead, it was a 'weekly get-together'. Today was to be their first, and Cordelia had asked both women to come along with ideas for how to get more readers and book loans.

She made some tea and hoped the first week had been enough for them to get to know her a bit. It was easy to see they were both hard-working, even though their personalities were very different. Mavis was a straight speaker. Cordelia knew she'd never need to worry that she wouldn't be told if she was doing something wrong with her. But Jane was more timid, a shrinking violet afraid to speak up. Cordelia decided she must find ways to help build Jane's confidence.

Cordelia had high hopes for their future together, if she could only deal with everything in the right way. Several times a day she reviewed how she'd handled things and watched both women and the readers to see if she was getting a positive response.

Rays of sunlight filtered through the grubby windows and the sound of traffic was never-ending, but all three of them were used to ignoring the noise.

Cordelia gave Jane and Mavis time to sip their tea, then said, 'Before we begin, I want to thank you both for being so kind and helpful to me last week. I don't know how I'd have managed without your guidance.'

'Especially with angry Bert!' Mavis said.

Cordelia smiled her agreement. 'Especially with angry Bert and a few others.' She opened her bag and took out three small cakes Margaret had left for her and Jasper. As she shared them around, she said, 'I can't promise cakes every week, but I can promise my gratitude and I hope you'll both tell me if you think I'm handling things badly or need more knowledge to help you.'

She took a small bite of her cake before she continued.

'I wonder if you had any time to think of ways to increase readership and book loans, like I asked. The area librarian has told me I've got to increase them by 20 per cent in six months.'

Mavis's eyes opened wide and she almost spat out her mouthful of tea. ''E must be joking! Does 'e think we sit around doing nothing all day?' She grunted. 'Get more loans indeed!' She huffed in disbelief.

Jane didn't seem to like to contradict Mavis, and sat looking down at her hands. Her nails were bitten to the quick, and she appeared to shrink to make herself smaller whenever she needed to say anything. Yet strangely, she was fine with library customers, even the difficult ones.

'Did you want to say anything, Jane?' Cordelia asked. 'I really want opinions and ideas from both of you.'

She paused to give Jane time to pluck up the courage to speak.

Jane bit her bottom lip, and half looked at Mavis. 'I've got an idea that I think will save us time and our readers will like.'

Mavis put her empty cup on its saucer with a clatter and looked at Jane as if almost daring her to speak.

To break the atmosphere, Cordelia picked up the old brown teapot and refilled Mavis's cup.

'What's your idea, Jane?'

'Well, it's something you mentioned on your first day, so I can't take any credit for it...'

Cordelia had already learned that sometimes getting Jane to speak was like pulling teeth. It required time and patience.

'Jane, there's no such thing as a silly idea. What have you got in mind?'

Finally, Jane looked up. 'We could do what the subscription libraries do and let people browse the books before they choose them. Then we wouldn't have to keep leaving the desk to find what they want. We'd just stamp the book and their card before they leave.'

Cordelia could see Mavis was trying to find an objection to the idea, her gaze moving from side to side.

'That's a great idea, Jane. Mavis, I'm sure you'll appreciate not having to walk so much. Your feet will be thankful.'

Mavis pulled a face. 'I suppose we could implement that without a lot of work. Might work.'

Cordelia almost jumped up and down with delight at this easy win. There'd be plenty of struggles to change other things, she knew.

There was also something else she'd noticed, something she hadn't seen before Jane was speaking. The third finger of her left hand showed a band of skin paler than the rest. The sort of thing that happened when a ring was removed. Cordelia tucked the observation in the back of her mind, knowing at some stage she would want to know why this was the case.

By the next day, she'd put up a notice announcing the change, and another on the desk. Only one person objected, old Mrs Smith who thought she should be waited on. Everyone else seemed relieved not to have to take home a book they knew little about.

Though one more person wasn't so thrilled. Mrs Montague-Smythe, the councillor.

'And why wasn't I consulted about this?' She almost spat out the words when she saw the notices the next day. Her tweed suit looked tighter than ever as she drew herself up like a turkey trussed up, ready for Christmas.

Cordelia invited her into the office, where Mrs Montague-Smythe continued to look round for things to criticise. She spotted a pile of ledgers on a chair.

'I hope they don't contain important, confidential information, just left there where anyone can see them.' She plonked herself on Cordelia's chair.

Cordelia stood next to her. 'That's my chair. I'm sure you'll find the other one more comfortable.'

She folded her arms and waited for the woman to move. It was a battle of wills, but eventually, the councillor scraped the other chair nearer and moved into it.

'As you will have noticed when we came in here,' Cordelia began, 'the office was locked. I am very particular about locking it whenever I leave, even for a short time. And everything is locked away before the end of the day, so nothing is left when the cleaner comes in.'

Mrs Montague-Smythe's lip curled. 'That's as it may be, but you have made changes to the library systems without consulting me.'

Taking a deep breath to control herself, Cordelia looked her straight in the eye.

'I'm delighted that you're so interested in the library, Mrs Montague-Smythe. It's an important resource for your ward. However, as you will be aware, I take orders from the area librarian.' She paused and waited for the expected explosion.

'Mr Wood's a very busy man,' Mrs Montague-Smythe replied, her voice icy. 'He doesn't have time to oversee every library.'

Cordelia smiled. 'Has he asked you to take on the job for him? If so, he hasn't informed me, and I'm sure you'd want me to be fully informed of all library matters.'

'Well, no...' was the reply as the councillor stood and picked up her bag. 'But mark my words...'

Standing too, Cordelia stepped towards the door. 'Mrs Montague-Smythe, I've been given a goal of increasing library membership and loans. I promise to keep you fully informed about how that is going.'

She escorted the woman out, making a big show of locking the door behind her.

8

THE NIGHTMARE BROTHER

Cordelia came out of her bedroom and groaned. Even from where she stood, the smell of alcohol struck her senses, making her nose wrinkle. Jasper's bedroom door was slightly ajar and she could see him lying on top of his bed, fully clothed. She grimaced and pulled the door shut as gently as possible. She wanted to get off to work before he woke up. He was always bad-tempered when he had a hangover and that was the last thing she needed when she had a busy day ahead.

Robert, Dr Fernsby, was starting his weekly doctor's surgery, and it was likely a lot of people would want to see him. Some belonged to benevolent clubs, putting aside a small amount each week for medical needs, but not everyone could afford that. It was likely that the chance of a free consultation would be very popular.

They'd pinned up notices about it for a few days and there had been a lot of interest. All the previous evening when she was trying to work on library paperwork, she'd tried to push thoughts of him from her mind, but the image of his face kept ruining her concentration. She scolded herself. They'd only had a short professional conversation, and she was behaving like a silly girl, thinking of him so much. She told herself she wasn't looking for love. After how her last relationship ended, she no longer wanted to risk that much distress again.

She walked into the living room and sighed. Before she'd gone to bed after an evening's work for the library, she had tidied up, ready for the morning. Now it looked as if a herd of elephants had crashed through it. A half-eaten sandwich was on the carpet, a full ashtray gave off bitter smells, and a chair was upturned. She opened a window to let in fresh air and shivered. Although it was the tail end of summer, the wind that hit her was cold enough for winter. Outside people were scurrying to work, shoulders down, men in their bowler hats, rolled umbrellas hooked on one arm, briefcase in the other hand. Women wore high heels, warm coats and smart hats, with handbags over one arm.

She groaned again as she turned back to the messy room. An empty whisky bottle lay sideways on the coffee table, its golden contents dribbling in a sticky circle on the antique wood. She wiped it off, straightened things, grabbed some tea and toast, and headed out of the door. As she walked to the bus stop, she tried to push thoughts of her brother's behaviour out of her mind. He must have had call-up papers by now, and somehow he'd never done his National Service. When she asked him if he had some health issue that meant he was unfit for service, he always changed the subject. She'd heard stories of men paying someone who suffered from real ailments to pretend to be them for the army medical. Surely he wouldn't have gone that far to avoid his duties? Yet why wouldn't he? He'd never been one to take responsibility seriously.

Shaking her head, she tried to focus on her surroundings instead. The wind was getting stronger, blowing pieces of paper about and causing people to clutch their hats as they walked. Trees blew about wildly and some leaves, anticipating autumn, flew away like migrating birds.

She'd never noticed before, but where men in the West End wore bowler hats, in the East End they wore flat caps. Women in the West End wore smart hats, in the East End they wore scarves, or knitted or felt hats.

Smiling at the observation, she straightened her hat and began to walk to the bus stop, looking forward to the day.

* * *

It was Derek's first day as a volunteer at the library. Cordelia had been in touch with him, reminding him of his promise when she visited him on behalf of his sister, Mrs Taylor. She was thrilled he had decided to help out. He had a lovely, lively personality and would help with the workload.

It was a few minutes before the library was due to open and she took the opportunity to introduce him to the other two.

'Derek, this is Jane and this is Mavis.' She waited as they smiled and said hello. 'You'll remember, girls, that Derek is our new volunteer. He is the brother of someone I've known for many years.'

Derek took off his flat cap, scratched his head, and nodded. He was almost completely bald.

'That's right, my sister's 'er—' He gestured towards Cordelia.

'We don't need to go into that just now,' Cordelia said, interrupting him. She wished she'd asked him not to let on about how wealthy her parents were.

Derek was well past retirement age and was a veteran of the Great War. His skin, pale and papery, was wrinkled and weathered, with age spots like freckles. Although his clothes were shiny with wear, they were spotlessly clean and his scuffed boots were polished to a shine. But these things were less noticeable than his ready smile and kind eyes. He had a cheerful demeanour, and Cordelia was sure he'd handled much worse than difficult library customers.

'Right, Dr Fernsby will be here in an hour. We need to get a row of chairs near the room he'll be using...'

'The room's ready,' Mavis said. 'I checked it already. How about giving everyone in the queue a number on a bit of paper, so Dr Fernsby can just call the next one in. Saves squabbling. You know what some people are like!'

Jane put up her hand. 'I had an idea. We want more readers. Why don't we put library application forms on each chair? And we could have some popular books for them to look at while they wait as well—'

'They'll nick them!' Mavis interrupted.

Derek leaned forward. 'Tell you what. I'm not much good for anything yet 'til I learn the ropes. Why don't I keep an eye on 'em, chat to 'em, like, and make 'em feel at ease? Mind you, I'll need a chair to rest me old legs. Three hours is a long time to stand up at my age.'

Cordelia felt any tension about this new venture evaporating. With the great ideas they'd had, everything should go swimmingly. Shouldn't it?

The clock on the town hall tower struck nine, and they scattered to their posts. Bert brushed past Cordelia as soon as she opened the door, leaving his trademark smell in his wake along with a cloud of cigarette smoke, and she was delighted to see Mrs Gregory and little Hetty come in next.

'We've had a change of system,' Cordelia told them. 'You can pick your own book now. When you've decided what you want, take it to the counter and someone will stamp it.' She looked at Hetty. 'Have you got your library card?'

She produced it from her little knitted handbag and proudly showed it off.

'Good girl,' Cordelia said. 'I bet you'll find a lovely book, or even two!'

Cordelia was on the desk stamping books when Robert appeared at nine forty, twenty minutes before his clinic was due to start. He wore a dark blue suit, a dazzling white shirt, a grey tie and a trilby. His dashing good looks and suit made him look like a doctor out of an American movie. She was glad she was wearing her favourite work dress, emerald-green with white spots and collar. Pinched in at the waist, it emphasised her shape, then it flared to below knee length. It was both businesslike and flattering. Although he behaved professionally, carrying a newspaper and his medical bag, she noticed Robert look at her appreciatively.

As he walked over, she felt her temperature rising and had to force herself to act naturally, clutching the edge of the desk as if it would keep her upright. She noticed he had a small scar, no more than half an inch, on his forehead and wondered what had happened to him.

Robert smiled and his arresting eyes held her gaze for perhaps a second longer than usual, or maybe she imagined that.

'We... we're all ready for you,' she said, her feelings causing her to forget her words. 'You've got six people waiting already. I know you've only got three hours. Is there a limit to how many people you think you can see in a morning?'

He looked at the people waiting for him. 'How about I talk to you after two hours? I'll be able to judge then. It's often difficult to predict how long people will need. If the queue gets very long, we can tell people it's not worth waiting.'

She introduced him to Derek, who was chatting away to another war veteran.

'Hello, doc,' he said with a smile. 'You're going to be the most popular person in the library. That's for sure. Plenty of people round here can't afford to see a doctor.'

Robert went into his room and, two minutes later, Jane took him a cup of tea. She came back out smiling.

Half an hour later, Derek sought Cordelia, his face pink.

'It's them women in the queue,' he said, avoiding her eye. 'They keep talking about lady things...'

Cordelia swallowed a smile. 'Lady things? What would that be?' she asked, wickedly feigning innocence.

He looked down at his feet. 'Well, you know, the curse and things. My missus, God rest her soul, never spoke about such things. Not fit for men's ears, she always said. What'm I going to do?'

Cordelia patted him on the arm. 'Go somewhere else down the line or tidy books. You've dealt with much harder things. I know you'll find a way.'

He went away unconvinced, shaking his head so much the few hairs on his head waved from side to side.

Feeling sorry for him, she found four romance books and approached the women in the queue.

'I wondered if you'd be interested in these?' she said. 'If you don't already belong to the library, just fill in the cards. I'm sure you'll find plenty of books you'd like.'

One woman glanced at the cover, then looked at Cordelia.

'Is this one a bit racy? I like a bit of excitement in my romances.' Out of the corner of her eye, Cordelia saw Derek backing away further and suppressed a smile.

A woman sitting next to her giggled and nudged her.

'You are awful. I'd never dare say that!'

Derek coughed and took another step back.

'I don't know this book,' Cordelia replied to the woman. 'But I usually find the picture on the cover and the blurb on the back gives you an indication of what to expect. I'll leave you to it now. I hope you find something you like.'

As she walked back to the trolley of books waiting to be returned to the shelves, she realised this was another way to get more readers. Once Derek knew his way round the bookshelves, he could judge the people waiting and put one or two books out he thought might interest them.

The first two hours of Robert's session flew by. Cordelia was glad she was too busy to think of the way his presence, the smell of his cologne, woody and citrusy, distracted her from her usual professional persona.

After two hours, he looked at the queue and nodded that he thought he could see everyone. But she was sure that once word got around, the queues would get longer. Perhaps they would only give out a certain number of tickets each time.

She made sure she was at the desk when he finished his shift.

He hurried out, looking at his watch, but when he saw her, he hesitated and walked over.

'I'm sorry, but I've got to rush off. I hope we'll have time to talk next week. Oh, before I go, would you mind putting up this poster?'

And he was gone, leaving her feeling empty, bereft.

She looked at the poster. It showed a smiling baby on a red background. Large letters above its head said:

DIPHTHERIA IS DEADLY – IMMUNISATION IS THE SAFEGUARD.
Ask at your local council offices or welfare centre.

Cordelia had read about the increase in this deadly disease. It produced a toxin that led to a thick film covering the throat, and, in the worst cases, literally suffocating the baby or child to death. The toxins could also affect the heart and other parts of the body. She tried to imagine watching that happen to your own child and felt chilled to the bone. Three and a half thousand babies died of it each year. She looked again at the poster as she put it up on the wall. Surely no one would be against such a life-saving vaccine?

9

COURAGE

Early September 1940

The earlier wind and rain had blown itself out during the day, and Mavis got off her bus a stop earlier than usual to go to her favourite butcher's shop. While she waited in the queue, she checked her bag to make sure she had her ration book with her. As usual, the talk was of shortages and the latest war effort. That morning, she'd heard about the continuing war in the air. They were calling it the Battle of Britain.

'Did you 'ear what Churchill said on the radio?' Mavis joined in.

'No, what was that?' the woman standing next to her asked.

'Well, it nearly brought a tear to my eyes. 'E said, "Never in the field of human conflict was so much owed by so many to so few." I 'eard them pilots don't live long neither. They're so blooming brave.'

As she approached the front of the queue, she felt a tap on her shoulder. She turned around to find a smiling young man in a Royal Air Force uniform standing behind her. He looked no more than twenty years old, with bright blue eyes and a cheery grin on his face.

'Excuse me, madam,' he said. 'I couldn't help but overhear the conversation about the Battle of Britain. I just wanted to say that we're doing everything we can to protect our country, and we won't stop until we've won this war.'

Mavis was taken aback by the young man's optimism and courage. She admired the bravery of the pilots who fought in the skies above Britain, but she had never met one in person before.

'Thank you for your service,' she said, feeling a surge of gratitude towards the young man. 'You and your brave colleagues are the reason we're able to stand in this queue and buy food.'

With a cheery grin, he saluted her and turned to speak to his friend.

A woman standing next to her nudged her arm.

'He's bit of all right, ain't he? I wouldn't climb over him to get out of bed.'

Mavis chuckled. 'You'll 'ave to get past me first!'

This late in the day, she expected the butcher would have little left, but she was a regular and sometimes he hid a piece of tripe or a couple of sausages under the counter for her. She was in luck, two sausages. They often seemed to have more sawdust than meat, but they filled the belly. And he slid a bone in her bag as well. She could use it to make a stew, getting the marrow out with a knitting needle. It always added to the flavour.

'Here you are, ducks,' he said with a wink. 'I remember how you helped my missus when one of the nippers was poorly.'

The butcher's friendliness and the conversation with the pilot couldn't help but increase her feelings of belonging in the East End.

As she tucked her sausages into her shopping bag and headed back outside, the sun broke through the clouds, bringing some welcome warmth to her face. She took a deep breath and allowed herself to feel hopeful for the first time in ages. Perhaps her poor country would pull through and beat the evil Nazis.

Walking down the street, she saw children playing with their carts, or playing hopscotch or jacks. Despite their hardships they still found fun and laughter in the everyday. It reminded her that amidst the chaos of war and uncertainty, there was still happiness to be had. She felt thankful for moments like these and resolved to remember them when she felt low.

Her step lighter, she continued walking, her mind on the vegetables she'd need for her meal, but she was distracted by shouting and screaming coming from round the corner where there were a couple of greengrocers' stalls.

She rushed round, fear guiding her steps.

The sight that met her eyes caught her breath. Two big schoolboys were harassing a smaller schoolgirl. One boy had hair so short it must have been shaven. The other had floppy, curly brown hair. Both had hatred in their eyes. Still in her uniform, the girl looked about ten years old. She had dropped her school bag and gas mask case.

Crouching down, she was trying to defend herself from their words and blows.

'Go on, apologise! You killed Jesus!' one boy was shouting as he shoved her over.

'Yeah, Yid girl, go on, say you're sorry!'

Mavis looked around and saw lots of people watching the scene. Some looked too scared to intervene, fear showing on their faces and through their tense body language. Others looked like they agreed with what the thugs were saying, seeming unperturbed by what was happening. One woman, to Mavis's surprise, raised her arm with a tight fist – a fascist salute.

'Blackshirt!' The word spread through the crowd like a virus, and they all turned to the woman, amazement and horror on their faces. She looked around, hoping for support, but seeing none, quickly hurried away.

Mavis felt a fury rising inside her. Her fists clenched, and her anger rose like a tidal wave. Her face began to flush and her chest tightened. How dare these boys bully this girl like this? Who did they think they were to treat a defenceless girl that way?

Without thinking twice or considering the danger she might be in, she strode forward and marched up to the thugs.

'What's going on 'ere?' she demanded, her voice loud and incensed. 'Leave that girl alone! Now!'

They looked up at her and sneered. Their faces were like pumpkin jack-o'-lanterns – twisted in angry grimaces. Their shoulders were tense and their fists were clenched, ready for violence.

'Oh, yeah, what you goin' to do about it, old lady?'

They were the last words they spoke. Mavis was only in her late thirties – no one was going to call her old and get away with it. She'd worked out they weren't much older than the girl. Their baby-smooth cheeks showed they weren't shaving yet, and they had the physique of boys on the cusp of adulthood, but not there yet.

Giving them no warning, she pulled her arm back and swung her bag at the first one's head. Then, as he tried unsuccessfully to duck, she did the same with the other one before he had time to move away. Her bag was heavy and made a gratifying thud as it hit each of them. Then, dropping her bags, she stepped forward and grabbed each of them by the ear, yanking them hard. Their heads bent forward as they tried to escape her grip, but she held on tight. They struggled, trying to pull her hand away, but her hold was not to be broken.

The young girl looked at her gratefully, and then ran away while she had the chance.

Mavis pushed the boys down and let go of their ears.

'Go on then, bugger off, you pair of cowards!' she shouted, swinging her bag threateningly again.

For a few seconds, it seemed as if they'd challenge her again, or even punch her, but then one of them shrugged.

'Come on, let's leave the old bitch. We can get 'er another time.'

They slunk off, shouting rude names at her.

As Mavis watched them walk towards a side street, heads and shoulders down, bodies rigid with anger, she muttered to herself, 'Lily-livered louts.'

A few people applauded her actions, and one woman came over and patted her on the back.

'Well done, love. You did good. Dustbin lids like them two need a good kicking. Wish I'd bin brave enough.'

Mavis scanned the crowd for any familiar faces of her neighbours and friends, but her gaze landed on the Jewish girl, who was hiding behind some people. She had pale skin and her lips trembled, but it was her eyes that held Mavis's attention – they were large and dark, filled with fear and desperation. The girl clutched her school bag tightly, her knuckles whitening as if someone might snatch it away from her at any second.

Mavis felt her throat constrict. She knew that feeling all too well – of having something precious taken away from you, with no way of getting it back. It was a feeling she had experienced more than once in her life. So she did the only thing she could do – she reached out her hand and looked the girl in the eyes. For a moment, it felt like time had stopped.

Uncertain, the girl stepped closer, and Mavis noticed her shaking hands and the tears that had started to well up in her eyes.

Mavis knew then that she had been right – she needed to keep her safe. Without a word, she took the girl's hand and pulled her away from the crowd, and they hurried off together, two strangers bound by an unspoken bond of understanding and shared fear.

'Come on, let's get you 'ome.'

'W... w... what?' the girl stammered, her voice shaking.

'You 'eard me,' Mavis said, her voice kind, but brooking no objection. 'Come on, let's get you back to your 'ome.'

'W... w... why?'

Mavis looked at her, puzzled. 'Why, what?'

'Why are you helping me? You don't even know me. I'm a Jew.'

Mavis shrugged. 'Why wouldn't I 'elp you? I don't care what religion you are. You were being bullied. No one should 'ave to put up with that.'

'I only live down there,' the girl said, pointing. 'My name is Eva. My mum will be waiting for me.'

Mavis was relieved that Eva lived in a different direction to the one the boys had taken.

'Come on, then, it's not much out of my way. I'll drop you at the door, then 'ead 'ome meself. Time I was cooking my dinner. By the way, me old mum gave me a good tip. Always carry a pot of pepper in your pocket. One you can easily reach. Then if you get bother like that, you can throw it in their eyes.'

Eva gave a little smile. 'I'll do that. Thank you.'

Mavis squeezed her hand. 'And another tip. Try to knee them in the goolies.' She paused. 'Do you know what they are?'

'I've got an older brother, so yes, I do.'

'And if they're too tall, kick them in the shins, hard, then aim your bag at their goolies.' She held up her bag. 'My bag's got me out of more than one scrape. You just saw that. With your schoolbooks, yours'll be 'eavy enough to do some damage.'

They walked together in companionable silence until they reached Eva's door.

'Would you like to come in?' she asked. 'My mother would want to thank you, I know.'

But Mavis's energy had drained like water down a plughole. Although she had seemed brave during the set-to with the boys, she was still feeling discombobulated, and just wanted to sit down with a cup of tea, or better still, a glass of stout.

'That's very sweet of you,' she said with a smile. 'But I gotta be on my way. Remember what I said now!' She gave the girl a hug and walked home. The stew would have to wait. She'd stop off at the fish and chip shop, thankful they weren't rationed.

As she queued in the chippy, she saw the woman who'd spoken to her after the incident.

'Fancy seeing you again,' she said. 'Too frazzled to cook, I shouldn't wonder.'

Mavis sighed. 'You're right there. And I was just thinking 'ow things have changed round 'ere of late. It was only, what, two or three years ago we was all out in the street together stopping that fascist Mosley and all 'is Jew-hating mates.'

The woman was getting her money out of her purse.

'Yeah, I was there. Bet you was, too. And we won, didn't we! We showed them bastards that we protect our own, Jews or not.'

'Well, 'e's inside now and damn good job, that is. The rotten British Union of Fascists is banned too. Yet 'ere we are with young lads treating that girl like that. It's almost like that awful man Hitler 'as got into their 'eads somehow.'

'Next!' the chippy man called, interrupting their conversation.

'One cod and chips and a pickled onion, please,' Mavis said. She turned to the other woman as she was leaving. 'Lovely to talk to you, sweet'eart. 'Ope we meet again.'

10

A TRAGEDY

When Cordelia woke up that morning, she stretched and smiled, thinking of the day ahead. It was Robert's day in the library, her favourite day of the week. As she opened the curtains, she saw it was raining outside, but she didn't care. She hummed a tune, grateful for her life. She had a job she loved and friends and family who cared for her. Working in the East End showed her every day how blessed she was.

She always dressed professionally for work, but decided to wear a bright red lipstick for a change. If she was honest with herself, it was because it was Robert's day. She looked in the mirror and smiled. Rosalind said she looked like Jean Harlow. She didn't, but the lipstick certainly made her look more glamorous.

The library day began as usual. Bert rushing in to read the papers, the old Jewish professor coming in to study whatever it was he studied, and the usual assortment of people she enjoyed meeting. She was especially pleased to see little Hetty with her mother.

Standing on tiptoes to reach the desk, Hetty slid her book across.

'I finished this,' she said proudly. 'I can read all the words.' She bit her lip. 'Well, most of them. You got another book for me?'

Her mother stood behind her, looking on proudly.

'Why don't you go with your mummy and choose another book? Or even two? You know where to go.'

Mrs Gregory, her mother, looked at the diphtheria vaccination poster.

'Oh, I keep meaning to see about that. Can the doctor here do it?'

'Not today, I'm afraid. Best to go to see your doctor. He'll arrange it.'

Jane was stamping someone else's book and muttered to herself, 'I must do that, too.'

Things were ready for Robert, and Derek, looking not quite his usual self, was sitting on a chair, waiting for more patients to arrive.

'You okay?' Cordelia asked. 'You look a bit pale.'

He clenched his fist and gently punched himself in the chest. 'Just a bit of heartburn. Get it sometimes. Must've eaten me porridge too quick.'

The familiar sound of Robert's steps made Cordelia turn round. He was flushed from hurrying.

'Sorry I'm a bit late. The road I usually go on got bombed last night.'

The patients already waiting stopped their conversation at this, but he said nothing more, picked up his coat and bag, and went into his consulting room.

There was a full house to see him. Cordelia was grateful to see that Derek was keeping those waiting amused as usual. She noticed, though, that he didn't have as much energy as usual, but shrugged it off.

''Ere,' he was saying. 'Fancy a joke to pass the time? I know a good 'un. We're in a library so I'd better say it quiet. This train, see, a passenger train, was packed to the gills. In this one compartment there was this old lady, a German soldier 'ome on leave, a cracker of a young French woman and a young French man.'

He looked around to make sure he had everyone's attention.

'Then the train goes into a tunnel, see, and no one can see a thing. But there's the sound of a kiss, clear as anything. Then the sound of a slap. When the train comes out of the tunnel, the German 'as a terrible black eye. So unlucky, 'e thinks. The French man gets the kiss and I get the blame. Well done, thinks the old lady. You stood up to that brute.' Derek paused for effect. 'But the young woman is confused. Why would that German kiss that old lady? The French man, though, 'e thinks, I'm a clever sod. I kissed the back of my 'and, hit the German and got away with it!'

He bent over double, laughing, and the others laughed with him.

But then he groaned and collapsed to the floor, clutching his chest.

For a few seconds they looked at him in disbelief, but then they all rushed to help. Cordelia had been at the desk and ran over. She could see Derek was in agony, and there was a film of sweat on his forehead. She ran to Robert's door and opened it without knocking.

'I think Derek's had a heart attack!' she cried and ran back, pushing the waiting people aside. 'Make room for the doctor to see to him.'

Before she'd finished her sentence, Robert was there, moving aside two older men who stood looking at the scene, transfixed.

Robert knelt beside Derek, and Cordelia couldn't help but notice how his muscles bulged beneath his shirt as he pushed down on Derek's chest, pressing on his chest regularly and counting one-two-three over and over again. Ashamed she should think of such a thing when Derek's life was in danger, she felt a flush creep up her neck, and she had to look away.

'Call an ambulance,' he barked at her, but Jane had already called one.

'It's on its way,' she said. 'I'll close the doors now.'

The wait for the ambulance seemed interminable. Cordelia sent the waiting patients away and moved some things around to give them some privacy. Some library users had come to see what was going on, but others seemed quite oblivious. Jane began to ask them to leave.

The whole time, Robert was pressing on Derek's chest, still counting one-two-three, one-two-three. He told Cordelia there was nothing she could do, and she paced up and down, feeling utterly useless.

Finally, the ambulance arrived, and the crew came in and took over. One continued pressing on Derek's chest while the other got a stretcher ready. They put him on it and carried him out to the ambulance.

Inevitably, there was a small crowd of people outside wondering what had happened, but the men were experienced in dealing with situations like that. After telling Robert and Cordelia which hospital they were going to, they took off at speed, their siren blaring and light flashing.

Back in the library, Robert collapsed into a chair and took deep breaths, trying to get his heart rate back to normal. Cordelia fetched a glass of water for him.

'Thanks,' he said. 'I didn't expect that this morning.'

Mavis came bustling over.

'I 'ope I'm not speaking out of turn, but you two look done in. Why don't you go to the café next door and 'ave a cuppa and a bun? You'll soon feel better.' She turned to Robert. 'Will Derek live, do you think?'

Robert shook his head.

'I'd like to think so, but it's probably a slim chance.'

* * *

They took Mavis's advice and went to Jim's café. Normally the smell of bacon from inside made Cordelia's mouth water, but she was too tense from what had happened to notice.

They ordered teas and buns and sat across from each other, unaware of the people around them. At first, neither spoke, alone with their thoughts and worry for Derek, but soon they relaxed.

'I'll phone the hospital in a while and see what's happened, then let you know,' Robert said.

As he passed her the sugar, his fingertips lightly grazed hers. A tingle of electricity shot up her arm and she had to fight the instinct to move away quickly. But she stayed looking at him, lingering in the moment as their eyes met. As they spoke – about Derek, about the library, about his work – she allowed herself to admire the way his blonde hair sometimes flopped over his forehead, and the twinkle in his eyes as he spoke animatedly about his job. Her heart fluttered despite her attempt to stay guarded, but she reminded herself that these were dangerous times, not conducive to courting or romantic entanglements.

'We'd better go,' Cordelia said, putting on her coat. 'I hope we'll have time for a cuppa again some time, but I must get the library reopened.'

He touched her arm lightly. 'Yes, I hope that, too. And I'd better get to the hospital. I've got a ward round in a couple of hours. I'm sorry I didn't get to see many patients this morning.'

'Next week,' she said, and, feeling bold, she bent forward and kissed him lightly on the cheek.

* * *

'It's not Jasper, Mother, it's *Mrs Taylor's* brother, Derek. He had a heart attack and died. That's why I'm here.'

Her unannounced arrival had thrown her mother into a state of panic, wondering what was wrong and expecting to hear that something terrible had happened to Jasper. But when she heard what had happened, all her mother could do was nod.

Cordelia took off her coat and then headed towards the kitchen, where she could smell some sort of meat cooking. Her mother made to follow her, but Cordelia signalled to leave this terrible task to her.

All the way home, she had practised what to say to her beloved friend. It seemed there was no right way to give such bad news. Whatever she said would cause great distress to the lovely woman.

Taking a deep breath, she knocked softly on the kitchen door and went in. Mrs Taylor was at the sink, her arms elbow deep in suds. The wireless was playing a lively song and at first she didn't hear Cordelia, who looked at her, remembering all the good times she had spent in this warm and inviting room. And she knew she would break this wonderful woman's heart with her news.

When Mrs Taylor looked up, she saw Cordelia and started.

'Oh, you gave me a fright, love. I didn't...' She stopped, her eyes narrowing as she looked intently at her. 'What is it? Something's wrong, isn't it?'

* * *

'She's gone home, Mother. I told her she could go straight away. She'll need at least a week to arrange her brother's funeral and empty his rooms.'

Her mother's eyes widened. 'But what will we do...?'

Cordelia shook her head, disappointed. 'Her only brother has just died and you're worried about your dinner. Is that right, Mother?'

Her mother went pink and blustered. 'Of course not. It's terrible for her, but has she...?'

'Yes, tonight's meal is ready and in the oven. I dare say we can manage to bring it to the dining room on our own. And Mrs Smith from the village will help out from tomorrow, no doubt, if you let her know.' Her mother's entitled response to the dreadful news left Cordelia struggling to be polite. 'I'm going for a walk,' she said and headed to her bedroom to change into her outdoor shoes.

* * *

Trying to suppress her irritation, Cordelia strode away from the house, breathing in the fresh country air – the slightly sweet scent of early fallen leaves, the rich earthy smell of the soil, damp after overnight rain, and, faintly, the woody smell of a bonfire somewhere in the distance. The trees stood tall and proud, branches reaching towards the sky, still holding their summer greens. The soft rustling of the breeze through the trees was like a gentle symphony, a melody of nature's calls, as if the trees themselves were whispering of the changing season soon to come.

After walking for ten minutes, Cordelia felt herself beginning to relax for the first time since she'd had to deliver such awful news to Mrs Taylor. Here, in the countryside, life seemed to carry on as if war didn't exist. People in the village still smiled and laughed, sheep grazed in the fields and birds chirped in the trees. There were no long queues in the food shops, as so many people grew their own vegetables or bought them from the farms surrounding them. It was almost like being in a dream – a dream of what life could be if the bombs had never fallen.

The pitter-patter of rain touched her face, causing her to gaze upward, where billowing clouds painted the sky in shades of grey. With no shield of an umbrella or raincoat to protect her, she reluctantly made the decision to retreat back to the house. Hurrying, her steps became more purposeful and her eyes fixed on the path ahead. She failed to notice the treacherous pitfall that lay beneath the cloak of long grass.

With a cry, she stepped into a rabbit hole, no larger than a fist, but big enough to make her twist her ankle. The pain was excruciating and as she pulled her foot free, she cried out again, her face a picture of agony. She tried again and again to stand upright but each time, the pain defeated her. Just as she was beginning to despair of ever getting back to the house, she heard a rough voice behind her. 'You looks in a right pickle there, Miss Cordelia, and no mistake. Want a lift in me wheelbarrow? You loved that when you was a little nipper.'

Cordelia had never been more pleased to see anyone in her life. There stood old Herbert, the man who had looked after the gardens for more years than she'd been alive. As always, he had a twinkle in his eye and a ready smile. He lifted his old gardening hat and scratched his head, seemingly unaware of the rain.

'Herbert! You're a lifesaver! If you help me up, I'd love a ride in your barrow.'

He was as gentle as he could be, but she still whimpered with pain as she got upright and almost fell into the barrow. Her legs hung over the side and she clutched her damaged ankle, trying to stop it being jolted.

'Hold on tight, girl,' Herbert commanded. 'I'll be as gentle as I can, but the ground's a bit rough hereabouts.'

He helped her into the house and her mother, alarmed, insisted she sit on the sofa with her legs up – surrounding her with pillows and covering her with a blanket.

'We must get Dr Curtis,' she said, ringing the bell for the maid.

Cordelia sat up straighter. 'You will not get Dr Curtis, Mother. I only need a bandage on my ankle.'

Her mother sighed. 'But you must stay until you are completely well. I insist.'

That could take several weeks, Cordelia knew. She also knew she'd go crazy spending all that time with her mother, no matter how much she loved her.

'I'll stay until the day after tomorrow, then I'll go back to London. James can take me. It'll make a change from him running you back and forth to the shops. I'll manage with a walking stick and taxis.'

The next evening, the last before Cordelia returned to London, her mother hastily arranged a dinner party. She invited some of Cordelia's old friends and an eligible bachelor, Atticus.

Cordelia had been dreading it all day. She looked forward to seeing her friends, of course, but knew her mother would contrive to ensure she spent time with this man with his awful name. But she put on her best dress as requested and limped downstairs, leaning heavily on her stick. She was deliberately late, having heard the others arrive.

As she opened the door, a braying voice dominated the room, and she knew it must be the man her mother had chosen for her. He wore a garish red waistcoat that clashed with his yellow shirt and grey jacket. As she looked in, he looked at her with a glint in his eye and she had to stop herself from shuddering.

Her mother immediately began to sing Cordelia's praises, which made her cringe. Her friends, seeing what was happening, caught her eye and she saw they were suppressing smiles.

Atticus, though, did not share Cordelia's virtues. He talked about himself incessantly throughout the first course, showing off, name-dropping and not even pretending to be interested in anyone else present. Cordelia let it go on for half an hour, then, her temper rising, she held up her hand.

'Atticus, you're being very rude. You have let no one else speak and I'm interested to know what my *friends* have been doing.' She emphasised the word friends. She knew she was being appallingly rude but she had spent her life being polite to men who assumed they were more important than the women in the room. Who expected everyone to listen to them, no matter how banal or stupid their comments were. Somehow, she found she didn't care. She realised she would never have said anything like this before working in the library. She hid a smile as she thought she probably sounded exactly like Mavis.

Atticus gaped at her, his mouth flapping like paper caught in the wind, and he stuttered, trying to take back control. But before he got the chance, Cordelia looked across to a friend on the other side of the table.

'What's been happening with you, Caroline?'

Atticus never regained the dominance he was used to, and was thoroughly ignored for the rest of the evening. To everybody's relief, he made an excuse and left early.

The group made sure he'd really gone, then burst out laughing, relieved that his presence no longer dampened their enjoyment of the evening. Cordelia's friends wanted to know all about her life in London and her new job, and they were aghast when she told them how many people there lived in poverty.

'Surely they can do more to help themselves!' Amelia said with a frown. 'There are always options.'

Cordelia bit her tongue. It wasn't Amelia's fault she had led such a sheltered life.

'I'm afraid they have very few options. Lack of money and education stop them moving forward.'

This led to a long discussion about life chances, and Cordelia was delighted that by the end of it they'd come to an agreement. Her friends decided that they wouldn't simply knit socks for the troops or help their mothers' fundraising efforts, they'd collect money to help the poor in Silvertown.

* * *

Cordelia got out of the taxi and began to limp towards St Matthew's church, using her stick for support. Usually she liked cemeteries – reading the old names on the weathered headstones led her to wonder about the lives of people who had lived long ago – but the wind had been building all morning, and it seemed to grow stronger with every step she took, allowing no time to look around.

As she stood near the entrance to the church, willing herself to go in, she reflected on how the place felt like a living thing. It blew her hat off her head and she fumbled to catch it before it fell to the damp ground. Around her, the ancient trees groaned as if in pain.

An elderly woman, someone she recognised from the library, came up beside her.

'Sad day, isn't it?' she said. 'We could always count on Derek to cheer us up.'

But the weather was too vile for them to stay where they were and they stepped inside, feeling the sudden stillness after the wildness of the wind. Cordelia paused briefly, letting her eyes adjust to the darkness, then she approached Derek's casket and placed a lily on it.

Mrs Taylor was in the front row. Cordelia bent and kissed her on the cheek before taking a seat in a pew further back. Funerals for the elderly were often not well attended, but Derek's was. His many friends had come to say goodbye to him.

They were singing the second hymn, 'Abide with Me', when there was a movement in her pew. Cordelia glanced round and, to her surprise, saw Robert quietly shuffling in. He sat next to her. He smiled at her and picked up the prayer book.

The vicar's sermon showed that he knew Derek well. He listed the many good things he had done for people in his community and his country, causing several people to get out their hankies and wipe their wet cheeks.

At the end of the service, everyone stood in silence as the pall-bearers slowly carried the casket out. Cordelia wanted to follow them to the graveside, but her ankle was beginning to hurt and she knew it would be too much for her.

Cordelia watched as the mourners walked towards the grave, feeling a wave of sadness wash over her. The wind had died down as if it had been exhausted by its own exertions and now everything seemed very still.

Robert had stayed behind as well.

'I'm afraid I don't have very long. I have a clinic in an hour.' He noticed her stick and bandaged ankle. 'I see you've been in the wars. What's the problem?'

Despite the solemnness of the day, she tingled at his nearness and unconsciously leaned towards him.

'It's only a sprain.'

His eyes grew wide. 'You're lucky it's not worse, then. But I can see that your bandage is coming undone. Let me redo it for you before I go.' He looked around. 'There's no one left to see. Put your leg on my knee,' he said softly.

Cordelia felt a familiar flutter in her stomach as she did as instructed, a more intimate thing than she'd ever imagined would happen. As he began to gently undo the bandage, she looked around the church as a way of keeping her attraction to him at bay. He was careful, taking his time as he unwrapped the cloths and exposed her bare skin. She could feel his breath against her leg, and it sent a shiver through her body. His fingertips were soft and gentle, and the warmth of his touch sent goosebumps rising across her skin.

When he'd finished, he stopped and gazed into her eyes, then gently leaned over and kissed her lightly on her cheek.

'There,' he finally said. 'That should do it. Are you going back to the library? I can give you a lift on my way to the hospital.'

'That would be lovely. It's Mavis's day off, so I'll have to miss the wake and get back to work.'

As they walked to his car from the church, he offered her his arm for support. His nearness made her heart beat faster, distracting her from the pain in her ankle. His presence was almost dizzying and her heart began to race. They walked in comfortable silence along the church path with its ancient flagstones. The sound of birds chirping and the church organ still playing seemed to blend together, creating a soothing background for the two of them.

In the car, the warmth enveloped them and Robert started the engine, apologising again that he had to head off quickly.

'What made you come?' she asked. She knew how busy his life was.

He turned on his indicator to go left, narrowly missing a cyclist who was wobbling all over the road. 'I didn't know Derek well, but he was such a lovely chap. Always ready with a smile and a joke. He probably did the patients as much good as I did, so I wanted a chance to say goodbye to him. And I've regretted so much that I didn't manage to save him.' He turned towards the library. 'If I'm honest, there was another reason, too.'

'What was that?'

Cordelia looked at him, but he was concentrating on the road and didn't look at her.

She saw him take a deep breath before speaking.

'I knew you'd be there,' he said and pulled over to the side of the road. 'Here is your destination, madam,' he joked.

He got out of the car, went round to her side, and opened her door for her.

After helping her up the steps, he smiled his sweet smile. 'I'll see you again soon,' he said, and to her surprise he kissed her hand, then got back into the car.

Cordelia watched him go, her mind in turmoil. He went to the funeral to see her? Did he really say that? It must mean he had feelings for her.

The sudden sound of loud boots on the library steps brought her back to the moment. She turned to see the man they called the Captain, in a green and yellow uniform, coming up the steps. He grinned and saluted at her, then held out his arm.

'Cor, you've been in the wars, girl,' he said, looking at her bandaged ankle. 'Come on, I'll 'elp you in.'

After a moment's hesitation, she put her hand on his arm, surprised to find he smelled of Lifebuoy soap, carbolic and antiseptic.

'Thank you, Captain,' she said with a smile.

'Always 'appy to 'elp a lady!' he said, saluting again, and headed off into the library stacks to find his next read.

11

THE BLITZ BEGINS

9 September 1940

'Have you been spending nights in shelters?' Cordelia asked Jane and Mavis when they had a moment mid-afternoon. It had been a busy day, with many women borrowing romances. Something to cheer them up, they said. Quite a few read several a week.

Cordelia had made all three of them tea, which they discreetly placed behind the counter, or as sure as eggs is eggs, customers like Bert would be demanding a cup.

Jane groaned. 'We go to the Anderson shelter next door. Eight of us squashed in there.' She looked at Cordelia. 'Have you ever been in one?'

Cordelia was too embarrassed to tell them about the very comfortable shelter in the basement of her block of flats. There were folding camp beds, pillows, clean blankets, a radiogram, books, magazines and tea and coffee. So rather than say that, she just asked what it was like in the Anderson shelters.

'Horrible,' Jane said with a sigh. 'The one we go to has bunk beds, but it's cold and damp, and if there's been a lot of rain, we can be standing in an inch of water. And if the bombing gets going, we'll be deafened. We can hear all the cars and things like they're in our garden.'

''Ere, you gonna stamp this book or what?' It was one of their regulars, Fred, looking at them expectantly. He wore an eyepatch but never said how he'd lost an eye.

Mavis stepped forward to help him. 'Sorry, Fred, we was just talking about Anderson shelters.'

He grunted. 'Nasty things. I 'ide under the stairs. Bit squashed, but at least it's dry. Still, we've bin lucky so far.'

He then saluted, tucked his book under his arm, and headed outside, buttoning up his jacket as he went.

'It's bin a bit quiet this week,' Mavis said and took a sip of her tea. 'Few more kids, though. I read one and a 'alf million kiddies 'ave been evacuated! Imagine! Where do they put 'em all?'

'But some have come back, haven't they?' Cordelia said. 'You must have seen some of them roaming the streets like I have. If the council always did everything as fast as they closed their schools, London would be perfect.'

There had been air-raid warnings most nights, but not until the evenings when the library was closed. And, thankfully, few bombs had been dropped so far.

But this was the day that pattern would change.

Cordelia was in her office, trying to balance the financial books, when the air-raid siren went. She frowned and looked at her watch. It was only four o'clock. She glanced around at the pile of papers on her desk. Her hands shaking, she threw them in the filing cabinet and locked it. Then she picked up her bag and gas mask and limped into the main library, using a stick for support and cursing her sprained ankle. Readers were already hurrying to the doors, and she could see that Mavis and Jane were running around, checking no one was left behind.

The rise and fall of the siren made thinking difficult, but soon her staff shouted, 'Library empty!' and they ran for the door together, breathless with fear.

They locked the library doors and silently hoped it would still be standing when the raid was over. If they were lucky, it would be another false alarm, and they'd be free to go home before nightfall.

Out in the street, it was chaos, with so many people, cars, and horses and carts, mothers with prams, owners of fruit and veg stalls, all heading for safety. The air-raid wardens directed them to the Underground station, blowing their whistles and helping the less mobile.

Using the station wasn't strictly permitted by the government, but that rule was ignored by many, all desperate for a place of safety. The trouble was, not everyone chose to go there, so people were dashing off in all directions, often getting in each other's way. Some headed home, and some to an alternative shelter. The barrow boys were pushing their carts to who knew where, and mothers pushed their prams while holding the hands of their bigger children. The noise of the feet and people's conversations were impossible to hear over the sound of the siren.

Overhead, it seemed as if night had arrived prematurely. The sky, thick with hundreds of German planes, was an absolutely terrifying sight. The earth shuddered beneath the weight of bombs falling, and flames erupted in many places, accompanied by sounds of destruction that shook their entire bodies. Brilliant searchlights criss-crossed through the cloudy afternoon light like jagged lightning as deafening guns fired from London parks. The sirens continued to wail in despair.

One much louder explosion momentarily stopped them.

'That's one of the factories in the docks,' Mavis said, shaking her head.

Slowed down because of her painful ankle, Cordelia urged Jane and Mavis to leave her and get to safety. But they refused and helped her, almost carrying her, their breathing heavy with the effort. They had to wait to go down the steps to the Underground because of the sheer volume of people doing the same. But at last they were descending, the stale air soon reaching their noses. But that was preferable to the smell of destruction they were running from. Cordelia sent up a grateful thanks that her ankle hadn't caused them to be caught in the bombing.

All three of them had heard tales of what the stations were like, but none were prepared for what they saw. It seemed like hundreds of people were already there, and from what they could see, many had been there some time, making themselves at home in this strange environment. It had the benefit of being warm and dry, but the stale smell got worse the further in they went and it made breathing difficult. To their surprise, there were mosquitoes in force, looking for a bloody feast.

There was only about a yard on the edge of the platform clear so newcomers like themselves were searching for space between those already there. The platform was so covered in people, those lying down almost looked like corpses, their bodies so close together it was hard to find an unoccupied half-yard of ground. Some people were alone, but many were in groups, often with children. Seeking a space big enough for the three of them, they sometimes had to step over people who'd sprawled out as if they had the whole platform to themselves.

It seemed like everyone had something to occupy them: some people were playing cards, others had flasks of tea and snacks, still others had magazines and books, and almost everyone had some form of bedding. Cordelia wondered how they'd all got settled so soon after the siren going off. Then she remembered hearing that some people spent a lot of their time underground for safety.

Mavis looked at the other two. 'We should 'ave brought blankets.'

'I only have a thick cardigan,' Cordelia said.

'Me too,' Jane replied, shaking her head.

They found themselves just enough space and sat down, huddled close together. Despite the depth of the platform, they could still hear bombs dropping and sometimes the earth itself seemed to shudder. They were terrified, but like everyone else on the platform, they acted as if being here with destruction happening over their heads was an everyday event.

'Right,' Mavis said in her no-nonsense way. ''Ow're we going to pass the ruddy time? And don't say playing "I Spy" neither!'

Cordelia opened her bag and produced a pack of cards. 'I've had these in my bag for ages. I'd forgotten all about them until I saw all the others playing. And if you two haven't got a book each, you're not the wonderful librarians I thought you were.'

'Course I 'ave,' Mavis said, and took out a copy of *The Scarlet Pimpernel*.

'Any good?' Jane asked, digging round for her book.

'Dunno, I 'aven't started it yet. But if this damn raid goes on all night, I'll 'ave it finished.'

They tried to play cards but found they all knew different versions of rummy as well as other games, so they gave up the effort and opened their books instead. But they'd barely read a page when a man at the other end of the station started playing an accordion.

'Any requests?' he asked.

'Something to cheer us up!' a woman shouted. ''Ow about "Jeepers Creepers"?'

The man played his accordion softly and began to hum, gradually getting more lively and loud, the melody rising up like a ghost in the air.

Cordelia watched as he looked up from his accordion and glanced across the station, his eyes sparkling in the dim light. Nearby, a group of friends sang along, their faces lit up with brief happiness despite the sadness that clung to their everyday life. Encouraged by the response to his music, the musician began to play other cheerful songs – 'Dancing Cheek to Cheek', 'I Got Rhythm', 'Tea for Two', 'Walking My Baby Back Home'.

The atmosphere, previously tense, lifted as they sang. Within thirty seconds, everyone was singing along; the music energising and soothing their weary hearts and minds. The man kept playing for half an hour, making their evening less frightening.

'I love that "Dancing Cheek to Cheek",' Mavis said. 'It reminds me of when I was young and stupid and loved dancing a bit too close to the lads.'

'"Rhapsody in Blue" was my favourite at the dances,' Jane said. 'I met a very special man dancing to that.'

''Ere,' Mavis said when the music stopped. 'You've never told us about your love life, Cordelia. We've got plenty of time to listen now.'

'Mavis!' Jane said, looking aghast. 'You're asking a very personal question. Cordelia may not want to talk about it.'

Cordelia shook her head. 'It's okay, it was a long time ago now. I met Edwin in Cambridge. It was the end of my first year and I was sitting by the river with a couple of friends, enjoying a break from revision before exams started. He and two of his friends were nearby when I noticed him looking over at us. One of his friends dared him to come to talk to us. I blushed so hard when he made a beeline for me and ignored my friends! He had this amazing smile that could melt hearts at a hundred paces and film-star good looks. We all chatted for a while, then the others drifted off and before long it was just he and I walking along the river, talking about our plans for the future. I felt as if I'd known him for years.'

'Never trust a charming man,' Jane said.

Mavis chuckled. 'Sounds like he slayed you, all right.'

Cordelia felt her cheeks flush with embarrassment. 'Yes. I was a fool, all right.'

'So you met this drop-dead gorgeous man. What happened then?'

'This is going to sound like a fairy tale. But next morning a massive bunch of red roses arrived at my room in Girton. You'd have thought it was Valentine's Day. I couldn't believe it. All the other girls were so jealous. There was a card with a romantic poem on it, too.'

'Wowza! So all you'd done was go for a walk and he sent you roses. I wish that would happen to me. No one has ever been that romantic with me,' Jane said, looking wistful. 'What was the poem?'

Cordelia looked away, remembering her confusion at the gift. It seemed too much for such a short acquaintance. 'I don't remember. I tore the card up.'

'Really? I'd have kept it to show my grandchildren. Anyway, he sounds just brilliant. What happened then? I'm surprised you didn't grab him immediately.'

Cordelia took another deep breath. 'Like I said, it started like a fairy tale: presents, flowers, beautiful cards, wanting to see me all the time... I had trouble getting him to leave me alone. It was flattering, but I was studying for my exams at the time and they were important, even if the rotten university wouldn't give us women degrees. I wasn't going to fail them just because I'd met a handsome man. And then...'

Mavis's eyes opened wider. 'Then...? Come on, I can't stand the suspense. Was he married? A mass murderer? A homosexual? After you for your money?'

'None of that. He had his own money from what I could see. He was certainly splashing it around. But he followed me when I went home for summer holidays. He said he had a friend nearby and he'd stay with him.'

Her story was interrupted when two little girls nearby began to argue over who owned the doll one of them clutched. Their mother solved the issue by taking it off them and putting it in her bag. 'Now, neither of you'll have it!' She handed them a comic each and told them to calm down.

But Mavis and Jane hadn't forgotten about Cordelia's story. 'So, where were you with your story...' Mavis said, then paused. 'Oh, yes, he didn't have any serious impediments to marriage as the vicars say, so what was it?'

'Well, he'd left a couple of messages for me which I'd ignored because I had this uneasy feeling about him. Strange, because I couldn't identify quite what it was. Then he turned up at my place, my parents' home as I now think of it. No warning, no invite. He just knocked on the front door, expecting to be made welcome. He'd brought with him the biggest box of chocolates I'd seen for ages.'

'What did your mum and dad think of him?' Jane asked.

'That's the thing. Edwin could charm the birds from the trees. Daddy was out and he soon had Mummy eating out of his hands. It seems she knew his mother from something or other years ago and that was good enough. I looked at her and could see she was hearing wedding bells.'

'So, come on, what was wrong with 'im?' Mavis asked. 'So far he sounds too good to be true.' She thought for a minute. 'Oh, I suppose you're going to say he was.'

'You're right there, Mavis. We met several times over the summer. We had meals out, lovely walks, picnics and drives to the coast. But then it got very strange. At first, I thought he was wonderful and he seemed to adore me. He was full of compliments about every single thing, my clothes, my looks, everything I said, but then...'

'Then...'

'Gradually it changed, and I could do nothing right without his approval. He told me what colours to wear, what length my dresses should be, who I should be friends with. And all the while saying he was giving me advice for my own good because he loved me so much and wanted me to be even more perfect. Wanted others to think well of me, too. Said he couldn't stand the idea that others may not see me as perfectly as he did. It was all so apparently gentle and kind that I barely noticed what he was doing at first and even took his advice on some things.'

Jane frowned. 'That doesn't sound like you, letting a man tell you what to do.'

'I know. Now I feel an absolute fool, but it was all so gradual, insidious. I can see that with hindsight. Not only that, but the advice, if we can call it that, was always given with protestations of love, presents, treats and all manner of good things. Sometimes it seemed as if he had taken over my mind. I'd lie in bed at night, going over and over everything, and couldn't make sense of it all. It was terribly confusing. I began to doubt myself about everything.'

Mavis grunted. 'It sounds ghastly. A fairy tale turned into a nightmare. Thank goodness you got rid of him. How on earth did you do it?'

'He had to go away for a few days, so I had time to take a step back and think. It gave me a chance to get things clear in my mind. Then an old school friend told me she'd heard of him and his tricks before. Tried to take over everything one of her friends did. She had a terrible time, nearly had a breakdown over it.'

'So you told 'im to bugger off? And 'e went?' Mavis asked, distracted by the girls who were fighting about the comics this time.

The all-clear was sounded and Cordelia was saved from having to say more about her sorry story. Some people were settling there in the Underground for the night, but others, like themselves, gathered their things together to leave.

As they made their way up the stairs, they found breathing increasingly difficult because of the dust showering them. And the air seemed to grow hotter, not colder as they expected.

Emerging from the station, they blinked in the daylight, and they looked around in horror.

'The whole town's burning!' Jane cried.

The streets were ablaze with orange flames that flickered and danced in the evening sky, making it look as if the whole city was on fire. The air was thick with the smouldering scent of burning buildings and the sounds of breaking glass and crackling fires echoed everywhere. People were running in every direction, screaming and shouting, while others like themselves stood frozen, staring in shock at the annihilation before them. They couldn't even make out where the familiar streets were, and the three women stood entranced, holding hands, looking around as they tried to take in what they were seeing.

They stayed like that until a warden shouted at them.

'Go! Get away from here! It's too dangerous to stay around here. You'll get in the way.'

Cordelia walked towards the library, thinking of the rest of the story about Edwin that she hadn't told her friends. Summer had been over by the time she told Edwin that she didn't want to see him any more. He wouldn't accept what she said, bombarding her with more gifts. She'd refused to see him and was glad when term started and she went back to Cambridge. Mistakenly, she assumed that was the end of it.

The trouble was, he was at the university too, and he still hadn't given up chasing her. But her friends rallied round when she told them what he'd been doing and they made sure he never got a chance to bother her. One or more of them was always with her when she went out, chaperoning her as if she were a Victorian lady. She returned all his letters and cards unopened and did the same with his gifts. It took several weeks, but finally he gave up. The weight of months of anxiety finally lifted from Cordelia's heart, like steam escaping off the last dregs of tea in her cup.

Her relief was enormous until she heard he'd replaced her with another student. She debated with her friends for ages on what she should do. She didn't want anyone else to suffer as she had, so decided to meet the girl.

Her heart racing in her chest, she'd stepped off the bus and walked slowly towards Fitzbillies café, where they'd arranged to meet.

Her mind was a jumble of thoughts when she pushed open the door and scanned the room. Spotting the student in the corner, she walked over, butterflies fluttering in her stomach.

Cordelia ordered tea for them both then sat opposite the young woman, whose name was Alice. She eyed Cordelia suspiciously, clearly confused as to why she was here and unwilling to begin the conversation.

Cordelia swallowed hard, her mouth dry. She had to do this. She had to tell Edwin's next victim the truth. Taking a deep breath, she launched into her story, explaining what Edwin had done to her and how he could potentially do the same again.

As Cordelia spoke, the young woman in front of her went through several different expressions. Suspicion turned to cautious interest then doubt and finally understanding before turning back to suspicion again. It looked at first like she was going to say something but then changed her mind. She didn't interrupt, though. She sat very still, took an occasional sip of her tea or dabbed at the corners of her mouth with a napkin and said nothing. But then her body language subtly changed, the way it does when you hear some completely unexpected news about someone you thought you knew well. Cordelia reached out and Alice took the hand she offered. Whether she believed Cordelia's story completely or not, Cordelia had done all she could. She wished Alice well and said her goodbyes.

She was so deep in her memories that she'd walked to the library without conscious thought, but was delighted to find it was still standing and intact.

Satisfied there was nothing she needed to do, she headed for home, having no hope that she would find any means of transport. It would be a long and difficult walk.

12

THE SCRAPBOOK

It was Saturday morning and Jane was relieved that her mother had gone out for the day. Time alone with little Helen in their own home was precious and she wanted to make the most of it.

'I've got an idea, sweetheart. How about we make a little scrapbook about your daddy and us?'

Helen frowned. 'What's a scrapbook?' she asked.

Jane tucked a strand of her daughter's hair out of her eyes and smiled warmly. 'It's a special sort of book you put precious memories in. You can write in it, or draw pictures, or even glue photos in if you want.' She was aware that soldier George had been gone for some time, and that Helen's memories of him would probably be hazy because she was so young. She took the photo of George off the mantlepiece and handed it to Helen. 'We've got some photos of Daddy we can put in. He's a brave soldier, keeping us all safe.'

'Even when I'm asleep?' Helen asked.

'Even when we're all asleep. He's working hard to stop a naughty man sending those bombs to us.'

She reached into her bag and pulled out a dusty beige scrapbook she'd found in the back of a cupboard at the library. The old book was faded and frayed, but showed few signs of use. There wasn't a title nor any writing on any of the pages.

Jane had been nervous about asking Cordelia if she could have it. Cordelia had no idea she was married, much less that she had a daughter. She thought Cordelia might ask why she wanted it, or say they needed the paper when it was so scarce. Instead, Cordelia had just told her to take it home with her.

She had already sorted out photos of Helen as a baby and even a few of George as a child. Sadly, she realised she only had a handful of him as an adult – one in uniform and two taken by a friend at their wedding. There were even fewer of her, but she'd found two of her mother. She laid them all out on the floor and sat beside Helen. 'How would you like to put them in the book?'

Helen looked blank. 'Um... I...'

Jane realised the question was too advanced for her. 'Shall we have a page for you, a page for Daddy, one for me and one for Nanny?'

At the word Nanny, Jane saw her daughter's body tense and she pushed the photos of her grandmother away. 'Mummy, why doesn't Nanny like me?'

Jane went cold. She'd thought she'd protected little Helen from the worst of her mother's nastiness. Helen's question showed she'd failed. 'Why do you say that, love?' she asked.

Helen's small body shook as she clung to her mother, her face screwed up with hurt. Jane had always been a comforting presence in the life of her daughter, but this time she felt helpless to stop the tears streaming down Helen's cheeks.

'Nanny's always angry with me,' Helen sobbed. 'And she shouts at me when you're not here. She says I'm an ugly girl and no one will ever love me.'

Jane felt a searing anger course through her. She had heard those words herself, many times, as a child. Her own mother had spoken those same dark, bitter words to her, until they felt like a part of her, ones that she could never quite shake. Now, it was like a horrible echo, those same words being spoken to her own daughter. She knew it was wrong, that it was dreadful to carry this hurtful legacy into the future, and she resolved to do something about it. She had very few savings, but moving into a single room somewhere might be an option. That would hardly be a wonderful place for her daughter to live in, but almost certainly better than being subjected to such bile from her grandmother. Jane sighed, even considering the other option, which was to let Helen be evacuated somewhere safe. Bombing was every night now and there was no way she could be sure of Helen's safety. She had to make a decision soon.

She soothed Helen, made her a drink of milk, then they settled down to work on the scrapbook. Helen insisted that the photos of her grandmother should not be in it.

Later, when Helen was tired and losing interest, Jane settled her in an armchair wrapped with a crochet blanket. She gave her her favourite book and within five minutes Helen had nodded off.

Quietly, not to disturb her, Jane opened her latest letter from George. She'd already read it twice and each reading made him seem nearer to her. Of course, it had taken a long time to reach her so there was no way of knowing what could have happened in the meantime.

She read again:

My darling Jane,

I have written two or three times lately so you may get a bundle of letters together. We have been very busy for the last few weeks and met with some success. I only wish I could tell you about it, but the censor would just cross it out. I'm very glad to say we are much better off for food. We have potatoes and other food stuffs – a better store than we've had for ages. But how I miss your cooking, my love. No one makes an apple tart like you!

You will remember that I had a chest infection, I am pleased to say that it is better now thanks to our wonderful medics.

Every day I pray that you and little Helen are safe. I have heard there has been a lot of bombing in London and feel terrified for you both. We soldiers expect such dangers. It is not fair that you should experience them, too.

When this wretched war is over, we could consider moving out of

London, perhaps to a small country town. I should be able to find work and the air will be so much healthier for our little one.

I'm afraid there is no more news at present, every day is much the same. But I love you and think of you both all the time.

All my love

George

Jane folded the letter again carefully and put it with his others, tied together with a red ribbon. Then, seeing that Helen was still sleeping soundly, she got out her pen and paper to write him a reply. She would make out that things were nowhere near as he feared, even though they were probably worse. There was no point in worrying him. She would have to sort out these things on her own.

13
CHANGE LOOMS

It was a blustery autumn afternoon and Cordelia hurried to the Underground station in Canning Town, holding on to her bright scarlet cloche hat with its bow on the side. The wind blew leaves and scraps of paper around her feet like a river current, pushing her towards the Tube entrance. Shivering, she increased her pace, longing to get out of the autumn chill.

As she walked from the library, she noticed the people around her yet again. Most had thin, inadequate coats for the cold weather. It was no surprise that the level of TB infections was increasing, especially as many people lived in unsanitary conditions. A barrage balloon caught her eye as a brief ray of sun shone on it. It seemed that there were more of them every week. Just yesterday a newspaper headline in the *Mirror* read 'London lit up by mass bombing'. And the *Daily Mail* headline was 'Terror from the sky'.

On the BBC news, they'd said the Germans were hoping to break the spirit of British people. So far, Cordelia thought, that wasn't happening. She overheard two people as she walked, talking about the night's bombing.

'My neighbours' house got a direct hit,' the woman said. 'Lucky we were all down the shelter. My house is going to need a lot of repairs, too. Thank goodness for the repair squads.'

But even as she listened to the sad tale, the woman wasn't talking as if she was defeated.

Cordelia felt proud of the attitude of the people she worked with. Would the women in the village where she'd grown up fare as well, she wondered.

As she went down into the Underground to travel to Mr Wood's office, she wondered why he had asked to see her. The air in the Underground got increasingly stale and her nose wrinkled as she smelled metals, grease, dust, cigarette smoke and sweat. It was so much worse when she got on the train that her eyes began to water, and she thought she should have caught a bus instead. But if an air raid started earlier than usual, being underground was safer.

She sighed and pondered on what Mr Wood wanted to see her about. He was her boss at the library, holding a senior position in the council, but she hadn't seen him since her interview. They spoke on the phone regularly, but he seemed to trust her to run the library without interference. She wondered if he knew about Mrs Montague-Smythe's meddlesome visits. Had she been in touch with him, trying to stir trouble? It certainly seemed like something she would do.

Relieved she only had to go two stops on the train, Cordelia edged her way through the crowds and sighed with relief when she breathed fresh air again. Or as fresh as it got. Even after just a few days of bombing, the air seemed to be filled with fine powdery grit. As she walked towards her destination, a newspaper headline caught her eye: 'Buckingham Palace hit!' it screamed. She could barely take in something so awful and hastily bought the paper, tucking it under her arm to read later. The king and queen must be safe, she thought as she walked, or the headline would be very different.

The entrance to the council offices was, like so many buildings, surrounded by sandbags. Somehow, they lessened the grandeur of the building with its imposing double doors. She went to the reception desk, where a young woman looked up from her typing. She had blonde hair styled after Jean Harlow and bright red lipstick.

She smiled and directed Cordelia to room 207 on the second floor.

The building echoed with the sound of busy footsteps, typing and murmured conversations. Cordelia's stomach tightened as she walked up the stairs. Silvertown Library was her first management post. Had she done something wrong? She mentally reviewed the number of new borrowers and books loaned and felt sure they'd met the targets she'd been given, so why had she been called in?

Finally reaching room 207, with its faded brass number plate, she tapped tentatively and was surprised when it was opened immediately.

'You must be Miss Carmichael.' She was greeted by a plump middle-aged woman dressed in a grey suit. She smelled of mints. 'I'm Mrs Simpson, Mr Wood's secretary. Mr Wood is expecting you. Go straight in. I'll bring you some tea.'

When Cordelia entered, Mr Wood stood up to shake her hand. She had almost forgotten what he looked like. He must be past retirement age, but with his lively face and pleasant smile, she was glad to see him. She felt herself relaxing instantly.

'Sit down, Cordelia. May I call you that?' he asked, straightening the pens on his desk. 'I'm sorry to ask you to come to the office, but—'

Mrs Simpson came in and interrupted with the drinks, leaving Cordelia almost holding her breath to know what the issue was. Mrs Simpson placed a tray with two bone china cups of tea in front of them, along with a sugar bowl.

Mr Wood put two spoons of sugar in his tea and stirred it before he continued.

'I have some news about the library and it is somewhat difficult.'

Cordelia's heart sank.

He took a sip of his tea. 'It's like this. As you know, many children have been evacuated and, as a result, many schools were closed and the buildings given alternative uses.' He looked up at her and she nodded in agreement. 'Now, because we had that long period of phoney war, quite a lot of mothers have brought their children back to the city. This means many children are without schools to go to, and we are worried about the long-term effects on them.'

His phone rang, and he answered it briefly before returning to what he was saying.

'One suggestion is that your library is closed down and used as a school.'

Cordelia's hand went to her throat as her breath caught. Close the library! That would be terrible. She thought of all her readers, and the people who came to see Dr Fernsby. They would all be let down.

'But...' she started, but before she could continue, Mr Wood held up his hand.

'I can see you don't like that idea, but all is not lost. I've been fighting on your behalf.'

She couldn't keep quiet any longer. 'So what can we do?'

'Well, as you know, something else that is much needed is more air-raid shelters. There are no Underground stations in Silvertown, so that is a major disadvantage. As you know, you have quite a big basement. If you were willing to have that used as a shelter, the library could continue as usual. It would be disruptive, of course, whenever a siren goes, but anyone already in the library would simply go downstairs and join any others coming in from outside. We wouldn't expect you and your staff to deal with it after closing hours. We can find ARP volunteers who will do that. What do you think?'

Cordelia's mind buzzed with the implications. There would be many panicked people rushing through the library, often with children. And she knew that Mavis would immediately worry about books being stolen, but that could be dealt with by one of them seeing everyone in.

She took a deep breath and spoke.

'It would be a lot of work. The basement hasn't been used for a very long time. All sorts of unwanted things have been left down there and it's very dirty and cold.'

Mr Wood smiled. 'I do understand, and I'm glad you are able to at least consider it. I've realised the work it would require, so I'm willing to allow the library to close for two days while changes are made.'

'But what about things we'd need? Chairs, carpets and so on. And tilly lights in case the electricity goes off. We don't have them. We can't expect people to sit for hours on the concrete floor, possibly in the dark.'

He nodded. 'Leave that with me. We have a lot of chairs from closed schools, although admittedly they're rather small for adults. I'll see what I can do to make people as comfortable as possible.' He paused. 'But I have to explain, and I wish to emphasise this. This may well be only a temporary reprieve. Many people in the council think the library would be ideal for a school. As you know, some churches are being used, but their spaces are not really suitable. The library with its various-sized rooms would be ideal.'

Cordelia's heart sank. So the problem might not be permanently fixed. She sighed. She'd better warn Mavis and Jane. Hopefully, they wouldn't start looking for other jobs, or that would be a great loss.

But for now, Mr Wood had come up with a solution that would keep the library open in the immediate future and the idea would still serve the community. She smiled and thanked him. As she stood to leave, Mrs Simpson appeared as if by magic to show her out.

But as Cordelia walked back to the train station, her mind began to wander. Would the basement be safe enough for people to stay there during an air raid? What if it was damp or had rats? She'd never really inspected it. There were always too many more important things to do. What if someone got hurt during the chaos of the siren and the rush to the basement? And was it even worth spending a lot of time on it if they might have to close down before long?

She rubbed her forehead, feeling a headache coming on.

Then she remembered the newspaper she had bought earlier. She took it out of her bag and read the headline again. Buckingham Palace had been hit! Her heart went out to the king and queen. They had been so brave staying in London when they had so many other homes in safer places. If the palace could be hit, what hope did they have in the East End, so close to the docks?

She shook her head, trying to clear her thoughts. She needed to focus on the library, on what she could do, not on the difficulties she faced. At least the library would continue to function until further notice, albeit also as an air-raid shelter during wartime. As much as she appreciated the need for more schools, she couldn't bear the thought of her library being turned into one. She knew how important it was to the community, especially during these tumultuous times.

As she made her way back, she mentally listed all the work that needed to be done to prepare the basement. She was confident that Mavis and Jane would be happy to help.

Mavis was waiting for her anxiously.

'What did Mr Wood want?' she asked immediately.

'Hang on a minute until Jane is free and I'll explain.'

Jane was serving the elderly professor. When she was finished, she stepped over to them.

'What did 'e borrow?' Mavis asked, surprised to see him at the desk.

'A book on philosophy,' Jane said. 'He's a lot cleverer than me and a lovely gent as well.' She looked from one to the other. 'What's happened?'

Cordelia waited until they couldn't be overheard, before eventually speaking.

'Mr Wood called me in to say the council wants to close down the library and turn it into a school.'

They both turned to her in alarm, eyes wide with surprise.

'What! They can't do that!' Jane said, speaking more firmly than she usually did. 'What about all our readers and Dr Fernsby's surgery?'

'Hang on,' Cordelia said, holding up her hand. 'It might not be as bad as that. Mr Wood has got us a reprieve, at least in the short-term. In return for letting us continue as a library, the council wants us to turn the basement into an air-raid shelter.'

'Short-term! 'Ow long's that then?' Mavis asked. 'Should we be looking for another job?'

Cordelia's face paled. 'No! Please don't do that, either of you. We can't manage without you. If it does look like we'll close, we'll do all we can to get the council to change their mind.'

Mavis folded her arms. 'Too right. There's plenty round 'ere who'd be 'appy to make them see sense.'

Jane nodded in agreement. 'Absolutely. We'll fight tooth and nail to keep this library open if it comes to it. It's a vital community resource and we can't let them take it away from us.'

Cordelia felt hugely relieved at their response.

'Thank you both,' she said, smiling. 'I knew I could count on you. You're stars, the pair of you. And who knows, maybe the air-raid shelter will attract more people to the library. We could hold readings down there.'

Mavis rolled her eyes. 'I don't think people are gonna be queuing up to spend their evenings in a dingy basement, Cordelia. But you're right, we'll make the best of it.'

'I didn't mean to invite people in, only if they're already down there. There's sure to be people who would be happy to read a bit. Or even just tell stories. It would pass the time.'

Jane suddenly furrowed her brow. 'Hang on, what about Dr Fernsby's surgery? If we had to close down, he wouldn't have a place to practise.'

'I know. It's all up in the air at the moment. We'll have to wait and see.'

* * *

'Ugh!' Mavis said and gave a huge sneeze. 'It's nasty down here. You'd think we were in the basement of an old castle that 'asn't been inhabited for centuries.'

The basement was dank with stagnant air and the smell of dampness and mildew. Cobwebs criss-crossed the ceiling, catching in their hair, and dust motes floated in the hazy light that spilled down from the bare ceiling light bulb that threw harsh shadows on the concrete walls. Bits and pieces of broken furniture, chairs, a stool and a small cupboard were heaped on one side of the room, looking like the remnants of a forgotten and forsaken past.

Cordelia laughed. 'As long as no monsters are hiding in the corners, I expect we'll be safe.'

It was the week following Cordelia's conversation with Mr Wood and, after terrible bombings every night that week, turning the basement into another air-raid shelter for local people was becoming increasingly urgent. Underground stations used for the purpose were full to the brim, and sometimes people were caught between two with insufficient time to run to either.

Cordelia's legs weakened beneath her as she thought of all the people who would soon be scurrying to find shelter in the library basement. She would have responsibility for all their lives. She had no idea if she was strong enough, but knew that with Mavis and Jane's help, they would succeed somehow.

'Two houses at the end of the next road copped it last night,' Jane said, a catch in her throat. 'They said everyone got out and into their Anderson shelters. I hope so. One house vanished completely into a pile of smoking bricks. The other one was sort of cut in half down the middle. You could see everything inside like a dolls' house.'

The three women were silent for a moment, thinking of all the destruction they saw day after day. Dust in the air that never seemed to clear; gas mains on fire in the street; hoses snaking across the road as firefighters struggled to get control of the situation, police keeping people at bay. Sometimes people ignored them and climbed on the ruins of their home. They searched for anything of financial or sentimental value they could find. Often they found nothing, but sometimes picked up a photo in a frame, a child's teddy bear or cushions all thick with grime. Sometimes, even the next morning, rescuers attempted to dig people out from the ruins, stopping regularly to listen out for cries for help – cries that, Cordelia feared, were the type that got more feeble with each passing hour.

Worse still were the sheet-wrapped bodies lined up against walls waiting for the undertakers' van to collect them.

'Come on,' she said, trying to snap her mind out of these dark thoughts. 'Let's not get maudlin. This mess won't sort itself out. Let's work through until four o'clock, then I'll treat us all to egg and chips at the café.' She looked around and sighed. 'I wonder why it's been allowed to get this bad?'

Next to her, Mavis bristled. 'It's not our fault. I've never been down 'ere and I bet Jane hasn't either. Mind you, seeing this mess, I'm beginning to wonder if Mr Bartlett ever 'ad. This looks like centuries of rubbish.'

Jane laughed. 'With the way he liked everything tickety-boo, he probably took one look and decided to ignore it. He was never one to get his hands dirty.'

Knowing they would certainly get their hands very dirty, they all tied up their hair in scarves and wore aprons to protect their clothes.

'Right,' said Mavis. 'Let's sort all this rubbish out into piles. Things we can use in that corner.' She pointed to the far-left corner. 'Things to be sold or thrown away opposite. Are we all feeling fit?'

Cordelia turned on the wireless. It was an old black box, with an antenna reaching up to the ceiling. She found an adaptor that allowed her to plug two things in the light bulb fitting, and soon the sound of cheerful music filled the basement. It was a small miracle, as the reception wasn't very good down in the damp basement. But something in the atmosphere shifted, and they soon found themselves uplifted by the familiar tunes from the Light Service.

It was an optical illusion, but the surrounding space seemed to transform. It had been filled with darkness and despair before, but now music and the faint light made it feel much less daunting. Even the objects that had been covered up with sheets, like the furniture in Miss Havisham's living room, seemed less depressing.

The three women sang along with the songs. There was still much to be done, but the music made them feel they could deal with the muddle and mess.

The old wooden desks creaked ominously as Mavis and Cordelia dragged them across the floor. They were scruffy, but they would be serviceable – large enough to store supplies, with enough drawers and nooks in which to tuck away what they'd need for people spending hours or even all night there.

As the desks were moved, several spiders came scurrying out from the deepest crevices, startling Mavis and causing her to jump back. When she did, the edge of the desk caught her hand, and she swore at the pain. Jane, ever kind and thoughtful, rushed to her side and quickly covered the small wound on her hand with her handkerchief.

'Should we leave some books for people to read while they're down here?' Jane asked. 'When we've done the worst of the cleaning, we can sort them into adults' and children's books.'

'Great idea,' Cordelia said as she lifted a pile of friable papers which began to disintegrate in her hands. 'If we find any as we're sorting through, we can put them in two piles.'

Underneath the papers she found an old-fashioned metal key, the sort with an elaborate shank and bow.

'Hey, look at this. Do you think there's a door to another room here?'

'Or an enchanted castle complete with a Prince Charming,' Mavis said. 'I could do with one of them. More likely a vampire out for our blood.'

'It could be the key to a chest full of gold and jewels,' Jane added. 'Or the doorway to another universe.'

They were letting their imaginations run riot.

'Or a library where all the books float through the air and put themselves away on the shelves in the right place every time.'

The three women smiled at each other, the dim light encouraging an intimacy not usually found in the busy working day.

'What scares you most?' Cordelia asked, after they'd tired themselves of hypothetical chat. The key remained an enigma for now, but she made a note to check her notes to see if Mr Bartlett had mentioned anything about other rooms in the library. Meanwhile she put the key in her pocket to put in her desk later so it didn't get lost. 'The claustrophobia of being in the shelter or the screech of falling bombs?'

'I'm terrified all the time during a raid. What will the world be like when this dreadful war is over?' Jane's voice shook as she spoke. 'Will any of us have somewhere to live?' She gave a small sob and wiped her nose.

'Have you got a boyfriend now, Cordelia, or shouldn't I ask?' Mavis asked, trying to distract Jane from her fears.

'No-one special,' Cordelia said. 'I meet men at the clubs I go to sometimes, but no-one interesting. But there's plenty of time. And I might have my eye on someone.'

Mavis was agog. 'Who's that then? Come on, tell us all. Is 'e tall, dark and 'andsome, and rich of course.'

Cordelia laughed. 'There's nothing to tell yet, and I may not tell you if anything ever happens!'

Mavis grunted as she lifted a pile of damaged books.

'I've 'ad one like you said. Proper con men they are, ain't they?' She wiped the dust off the books. 'These need repairing, but it'll be months and months before they're done.'

'What about you, Mavis?' Jane said. 'It must be a very long time since you were widowed. Have you had any blokes since then?'

Mavis laughed. 'Chance'd be a fine thing. I never seem to meet anybody. Anyway, when Ken was little, I didn't think it was right to have anyone but 'is dad.'

They worked on for another hour, getting increasingly grubby, making small talk to pass the time. Then Cordelia moved a cloth on an old desk and released a cloud of dust. She sneezed several times.

'That's enough for now. Come on, girls, let's go upstairs and make some tea.'

'I thought you'd never ask,' Mavis said. 'Me back's killing me.'

* * *

Mavis washed her hands and filled the kettle, putting tea leaves in the pot while they waited for it to boil.

'Mavis,' Jane said, 'there's a dance on this weekend at Tate's Social. Fancy coming? I've got no one else to go with and I'd love an evening thinking of something other than being killed.' She paused. 'Mind you, they start it early so we can get a few dances in before the rotten siren starts off.'

As she put the milk in the cups and placed the tea strainer ready to pour, Mavis wondered how to respond.

'You know,' she said, unsure whether she should say anything, 'I think I'd like to go to a dance if I can even remember what to do. It's been so long since I've been to one.'

She paused, wondering what to say next. She knew that a golden rule for telling lies was to keep it simple. She'd long ago decided to say that she didn't like talking about her supposed late husband. Not that she'd ever been married. The trouble was, Ken believed she had been married and that her husband had just left her. Better not to mention it at all.

'Excellent,' Jane said, removing a cobweb from her shoulder. 'It's this Saturday night. Do you want to come too, Cordelia?'

Cordelia took a sip of her tea before responding. 'Thanks for the offer, but I'm going out with my friend Rosalind. Anyway, do you mean Tate & Lyle, the sugar factory? They have dances?'

Jane nodded. 'They have a good social life for their staff and let others join in. My cousin works there. She says it's a great place.'

They'd just finished their tea when the air-raid siren shattered the peace. It was much earlier than usual.

Through the window, they could see the sky light up with anti-aircraft fire and the explosions made them all jump. The noise of the guns was deafening, and the heavy shells made the ground beneath them tremble. But worse was the noise from the huge guns they knew were mounted on mobile railway platforms. Their reverberating sounds shook the air and sent shivers down their spines. The noises thundered even down to the basement as if it were chasing them, determined to kill them. They could hear shrapnel falling like rain, tearing through the sky, sure to be a danger to anyone not in a shelter.

The three women huddled on a dusty old settee they'd uncovered, as if being close together would keep them from harm. They felt each other trembling with every loud blast, wondering if the next would flatten the library, trapping them underground.

'Well, we didn't expect to test out our shelter so soon,' Cordelia said. 'It's a good job it isn't open to the public for a couple more days.' The electric light swung wildly with each thud and she got up to fetch one of the tilly lamps that Mr Wood had already provided. 'Come on, girls, let's have a bit of light and tell ghost stories or sing hymns or whatever to pass the time.'

'Or read books,' Mavis said. 'We've got plenty of choice.'

Cordelia stood up to fetch one, took a few steps, then her scream shattered the air.

The others jumped up. 'What is it? What's 'appened?' Mavis asked.

Cordelia was shaking. She pointed to a pile of papers ahead of her. 'A huge spider! As big as my hand!' Her voice trembled.

Mavis looked at her, her mouth hanging open in surprise. 'What? You scared of a little spider? Strong woman like you?'

'Even strong women can have weaknesses,' Cordelia whispered. She backed away and went back to the settee, putting her legs up on it as if the spider would chase her there.

Jane found a cup and captured the spider.

'There,' she said, 'I'll put it outside once the raid has finished.'

At the sound of the all-clear, they went back upstairs, made more tea, and Jane set the spider free outside.

'Interesting, ain't it?' Mavis said with a grin. 'Timid Jane's not scared of spiders but you are, Cordelia. Just goes to show, don't it? We all 'ave our funny bits.'

14

BETRAYAL?

Cordelia and Rosalind could almost feel the excitement, the energy, emanating from the building as they descended the steps into the nightclub. As they approached the entrance, the beat of the music increased in volume, and they were both overwhelmed by the sheer energy. It was a kaleidoscope of colour and lights, with fabrics, surfaces and furniture in shades of deep purples, pinks and blues.

They walked inside, their heels tapping against the polished marble floor, and their eyes roving around the sophisticated room. Everywhere they looked, couples swayed to the rhythm of the music, or sat at small round tables enjoying cocktails. Cordelia couldn't help but think this was so different from the dance Jane and Mavis would be going to.

Rosalind was dressed to the nines in a rose-pink sequinned dress with narrow shoulder straps and a wide skirt, creating a powerful silhouette. Her dark hair was curled and swept up, away from her classic, porcelain-like face. Cordelia, on the other hand, had opted for a more subtle look: a vintage black dress, straight and figure hugging.

They found a small table in the corner, and took in the sights, sounds and smells of the club. They could feel the music pulsing through their veins and the night seemed as if it might stretch on forever. They were ready for an adventure.

'You look like a million dollars,' Cordelia remarked, a touch of envy in her voice. 'Bit different from your bus driver's uniform.'

Rosalind stood up and twirled around, her skirt billowing around her.

'We girls must always look the part,' she said, with a wink. 'Can't go to a nightclub in any old thing, now, can we?'

Cordelia's ankle was almost healed, but she didn't plan to dance much. Anything more than a slow mooch would be likely to set it off again.

As they settled themselves at the table, the singer was singing 'Moon River', her voice, slow and seductive, hanging in the air like fog, but not so thick that it hid the sea of glimmering sparkles from the singer's dress and the mirrorball overhead.

They hadn't been sitting more than five minutes when a waitress, dressed in a skimpy black dress with a white apron far too small to be of use, came to their table. She offered them two glasses of champagne from a tray.

'Compliments of the gentlemen over there,' she said, pointing to their right.

They glanced across and saw two handsome Air Force officers looking in their direction. They smiled and held up their glasses in a way that suggested they wanted to join them.

'What do you think?' Rosalind asked. 'Fancy some male company? It's been a while since you had any.'

She was right. But drinks with airmen who might be dead soon sounded more like doing them a favour than her.

'Okay, let's call them over,' she said.

The officers picked up their glasses and walked towards them. Rosalind's eyes lit up as they always did when attractive men were near, and she was especially attracted to men in uniform. Cordelia was more cautious, not wanting to seem too enthusiastic until she had weighed them up.

The men introduced themselves. The fair-haired one was Timothy, proud to tell them he was from Yorkshire. His friend, Jim, who was prematurely bald, came from the same town.

'We signed up together,' they explained. 'Let's hope we don't die together until we are old, old men.'

The conversation soon turned to the latest news about the war.

'It's not just London that's copping it,' Timothy said. 'Southampton's been hit badly too. The bastard Germans go for the ports, of course, just like they do in London.'

'They got Coventry, too,' Jim said. 'Completely flattened by all accounts, even the cathedral. But what are we doing, depressing you lovely ladies with this type of talk? Anyone fancy a dance?'

A slow number had started, so Cordelia accepted the chance to dance with Jim, warning him about her dodgy ankle. The singer began to sing 'Dancing Cheek to Cheek' and Jim held her tight as they danced, a little tighter than she was comfortable with, so she pulled away slightly. But that didn't stop her enjoying the music and once or twice Jim held her arm up and twisted her round. She was delighted to find her ankle seemed to cope with the movement.

The song gradually reached its crescendo, and then melted away like a dream. Cordelia felt a wave of euphoria wash over her. Life had been too serious for too long and it was a relief to just let go and enjoy the moment. She looked up into Jim's eyes, and saw that he was just as moved by the music as she was. They shared a moment of silence, almost as if to pay tribute to the beautiful song, before they started to make their way back to their table.

But then everything changed.

Being underground in the club, they didn't need to go to an air-raid shelter when the inevitable sirens began. The club provided a refuge from the reality of war raging outside, at least for a while.

But something she saw made her eyes widen and her stomach clench with a different sort of fear. Through the crowd of dancers, she saw him. Robert. He was dancing with another woman. Cordelia was struck by the woman's beauty, by the glittering emerald-green dress she wore and her perfect teeth as she laughed at something Robert said. They looked every inch a couple.

She felt her heart sink in her chest as she watched them, the heat of humiliation rising inside her. She wanted to leave immediately, but instead she seemed frozen to the spot as if her feet were glued to the ballroom floor.

How foolish I've been, she thought, thinking that Robert was interested in me. We've never even been on a date.

She was annoyed with herself for the surge of jealousy that swept through her. She longed to go to him and demand an explanation, but what would she say? She didn't own him, and he owed her nothing. He'd probably be amazed that she had read so much into their tentative relationship.

She stumbled and Jim, worried, asked if she was okay. He probably thought she had had too much to drink. But she couldn't take her eyes off Robert and the woman, even though she wanted to run and hide, her heart aching with sorrow.

Taking Jim's hand, she led him back to their table.

'I'm sorry, Jim, my ankle is playing up. I need to sit for a while. Would you get me another drink? Something strong.'

When he went to the bar, she moved so her back was to the dancers. She didn't want Robert to see her or to know she'd seen him. Her temper was rising and her muscles quivered. Had he been lying when he said he'd gone to the funeral in the hope of seeing her? Was he a Lothario who had many girls at his beck and call?

Trying to calm herself, she leaned forward, her head in her hands.

'Are you okay? Got a headache?' Jim asked, sitting down next to her, looking concerned. 'I got you a Martini, I hope that's okay.'

She forced herself to look up and smile. Her anger and jealousy should not ruin the evening for Rosalind and the two pilots.

But what if Robert saw her? Would he come over and explain or simply ignore her? Her chest tightening, she caught Rosalind's eye and gestured that they go to the ladies' WC.

Once there, Cordelia and Rosalind waited impatiently for two other women to go. They took forever, fixing their hair, reapplying lipstick and gossiping about their friends. But finally they left.

'Robert's here,' Cordelia said, fury in her voice. 'He's dancing with another woman. I'm going to go and give him a piece of my mind. Telling me he only came to the funeral to see me, when he's got another woman. How dare he!'

She picked up her bag and took a step towards the door, but Rosalind grabbed her and pulled her back.

'You're going to do what?'

'Give him a piece of my mind. It's the least he deserves.' Cordelia was struggling to speak, she was so angry.

'Hang on. You mean you're going to make a big scene in the middle of the dance floor because a man paid you a nice compliment? Did he propose and you forgot to tell me?'

Cordelia grunted. 'Of course not.'

'Did he ask you to be his girl?'

There was a long pause. 'No. But—'

Rosalind turned her round and made her face the mirror. 'Right, now say to yourself, "I'm being unreasonable. Robert is not mine. I have no rights over him."'

Ignoring her, Cordelia hissed, 'But I thought we had a special relationship. He shouldn't be out with another woman.'

Her fists were still so tight her nails cut into her palms.

'Shouldn't? Shouldn't? You're kidding yourself, Cordelia. I'm amazed. You're usually more sensible than this. You must have it bad to be reacting this way. Anyway, you're here with another man!'

For a moment, Cordelia hated her friend with a fierceness that frightened her, but before she could say or do something she'd later regret, two other women came in. By the time they'd gone, she'd calmed down.

'You're right. And you're a good friend to make me see sense. Come on, we'll get back out there and dance the night away. Damn him!'

15

ROMANCE IS IN THE AIR

'Care to dance?' the tall soldier asked Mavis. He had a friendly smile and a small scar on his chin that somehow added to his mature attraction. She hadn't expected to be asked to dance. After all, at thirty-seven, she was older than most women there. But he was one of the oldest men too.

'I'd love to,' she said, relieved the band wasn't playing a fast number. 'Putting on the Ritz' was one of those songs you could dance to any way you wanted.

As she walked on to the dance floor, she had butterflies in her stomach. It was so long since she'd been in a man's arms. Even for a dance, she felt sure she'd do something stupid. It was not a feeling she was used to.

'Do you come here often?' he asked as he held her in his arms.

She couldn't help but laugh. 'Did you make that line up?'

He had the good humour to laugh at himself. 'I'm a bit out of practice with the ladies, I'm afraid.' He twirled her round. 'My name's Joe. I'm in the army.'

She laughed again. 'I'd never 'ave guessed from your uniform!'

His ears went pink. 'I told you I never know what to say to the ladies. Take pity on me. I get in a right two and eight.' He spun her round. 'I'm home on leave for a week. I want to forget all about the war for a few days.'

She thought how lovely his eyes were, honest and trustworthy.

'Well, you're in the wrong place then in London, I'm afraid,' she replied, but her words were lost as his arm round her waist tightened slightly and they moved together across the dance floor without a hitch. Mavis was surprised she could remember how to dance at all, although he was so good, he made it easy for her to follow. But she felt a bit unsure of his closeness, and he seemed to sense that. He loosened his hold a little and smiled at her, holding her eyes with his.

'Can I buy you a drink when this number's over?'

The room was already hot and smoky, even though the dance had only been on for half an hour. Everyone was making the most of it until the wretched air-raid alarm went, as it surely would.

'I'd love a lager,' she said when they found chairs away from the band.

When it came, she rubbed the glass across her forehead to cool it down and sighed with pleasure.

Jane was dancing with a man who wasn't in uniform, and she caught Mavis's eye to let her know all was well. He looked familiar, but she couldn't place him.

'I'm Mavis,' she said, giving Joe her full attention. 'It's years since I've been to a dance. I hope I didn't step on your toes.'

'Not once,' he said. 'But I'm glad of a chance to rest my feet.' As he spoke, a woman walking past tripped and spilled a few drops of her drink on his sleeve. She was tipsy and made a great play of brushing the liquid off, apologising many times, kissing his cheek and leaving a lipstick kiss behind. He just smiled, and when she'd gone, he said, 'First kiss I've had for a while.'

'Poor you!' Mavis said, and, feeling very bold, planted a quick cheeky kiss on his other cheek.

He put his hand over where she'd kissed him.

'I'll never wash that side of my face again,' he said with a grin. 'But I'll scrub the other side raw.'

They sat in companionable silence, watching the dancers and sipping their drinks.

'You married?' Joe asked after a while. 'Husband away fighting?'

'No 'usband. I'm a widow. I've been on me own for a long time.'

He blinked in astonishment. 'You're kidding. A good-looking woman like you? What's wrong with the blokes around here if they haven't snapped you up?'

She hadn't been called good-looking for a long while. She was a little overweight, although rationing had almost entirely taken care of that. And she hated the grey she saw in her brown hair every time she looked in the mirror. But that wasn't why she'd been shy of getting involved with anyone. It was because she knew Ken would find it difficult. But as she looked at this kind man, she thought perhaps she could consider it now. Ken was away at war and if she was lucky, he wouldn't want to live back with her when the war was finished.

'Perhaps I didn't want to be snapped up.' She smiled and raised an eyebrow.

Jane and her dance partner came over at that point, interrupting their conversation.

'Mavis, you recognise Ralph, don't you? He's the postman in my mum's street.'

'Of course,' Mavis said. 'I knew I knew you from somewhere. This is Joe. He's 'ome on leave.'

Ralph shook Joe's hand. 'Well done, Joe. I tried to join up but I've got a dodgy ticker so they wouldn't have me. Still, I'm an air-raid warden. Do my bit that way. Not as brave as you, though.'

Jane put her hand on his arm. 'Being an air-raid warden is very brave, if you ask me. Out there all night when the bombs are being dropped, putting out fires, rescuing people. Takes a lot of courage.'

Ralph patted her hand. 'I'll get us some drinks. Back in a mo.'

The air-raid siren cut across their conversation, its waxing and waning drone filling everyone with dread.

'It gets earlier and earlier every day!' Mavis said. 'Come on, to the shelter!'

They picked up their bags and gas masks, called to Ralph to follow them and joined the crowd trying to get out of the door.

'Where are we going?' Joe asked. 'I don't know shelters around here.'

'Jones's Department Store!' Mavis shouted above the noise. 'I've 'eard we can go in there. Nearer than the Underground.'

Outside, the sound of bombers overhead and the siren blotted out all other sounds. People were running here and there, being guided by the wardens. The store was only a hundred yards away, and they joined the queue to get inside. It was still shop opening hours, and the staff had stopped their normal work and were guiding people down into the basement. As they waited, anxious to be safe from the bombs dropping in the area, fires from incendiary bombs sprung up here and there; wardens and police officers shouted directions; and an ambulance rushed past, its siren blaring. More incendiary bombs dropped on the roof of the shop opposite and home front wardens rushed to try to put them out.

'I'm going to have to go,' Ralph said. 'They'll need all hands on deck. I'm really sorry, Jane. But I hope I'll see you soon.'

And with that, he was gone.

* * *

Jane followed the crowd down the store steps to the basement and looked around.

'Not exactly the basement of John Lewis,' she heard someone say. 'I hear it's quite comfortable there.'

One of the shopworkers who had shown them in was with them.

'The storeroom's over the other side,' she said. 'Pity we can't reach it. There'd be sure to be stuff we could use there.' She paused. 'But I suppose that would be stealing.'

In one corner of the space sat a collection of mismatched chairs, their fabric sagging and woodwork scratched. Between them stood an old table, its surface battered after years of use. On it was a large jug of water and some glasses and cups that had seen better days. Layers of worn rugs and carpet scraps patched together gave the cold, damp floor a vague semblance of warmth.

Two bare light bulbs lit the space, and every time a bomb dropped, they danced about, casting eerie shadows around the room, making the space seem even more claustrophobic than it already was.

The fear in the air was so thick they could almost taste it. Some people were holding themselves tight, not speaking, while others whimpered or comforted each other. One man let out a loud scream, making them all jump.

Looking round nervously, Jane, Mavis and Joe found chairs together.

'I wonder how long this'll last,' Jane said, biting a nail. 'I'd like to get back to my own bed tonight.'

She wasn't about to get her wish.

As the bombardment above them intensified, the basement shuddered, and it seemed as if the whole building would collapse any moment. Joe put his arm around Mavis, who leaned towards him as if it was the most natural thing in the world, and Jane wished Ralph was there to reassure her. Then she felt guilty for thinking of him when all her thoughts should be of George, her lovely husband, away fighting for king and country.

Seconds later, a deafening crash shot through the basement, followed by a shower of dust. For a moment no one spoke, everyone's eyes wide with terror as they looked around to see if the walls or ceiling were collapsing, but all looked safe.

For a minute.

Another deafening crash and a large section of the wall near the door they'd entered through collapsed, terrifying them all. All that was left was a pile of debris: bricks, plaster and beams completely blocking the way out.

'That's the exit!' a man shouted, his voice harsh with horror. 'We're trapped!'

One man stepped towards the debris, determination in his every move. 'Come on, let's pull it out and get the hell out of here.'

But his friend pulled him back. 'The air raid hasn't stopped yet. We're safer here for now. Come and sit down again.'

People huddled together, trying to take in what had happened.

The ground still trembled beneath their feet as they heard more deafening crashes above them.

'That must be the rest of the shop collapsing!' Jane cried out. 'We must be under tonnes of stuff.'

Small pieces of masonry rained down on them like hailstones and chunks of wood flew about, some narrowly missing people by inches.

The sound was thunderous and grew louder by the second, like a never-ending thunderstorm inside the shelter. Suddenly, a heavy beam came crashing down. They scattered, trying to avoid its path, but an elderly man wasn't fast enough. It fell on top of him, trapping him completely.

He lay there, unmoving. Jane thought she saw him bang his head when he fell.

One woman went to him.

'I'm a nurse,' she called out as she checked for a pulse. 'He's alive, but he's unconscious. Probably a good thing. He's going to be in a lot of pain when he comes round. Come on, let's get this beam off him.'

Several men immediately stepped forward and even as the noise and chaos of the explosions continued to scatter plaster off the ceiling onto them, they began to pull the heavy beam off the man. It was heavier than they expected and they grunted and groaned as they pulled. One of the helpers, a burly fellow with an unruly shock of black hair, shouted orders, guiding their movements. The beam was slowly and painstakingly lifted, inch by painful inch, without causing the man any further injury, and after what felt like hours, the beam was finally removed.

They all breathed a sigh of relief and then those watching burst into spontaneous applause, to which the helpers grinned and bowed.

The nurse touched the man's forehead and his arms, feeling for a pulse. 'He's still alive,' she said softly.

'Should we move him?' someone asked.

She felt the old man's pulse again. 'I think we should leave him where he is until we're freed and the ambulance people can assess him properly.'

'If we don't die first!' a woman muttered.

The nurse turned to her, her eyes narrowing. 'You saying things like that helps no one. Do something useful. Find a light rug or something to keep him warm and get a glass of water. He'll want it when he comes round.'

The woman's shoulders tensed up as she shuffled across the room and reluctantly retrieved what the nurse had asked for, her hands shaking as she placed a rug over the old man. As she carried the glass of water across the room, an enormous bang shook the walls again and made them all jump in horror. The water sloshed around in the glass, some spilling onto the floor. One of the light bulbs flickered before plunging them into semi-darkness. Every breath was held in tension and fear as they were shrouded in an eerie gloom. Some people were whimpering and one woman began to cry.

A man stepped forward towards the pile of debris. 'Come on, you lot. Let's shift this so we can get out.'

Jane, usually the quiet one, stood up.

'We need to wait. The raid is still on, and it sounds like the shop has collapsed on top of us. If we start disturbing that pile, who knows what'll happen!'

'She's right,' someone joined in. 'We're safe here. Leave it well alone.'

'We were with a warden when we came in here, so he knows we're here,' another voice added. 'We need to just sit tight and they'll get us.'

The sobbing woman looked up. 'Yeah, but how long'll that be?'

'Right!' shouted Mavis, fed up with the gloomy talk and making them all jump. 'Nothing we can do to 'elp ourselves just now, so let's 'ave a good old sing-song. Cheer ourselves up. What's it to be?'

There was a moment's stunned silence. 'How about "Run Rabbit Run"?' someone suggested.

After a hesitant start, the sound of ragged singing competed with the continuing sound of bombs, falling masonry and plaster. Somehow, the voices joined together as if in defiance of the enemy above trying to kill them and flatten their city. It was as if they'd gained a sense of unity, of strength in the face of their awful situation.

As the song faded away, Joe spoke up. 'We won't be conquered. We'll fight to the end. Those damned Hun will never occupy our country!'

People cheered and Mavis quickly led them into more songs until people were tired. It was late evening and most of them would normally be in their beds. They did the best they could to make themselves comfortable and several people managed to fall asleep.

A while later, Mavis nudged Jane to get her attention. When Jane looked at her friend, she noticed she had dark rings under her eyes from exhaustion.

''Ay, the bombing's stopped,' she said quietly.

'You're right,' Jane replied, feeling exhausted. 'Hard to notice with the sounds of all the falling stuff and the sirens. It's going to be a long time 'til they dig us out. Ralph'll make sure they know we're here. Might as well get some shut-eye.'

The air in the basement grew more stale as the hours passed and the captive people moved about like ghosts in the half-light, speaking in hushed tones. Some had food and shared it with others, but most wished they'd been better prepared.

The hours ticked by slowly, and although their anxiety was palpable, some, including Jane, did manage to sleep again. They had been in the semi-darkness for what felt like years, not knowing how long it would be until they would be rescued, or even if they would.

Then, after what seemed like an aeon of anxious waiting, they heard what they longed for – bricks being moved and muffled shouts from above. At first the voices were too faint to be made out, but then they heard the unmistakable words, 'We're coming for you! Sit tight!'

They erupted into cheers and Jane noticed several people wiping tears from their eyes. Even though they knew they had no choice but to sit tight, they could now believe their ordeal would soon be over.

It took half an hour before the first gap in the fallen bricks appeared and they saw the daylight they had feared they might never see again.

As Jane emerged, Ralph rushed up to her and wrapped her in his strong arms, stroking her hair out of her eyes, wiping away a smut on her forehead. She could feel his heart beating against her chest and the warmth of his breath on her cheek. She felt tears of relief and thanks stream down her face. Ralph wiped them away, and tenderly pushed back her dust-filled hair so he could see her properly. If only, she thought, she wasn't married, then she could go out with this lovely man. But instantly she felt guilty. Ralph was certainly kind and caring, but she barely knew him. She certainly wasn't going to risk upsetting her marriage for him or anyone else.

She squinted in the sunlight, blinking away the dust that filled her eyes. After so many hours underground, she barely noticed it was a chilly day with a cold wind. Instead, she saw Ralph's kind eyes, the weak sun, and the relieved, smiling faces of the other rescuers and the WVS ladies offering tea and sandwiches.

Several survivors cried out with relief, beginning to process what they had been through. The brave men who had worked tirelessly through the night, pulling them out of harm's way, wiped their faces, their work done. This time.

Many were hugged by way of thanks despite their filthy clothes and dirt-streaked faces. A small crowd of friends and family who'd been waiting patiently rushed forward and wrapped their loved ones in blankets, holding them tight. Jane looked around for her mother, forlornly hoping she would be there. She wasn't. Jane knew she was being irrationally disappointed. Her mother would not have known where she was, but that didn't stop her familiar feeling of being unloved by the person who should have loved her most.

As they began to make their way back home, some noticed the surrounding devastation, the flattened buildings, the fires still burning, another rescue team working on a different flattened house, but others were too numb, tired and dazed from their experience to see. But they all coughed from the smoke and dust that was getting into their lungs and making their eyes gritty.

Mavis and Joe, who were holding hands, watched Jane and Ralph.

'Those two seem to be getting on okay.'

Mavis nodded. 'Don't worry, Jane would never two-time her 'usband. She loves George too much.' She put her hand over her mouth. 'Oh. I shouldn't have said that. She doesn't know I know she's married. Not many secrets in Silvertown, though!'

Joe hugged her tighter. 'Well, Mavis, it's been a hell of a way to meet someone, hasn't it? Awful night, but I'm not complaining because I got to spend it with you.'

She smiled and kissed him lightly on the cheek.

'I couldn't agree more. How many more days' leave have you got?'

'Five. And I hope to spend every one of them with you. Would you like to come for a walk and a bite to eat tomorrow?'

16

CLEARING UP

It was one of those autumn days when the weather makes you happy to be alive, even when everything around you is falling apart. The sky was a bright midsummer blue and although there was a chill in the air, there was no wind. Sitting in the sunlight, you could even feel the warmth.

Mavis and Joe decided to go for a walk before they had something to eat. 'Where shall we walk?' Mavis asked. 'There were precious few parks or anything before the war. I don't think there's any left now. Even Lyle Park is gone.'

Tentatively, Joe tucked her arm through his. 'I hear the market is still okay. We could head that way and look for a bargain or two. And there's always some good food stalls. How about it?'

Rathbone Market was overflowing with life and colour. Everywhere they looked, people were gathering around the stalls, buying and haggling for the day's supplies. The smells of fresh fruit and vegetables filled the air, mingled with the scent of frying onions from the hot food stalls.

At one stall, a man in a brightly coloured waistcoat was shouting out his wares.

'Lovely tomatoes! Come and get them!' He waved his arms in the air, trying to be heard above the hubbub of voices and footsteps.

Joe and Mavis made their way through the crowd, stopping at several stalls. Joe bought some apples for later and a small posy of wildflowers for Mavis. At another stall, he spotted a pretty silver antique brooch and impulsively bought it for her.

Initially, she hesitated. 'But Joe, we hardly know each other and here you are buying me a lovely brooch! I can't possibly accept it.'

'Mavis,' he said, 'I hope you will get as much pleasure from wearing this brooch as I've got buying it for you.'

Eventually, Mavis accepted it with delight, and as Joe fastened it to her coat, she kissed him on the cheek, enjoying the unfamiliar feeling of being close to someone.

They spent almost an hour wandering round, then found a small corner table in the Carpenters' Arms pub. Both with a pint of lager in hand, they began to relax and talked more intimately about the things that really mattered to them.

'Do you think it's the war that makes us talk so freely when we've only just met?' Mavis asked.

Joe kissed her cheek. 'I don't know, love, but I do know it's lovely sitting here being with you. This is the best time I've had since I don't know when.'

They were just leaving when the wretched air-raid alarm sounded again.

'Bugger!' Mavis cried, her heart pounding once more. 'Not so soon. Not in broad daylight!'

Holding hands, they joined people running for safety to the nearest Underground station in Canning Town. The raid was a short one, only two hours, but for the whole time they heard the crumps of bombs dropping.

'I wonder what factories they'll 'it this time,' a woman near Mavis said. 'I hope it's not Tate & Lyle. Life's 'ard enough without 'aving no sugar going in me Rosie Lee.' She paused for a minute. 'Nor Keiller's marmalade, come to that. Scarce enough as it is.'

When the all-clear sounded, they made their way out of the station, tentatively, fearful of what they would find. And once on the road, they stopped, mouths open as they looked at the devastation. Great sprays of broken glass spread across the road along with dead birds, a dead cat, and a huge amount of debris from fallen buildings.

Hardly knowing where they were going, they walked carefully towards the streets where Mavis lived. The smell of gas and smoke made breathing difficult.

'Are you sure you want to do this?' Joe asked. 'We could try to get a bus to the West End or somewhere.' He paused. 'Mind you, it's going to be a while before the buses are running again with all this glass around.'

Fires still raged here and there, and the sounds of falling masonry competed with the wail of ambulances and fire engines. Incident teams were already at work, searching for survivors or bodies, cordoning off properties that were likely to collapse.

Two streets away from Mavis's home, they were stopped in their tracks. A whole street was gone, replaced by mountains of rubble still smoking and emitting clouds of dust.

Joe clutched her hand tight.

'I don't know about you, Mavis, love, but I feel a bit sick seeing that lot. You don't have to, but I need to go and help the incident teams. I couldn't live with myself if I didn't. There's probably people alive under that. You can go on and I'll see you tomorrow.'

'No, I'm coming with you,' she said, rolling up her sleeves.

The incident team directed them to what remained of houses on the left and they joined four other volunteers. They moved planks of wood, mounds of clothes, mattresses, shoes, two table lamps, broken chairs and an endless amount of bricks and mud.

Twice they heard a loud shout of 'Here!' and helpers ran to the sound, where they frantically threw aside debris to free the person, dead or alive. A while later, ten minutes, twenty, half an hour, ambulance men would come by with a stretcher and take back a survivor or victim. Each time, Mavis couldn't bring herself to look if the person's face was covered or not.

Despite the constant chaos, there was an undeniable feeling of camaraderie among the rescuers, both paid and volunteers. Some worked tirelessly without rest, while others took a break sitting wherever they could, an air of quiet fortitude holding them together.

Every now and then, the Red Cross van would come round and give them hot tea and a chance to catch their breath.

Joe and Mavis found two filthy broken chairs and sat down, cradling the mugs in their hands, trying to get them warm again.

Joe looked at Mavis, her hands torn and clothes covered in dirt and mud.

'Well, girl, bet you wasn't planning to look like this on our first date.'

Mavis gave a weak smile. 'Cheeky sod! Well, I didn't expect you to bring me here on a first date neither.' She spotted one of the incident team and beckoned him over. 'Do you know if Argyle Street is still standing?'

She held her breath as she waited for the answer.

'It was, last I heard,' he said, then moved on to organise some new volunteers.

Joe put his arm around Mavis's shoulders. 'That's good news. I'm really glad for you.'

'But what about you? Where are you staying?'

He pushed his hair back from his forehead and wiped the dust from his face. 'Don't worry about me, I'm staying with a friend in Barking. It should be okay.' He drained the rest of his tea. Then he reached out and squeezed Mavis's hand softly. 'Now c'mon,' he said, standing up, 'we got more work to do.'

Mavis nodded, feeling a wave of admiration for him. Everything about him told her he was a man worth holding on to. An inspiration, even in the worst of times.

She got up and, together, they headed back to the ruins.

After another hour of digging, they uncovered an arm sticking out of the wreckage. Mavis stopped and put her hand to her heart, but Joe acted instantly, bending forward, feeling for a pulse.

'Too late,' he said, more to himself than anyone else.

He opened his mouth to shout 'Here!' But before he could, a little voice behind him said, 'That's my mummy's watch. Where's my mummy?'

Mavis and Joe looked at each other instinctively, silently understanding the roles they needed to take.

Mavis stood up and, moving towards the little girl, reached to hold her hand.

Joe shouted, 'Here!' and as other rescuers rushed towards them, Mavis took the little girl away. Away from her dead mother, away from what had been her home, away from her past, which was now gone.

Mavis held her hand tight, and she pulled her away from the wreckage. She felt the girl's tiny fingers trembling in her hand and tried to squeeze back reassuringly. She paused and squatted down to be at the little girl's level.

'What's your name, sweet'eart? Mine's Mavis.'

The reply was barely more than a whisper. 'Joyce.'

They walked on in silence, away from the chaos. Suddenly Joyce stumbled, almost pulling Mavis down with her. Mavis scooped her up and held her tight, feeling the little girl's tears against her neck.

'Don't worry, sweet'eart,' she murmured. 'We'll take care of you now.'

'I want my mummy!' Joyce sobbed and Mavis stroked her hair in an attempt to soothe her.

They walked towards the ambulance where Mavis explained the situation.

'Where's the reception centre at the moment?' she asked, hoping it hadn't been blown up along with so much else.

'Coolin Road school,' the man said. 'Shouldn't take you long to get there, but be careful of all the stuff on the roads.'

She smiled her thanks and began walking. Rubble was spread across all the major streets. Shops and homes that just hours earlier had been full of life were now unrecognisable, just piles of bricks and debris, still smoking. Smoke was everywhere, from the bombs, from the fires caused by incendiaries, from gas leaks, from the factories. It got into their throats and stuck to their clothes and skin. It made their eyes water and their noses run. Sandbags that were supposed to protect the buildings were thrown across the road like children's toys, along with tree branches, bricks and wood. So many roads had been damaged that it was sometimes difficult to be sure she was going in the right direction.

At the first junction, she lowered Joyce to the ground gently.

'There's a paper shop there and I know they sell sweets. What sweets do you like?'

'Sherbet lemons,' Joyce whispered.

'Come on then, let's see if they've got any. I think I've got enough coupons.'

She led the little girl in and they bought the sweets. 'Would you like a comic as well? *The Beano*?'

Joyce nodded and Mavis paid for it. As they walked on, the comic tucked under her arm, she asked, 'What's your other name, Joyce? Your last name.'

Joyce was sucking her sweet and, as she hesitated to answer, Mavis wondered if she was old enough to know her surname.

'I don't know, but the rent man calls Mummy Mrs Jameson.'

'Ah, so you're Joyce Jameson. That's a very nice name. Does your granny live near you?'

Joyce shook her head. 'I don't 'ave a granny.'

Mavis felt overwhelmed with sadness for the little girl and wondered if she had a father. If she did, he was probably away at war.

They'd come to a busy road and a rag-and-bone man went by, his horse tossing its mane and neighing loudly. Joyce laughed and did her best to imitate the sound the horse made. She skipped along, the pink ribbon in her brown hair bouncing as she did. Seeing her happy, if only for a moment, gladdened Mavis's heart.

She looked around at the damaged buildings and realised that there were probably many children like Joyce who were left without a home, let alone a family. The war had ravaged everything they held dear, leaving them with nothing but pain and heartache.

She was relieved to find the reception centre was still standing, although bursting at the seams with people who had been made homeless over the previous few days. They sat around on chairs or on the floor, clutching blankets the Red Cross had given them. Many looked dazed, unable to understand what was happening. Others were chatting or even playing cards. As ever, the WRVS ladies were there, handing out tea and fish paste sandwiches.

Holding Joyce's hand tight, Mavis walked over to a woman in the familiar WRVS uniform.

'I found this little girl next to a bombed house.' She turned her face away from Joyce and spoke quietly. 'Her mother is dead. She says she doesn't have a grandmother.'

'Oh dear. Poor thing. Go over there.' She pointed. 'See Mrs Wheeler, she'll look after her.'

For the first time, the woman looked properly at Mavis, who was still covered in dust and looked dishevelled.

'Are you okay?' she asked. 'Have you been injured?'

Mavis shook her head. 'No. But I've been helping the incident teams near Joyce's house.'

The woman smiled and patted her shoulder. 'Brave woman, we need more like you. Go and see Mrs Wheeler, she'll take care of you.'

They went to Mrs Wheeler's table and Mavis explained the situation. Mrs Wheeler reached behind her and pulled a teddy bear out of a large bag. It was obviously second-hand but in good condition, with a red ribbon round its neck.

'Would you like a teddy, Joyce? You can keep it. I think you'll be a very good friend for him.'

Joyce beamed and snatched it, clutching it tight. 'Is it really mine? I can keep it?'

'You can,' Mrs Wheeler said, smiling. 'Have you got a name for it?'

Without hesitation, Joyce said, 'Janet. It's my mummy's name, so she'll be pleased.'

The two women looked at each other and looked away, struggling to keep tears at bay.

'You play with Janet, Joyce,' Mrs Wheeler said. 'I just need to speak to this lady.'

She made notes of everything Mavis knew. Joyce's name and address was the total sum of it.

'Do you know why she was alone in the street?' Mrs Wheeler asked.

Mavis felt guilty. 'I didn't think to ask. She was probably out playing with friends, but I don't know.'

When they'd finished, Mrs Wheeler patted her arm.

'Don't worry, we'll take good care of her. If you want to know where she ends up, just get in touch with our head office.'

Mavis's feet dragged all the way back to where Joe was, sadly thinking of everything the little girl had lost, even though she wouldn't understand it yet. Maybe that was a blessing. But one thing Mavis was certain of: she fully intended to keep in touch with the little girl and do everything she could to help her.

When she got back to the bomb site, Joe was again sitting drinking tea on the wobbly chair. His shoulders sagged and he looked absolutely exhausted. Next to him was an untouched slice of bread and butter.

Mavis went up to him and hugged him, ignoring the fact that they'd only met the day before.

'You've done your bit,' she said. 'Why don't we call it a day?'

He nodded. 'That's what the rescue leader said. The worst is done. I think we should sit here a few minutes and then head for home. Hopefully tomorrow we can have that date after all.'

17

DISASTER

'Look at the mess you've made! You're a bad, terrible girl!' Jane's mother yanked little Helen's arm so hard she fell over. But she still managed to give her a resounding slap round the side of her head. Helen screamed, clutching her ear. 'It's time you understood what being tidy means! I'm sick of you and your mess,' Jane's mother hissed, letting go of her arm and leaving her to cry.

Jane had been at the door, about to leave for work, when her mother, who had slapped her like that many, many times, turned on her innocent daughter.

'Mum, she's only little. She doesn't—'

Hilda glared at her. 'Doesn't what? Listen to a word I say? She's got to learn right from wrong. Go on, you bugger off to that posh job of yours like you do every day. Leave me with the brat like you always do.'

The clock was ticking away and Jane had to leave, but her heart broke at the idea of leaving her little one with this awful woman. The woman who had given birth to her, but couldn't love her. Who, in return, was impossible to love as a daughter should.

But she couldn't take her lovely daughter to work. She was supposed to be a single woman, and if anyone in authority found out she wasn't, she'd be out of a job. Her mother would be pleased if she ended up sitting behind a sewing machine all day with rows of other girls, never using their brains, just cogs in the boss's ambitions. Underpaid and overworked.

With a sob, Jane hugged her daughter and left. It was like this most days and was always like this with her mother. Her only respite was when she was with George. Those precious months after they got married and before he went to war.

Tears trickled down her face as she got on the bus, trying to hide her sobs and frantically trying to think of a way out of the situation. She'd applied for a nursery place for Helen, one of the new ones the government was setting up to get women into the workplace. There was a chance Helen would be able to start there soon, and she hoped she would be happy there. But that still left her needing somewhere to live. Her savings were modest, her mother demanding almost all the money she brought into the house. But she had a tiny nest egg hidden under a floorboard in her bedroom. It was nearly enough for a few weeks' rent somewhere else.

She knew the effects of growing up with someone who constantly told you you were no good. If she was honest with herself, that's why she was so timid. Her mother's harsh voice was always whispering in her ear that she was useless, ugly, unloveable, making her doubt herself all the time. Though George had begun to counter her mother's brainwashing when they met, immediately pointing out there was no basis for the insults. And his love and kindness had made her feel worthwhile and loveable for the first time in her life.

The library day started as usual. Bert rushed in to read the papers and the increased number of early customers was a sign the steps they were taking to increase reader numbers were beginning to work. Cordelia was mostly in the office, and Jane was aware that Mavis had glanced at her several times since they opened.

Finally, when they had a quiet moment, Mavis took her aside.

'Come on, then. What is it? It's obvious something's been up with you all morning.'

Jane looked down and bit her bottom lip. 'It's... well, I can't say...'

Mavis looked around, then spoke quietly. 'Is it that girl of yours?'

Open-mouthed, Jane looked at her.

'You know about Helen?' she asked in a whisper. If Mavis knew, and told Cordelia or, worse, that dreadful Mrs Montague-Smythe, she'd be out on her ear.

'Course I do. I don't miss much that goes on around 'ere. I knew when you got married and all. You don't 'ave to worry about me telling anyone. Daft rule if you ask me, saying you can't work 'ere if you're married. You can work in a horrible factory filling bombs, but not in a library! It's stupid.'

Jane grasped her hand.

'Thank you so much,' she said. 'I've been so worried and my mum...'

Mavis folded her arms. 'Let me guess, she's being as big a cow as she's always been. I've known her of old.'

It was as if her words conjured up the person. The library door swung open with a bang and in walked Jane's mother, dragging a crying Helen behind her. She marched up to the desk and glared at the two women.

''Ere,' she said, looking at Jane. 'I've 'ad enough. I'm leaving the little blighter with you now, and I expect you both and all your stuff out of my house before the end of the day! Good riddance to bad rubbish, that's what I say.'

And leaving Helen there crying, she stormed out of the door.

Jane rushed round the counter and picked up the crying girl, whispering soothing words in her ear. She looked at Mavis, a question in her eyes.

'Why don't you—' she began, but never finished her sentence because the office door opened and Cordelia came towards them.

She looked at Helen and gave what she hoped was a reassuring smile. 'You're an unhappy girl.' She looked at the two women. 'Who is she? Has someone abandoned her here?'

As Helen clung on to Jane's legs, still sobbing, Mavis and Jane looked at each other. Mavis gave Jane a subtle nod and looked at Cordelia.

But they were interrupted by a frail elderly woman in a knitted tea-cosy hat coming in to register at the library. She had the sweetest smile and smelled of mothballs.

'Do you have plenty of crime books?' she asked. 'I like a good murder, I do.'

'Let me help you,' Mavis said and indicated to the other two to leave her to it.

Heavy-hearted, Jane decided there was no point in lying. It was obvious Helen was with her. Her precious daughter.

'Can we talk in private?' she asked, her stomach in knots.

Cordelia nodded. 'Come to the office.' She looked at Helen. 'You too, young lady.'

The office was only twenty paces away, but Jane felt as if every step was taking her towards a guillotine. The end of the job she adored. She loved spending her working day with books and the fascinating mixture of people who came in. She especially loved her new unofficial role in charge of the children's section. It didn't pay any more, sadly. Cordelia had explained there was no money in the budget to give her a rise. But it gave her so much satisfaction seeing the children enjoy selecting a book or listening to her read an exciting story.

Cordelia opened the office door and stood back for them both to enter.

Jane looked around the familiar office with its smell of old books, and Cordelia's cluttered desk. She couldn't shake off a feeling of dread as she sat down, Helen on her knee, clutching her tight as if she might leave her.

Instead of going behind her desk, Cordelia sat on another chair facing Jane.

'What's up? You can tell me. I heard a woman shouting, but couldn't make out the words from here. Is this her daughter?'

Fear made Jane avoid Cordelia's eyes.

'It... it was my mother. She can be loud sometimes.' She squeezed her little girl tight. 'I've got to tell you the truth. I'm married and this is my daughter, Helen. My husband, George, is away in the army.' She paused. 'I suppose you'll have to sack me now you know that.'

Cordelia took a deep breath. 'Jane, I worked out ages ago that you were, or had been, married. I saw the white mark on your wedding finger.'

She was interrupted by her phone ringing.

'Silvertown Library, Cordelia Carmichael speaking. How can I help you?' She listened for a minute, then said, 'I understand, Mrs Montague-Smythe. I'll have those figures ready for you.'

She put the phone down with a sigh.

'She's coming in this afternoon. Now, about your situation...' she said, looking at Jane again.

'She's thrown us out as well. My mum,' Jane said, her words tumbling over each other. 'I'm hoping Mavis will put me up for a night or two until I can find some rooms.' She began to sob. 'What am I going to do? I need this job and now we have nowhere to live.'

Standing up, Cordelia put her hand on her shoulder.

'Jane, I think the no-married-women rule is ridiculous. Unfortunately, I have to stick to the rules...'

Jane's mouth dropped, and she sobbed again.

'But...' Cordelia continued, 'I am sometimes very deaf and I haven't heard anything you've just said.' She went to her desk drawer and took out a sweet. 'This is for you,' she said, handing it to the little girl, who clutched it as if afraid someone might snatch it from her. 'So I suggest, Jane, that you take the rest of the day off. I'll mark you up as sick. Tomorrow is your day off. That'll give you time to sort things out.' She smiled. 'Then you can come back the day after tomorrow, your usual single self. How does that sound?'

Jane felt a wave of relief wash over her. It was as if a heavy burden had been lifted from her shoulders. She nodded and began to thank Cordelia.

'No need to thank me,' Cordelia said, moving towards the door. 'I'm relieved to keep you working here. You are a real credit to the library.'

Cordelia went and took over the front desk as Jane spoke to Mavis, who handed her a key. A tear in her eyes, Jane squeezed her arm and put the key in her pocket.

Then, clutching her daughter's hand, she led her out into the street.

Outside the library, she tried to control her racing heart. In her mind, she pictured the scene at home. Her mother's home as it was now. Her mother would have thrown their belongings into her old cardboard suitcase any old how. It was likely she'd also throw away things without checking with Jane if she wanted to keep them. Would her mother be there, standing inside the door with her arms folded over her chest, ready to give her another piece of her mind? Having her little granddaughter standing there wouldn't make her soften her words. She'd never had a kind word for her in her life.

When Jane thought about her childhood visits to Grandma Nellie, her mother's mother, it helped her to understand her mother's harshness. As soon as she'd arrive, her grandmother would push her outside, saying, 'Go and play and don't bother me.' It didn't matter what the weather was, rain, storm or shine, she wasn't allowed back in the house. Often she'd shelter in the library to keep warm and dry. Perhaps that's where she got her love of books. There certainly weren't many in her home. The librarian had given her a borrower's ticket, and she had it still, one of her most prized possessions.

She saw other grandmothers being loving towards their grandchildren, which made her feel sad and envious. Had she done something wrong that neither her mother nor grandmother loved her, would never give her a hug or even read her a bedtime story?

Mealtimes with Grannie Nellie were always torture. They were conducted in absolute silence and Jane had to eat everything on the plate, no matter how awful it looked. The kitchen table had seen better days. It was dark oak with claw feet, and always covered with a white starched cloth that Jane was terrified of dirtying with her clumsy hands.

Grannie Nellie would sit at the head of the table, dressed in a long, drab dress. Her face would be as stern as ever, and her long grey hair pulled into a bun, though strands of grey and white escaped here and there, like cobwebs in an abandoned window.

Jane was always aware that her grandmother was watching her every move, so she'd gingerly move her fork from her plate, careful to keep her elbows off the table and her back straight. Every so often, Grannie Nellie would murmur something like, 'Eat up!' Jane had known that if she didn't comply, she'd be in trouble. She always called her Grannie and tried to be as polite as she could. She wished Grannie would talk to her sometimes, but the only words she ever spoke were blunt, direct instructions. 'Do this.' 'Don't do that!' 'Stop!'

So she'd take a deep breath, and take a bite of whatever it was she was given, trying not to make a face if she hated the taste. She'd wash it down with a sip of milk, before returning her gaze to her plate, not daring to look at her grandmother. Each mealtime, the minutes ticked by slowly, and Jane would feel the tension in the air grow with every passing second, until finally her grandmother got up from her chair and announced that it was time for bed. Jane would eagerly follow, relieved to escape the cold silence.

Pushing aside the memories and glad she didn't treat her girl in the same way, she held Helen's hand and headed towards the bus. The road was busy even though there were fewer cars on the road each day now petrol was rationed. The coalman's horse and cart passed by, and he smiled and tipped his hat at her. She forced a smile back.

When their bus came, her gloomy mood brightened a little when she saw who the driver was. Cordelia's friend, Rosalind. She had called in at the library once and been very friendly towards everyone, even if she did have a cut-glass accent.

She spotted Jane and waved cheerily.

As they found their seats, her mouth still full of the sweet Cordelia had given her, Helen asked, 'Are we going home?'

Jane put on her brightest voice. 'I've got a lovely surprise for you. We're going to stay with Aunty Mavis for a while and then find ourselves a new home until Daddy comes back from the army. Tomorrow is my day off, so we can sort it all out and get you started at the nursery. You'll have lots of friends to play with.'

She'd never been to Mavis's house and had no idea if she had room for them. But they could sleep on the floor if necessary. She sighed and hoped she could find alternative accommodation quickly.

She wondered if Helen would be upset about the move. Even if her grandmother was horrible to her, it was what she knew. But she needn't have worried.

When she told her, the first thing she asked was, 'Has Aunty Mavis got a cat?'

Children just seemed to accept whatever happened to them.

'No, but the cat that lives next door often visits her. She talks about him a lot. His name is Tiger.'

As they got off the bus, they heard a humming noise from the sky that got louder and louder. It seemed everyone in the street was looking upwards, all looking as frightened as Jane felt. The street got darker, as if a cloud had covered the sun, and everything seemed to shake with vibrations. There were hundreds of planes, all in formation, enough to blot out the weak sun, throwing them all into premature twilight. Jane's heart pounded at the terrifying sound. Were these German bombers? Were they all going to die? There had been no air-raid alarm. She clutched Helen's hand, ready to run to the nearest shelter, when she heard an ARP man shout, 'Don't panic! They're ours. Look at the circles on the wings!'

'Coo, that's exciting, Mum,' Helen said as the formation gradually passed by them and the sound lessened. 'Will we see any more? I like aeroplanes.'

Jane's footsteps dragged as she approached her mother's home and she couldn't resist looking around to see if she was nearby. But the street looked much like normal. Mrs O'Connor next door was chatting on the doorstep with another woman, her hair done up in a scarf knotted at the front, and her wrap-around pinny with its faded red and pink rose pattern stretched at the front. Jane didn't stop but caught a snatch of the conversation – *he's not going to be happy when he gets back from war to find he's got another kiddie.*

Two boys were enjoying war games with sticks for guns, and a couple of girls were skipping, singing songs as they did.

'Is Granny in?' Helen asked as Jane got out her key.

She bit her lip. 'I don't know, love. We'll see.'

But to her relief, her mother was nowhere to be seen. As she'd anticipated, her case sat on the floor by the door, already packed. No note or any other acknowledgement of what had happened.

'Wait here!' she said, and hurried to their room. Her heart beat fast as she looked at the multicoloured rag rug that covered the loose floorboard where her savings were hidden. She'd spent months making the rug out of bits of old dresses she'd got from jumble sales.

Was the rug in the same place or had her mother found her secret and taken everything? She tucked her hair behind her ears and, holding her breath, she knelt down, moved the rug and struggled to lift the floorboard. In an effort to make sure her mother never found her hiding place, she'd made sure it was a tight fit. She broke two fingernails trying to lift it, quietly praying for divine help. None came. Frustrated, she ran downstairs and fetched a knife.

Helen was quietly looking through a book she'd borrowed from the library. It was about a bear and she was running her finger along the words and pretending to read them. Jane had read it to her so often she knew it by heart. She kissed her cheek, then ran back upstairs, breathless with worry.

She wriggled the knife in between the floorboards, trying to lever one up, back and forth, back and forth, hoping the knife wouldn't break. Surely her mother hadn't lifted the board, and put it back so firmly? The thought made her hold her breath again. Then, with a little cracking noise, the board lifted. She put her hand into the darkness inside.

All the tension she'd been holding in evaporated as she realised the money was still there, wrapped in an old piece of material. Her relief was so great, she almost collapsed onto the bare boards. But a sense of urgency made her get up again, which she did, brushing down her skirt. She had to get them both out before her mother returned. She quickly tucked the money into her shawl, put the wood back in place, ran downstairs, picked up the suitcase, and hurried out of the door with Helen as fast as she could.

Mrs O'Connell next door was just about to go into her house.

'I've spent so much time enjoying the craic with Mrs Cohen, I'll be behind with everything to be sure, to be sure.' She noticed Jane's suitcase and frowned. 'You leaving us then?'

Jane nodded. 'Yes, we're going to stay with a friend. I'm sure I'll see you again.'

She pulled Helen away before Mrs O'Connell, who could talk for Ireland, engaged her in more conversation.

* * *

Tiger was sitting on Mavis's doorstep when they arrived, looking round as if hoping for food or someone to make a fuss over him. Helen immediately sat on the ground, chatting and stroking his fur.

Mavis's home was as neat and spotless as Jane would have guessed. Like her mother's place, the attic floor was rented by a couple, and Mavis had one bedroom, plus a tiny box room with a small single bed in it. She looked at the box room and decided that it was big enough for her and Helen to share for a few nights.

The living room had a settee, an armchair, a small dining table and three dining chairs. Two cushions with knitted covers were on the settee and their colours, pink and grey, matched the thin curtains. The kitchen was off that, and the toilet was outside, shared with the house next door. Jane put their things in the box room, then took her daughter's hand. 'Come on, little one, we need to go to the shops. We can't eat all of Aunty Mavis's food, can we?'

Helen was restless in the queues for meat and veg, and Jane tried to distract her with nursery rhymes and I spy. Then, tired and feeling drained herself, she led her to Mo's café, where they both cheered up after having a drink and a bun.

'Right, nursery next!' she said, wishing she could have a sleep instead of running all these errands. The scene with her mother and everything she'd had to do since had sucked away all her energy.

The nursery was in a Methodist church and many of the staff were church volunteers. Jane and Helen arrived mid-afternoon, and the children were sitting at wooden tables, their backs upright as they'd obviously been told. The room was decorated with bright Bible story pictures – Jesus healing the sick, feeding the five thousand, the wise men arriving at the manger, and posters with positive messages: *God loves a cheerful giver*, *A happy heart makes the face cheerful*, *A joyful heart is the best medicine*.

Although the children were silent as they ate, they looked quite content, which reassured Jane. Helen spotted some toys in the corner, and, tugging away from her mother's hand, went and picked up a rag doll. She was soon holding it and singing it a nursery rhyme.

'We like our children to be well behaved and also happy,' Mrs Johnson, the head of the nursery, said. She looked in her notebook. 'I see you've registered little Helen. You're in luck. Two children left in the last few days. Their mothers felt they'd be safer if they were evacuated out to the country.'

Her words plucked Jane's heartstrings. There had been dreadful bombings for several nights in a row and everyone feared it wouldn't stop until the whole East End was razed to the ground. The newspapers and wireless talked endlessly about the 147 Nazi planes shot down during the Battle of Britain. It seemed good news sold newspapers. But people in the East End were shocked that the terrifying damage done by bombs to their area was hardly reported.

Should she let her beloved daughter go to the country? She looked at her and her heart ached at the thought of not seeing her every day, not being able to hug her or listen to her little stories.

* * *

Jane and Helen had enjoyed staying with Mavis, rubbing along together well, but she didn't want to outstay her welcome, especially as Mavis's son might be due home on leave before long. Mavis had been a kind and thoughtful hostess, not once complaining about sharing her small home with the two of them.

But now it seemed likely that Ken, Mavis's son, was getting weekend leave. Mavis had been tactful when she spoke about him, but Jane could read between the lines. It was clear that he was a difficult character who wouldn't appreciate the presence of two extra people.

So they had to find a new home and quickly. Jane had been looking without luck, but now she had to seek somewhere without delay.

Since bombing had started in earnest, it was harder and harder to find anywhere to rent. Thousands of people had been made homeless. Some were lucky enough to have family and friends to stay with, a few decided to leave London altogether, but most wanted to stay in the East End. It was their home, where they'd had their children, where they had been born and where their work was. The area was in their blood.

It was a chilly day, with heavy clouds and a cutting wind. Jane wrapped Helen up well and tried to make fun of their outing.

'We're going to see lots of places. Do you want to bring Teddy to see what he thinks of them? It'll be interesting to see other houses.'

But Helen wasn't convinced. Once she felt the cold, she whinged to go back indoors. Jane had to bribe her with the promise of a hot drink and another bun when they finished.

She began by looking around the area where Mavis lived.

So many of the houses were run-down, it was hard to keep her morale up, never mind Helen's. Often, landlords didn't care enough to look after their properties, but they were fast enough collecting their rent.

The first door she approached merely had a 'Rooms to let' sign in the window. The window itself wasn't clean and the tiny front garden was full of weeds and rubbish. With a sigh, she knocked on the door, clutching Helen's hand tight.

The landlord opened the door and looked the two of them up and down.

'Got a kid then?' he asked, as if it wasn't obvious. 'I don't like kids. Too noisy.'

With that, he slammed the door in their faces.

'He was a rude man, wasn't he, Mummy?' Helen said, sucking her thumb, something she only did when she was very stressed.

Pulling up their collars against the cold, they walked on to the next street. The next door they knocked on looked no better than the last, but Jane felt she had to try.

An elderly woman opened the door, dressed in widow's weeds, like something from a Dickens book.

'You looking for a room, then?' she asked in a voice so quiet it was hard to hear.

But Jane didn't answer. The smell from the hallway was enough to make her want to gag, and she could see mice running about the skirting boards.

'It's okay, thank you,' she replied, and pulled Helen away.

The third house looked more promising. There was no front garden, but the front door was clean. Jane knocked, noticing the paint was peeling around the letter box and the keyhole.

A tall, thin man with thick grey hair opened the door and looked her up and down. 'Looking for rooms, are you, darlin'? Got two that might suit you and that little one.'

As they walked up the stairs, she was sure he was trying to look up her skirt, not that it was short. His attitude gave her an uneasy feeling and she could smell his sweat, even though she was not close to him.

He led her into the first of two rooms. It was basic, with minimum furniture and curtains so thin you could almost see through them. The man gestured around the room, acting as if he were offering a palace.

When she kindly dismissed the offer and turned to head out, Jane's heart sank as she looked up to see the landlord standing in front of her, blocking her way. His eyes travelled up and down her body, and she got an unsettling feeling in her stomach.

'Well,' he said in a gruff voice, 'it's a good place and a lot of my lady tenants like to get a good reduction in their rent. Paying in kind, you know what I mean.' He stopped and looked her up and down again like she was a joint of meat. 'You're a looker. I'm sure we could come to some sort of arrangement.'

She had heard enough. She made to move past him, holding Helen's hand, but he stepped in her path, blocking her way once more. He looked her up and down again and this time it was more obvious what he had in mind. His breath reeked of ale, stale food and cigarette smoke.

She tried to sidestep him, but he blocked her again, moving even closer.

Helen, sensing the tension, began to cry.

'Shut up, brat!' he hissed, not even looking at her.

Jane felt a wave of revulsion come over her, but knew she had to keep calm. She attempted to move round him again, expecting him to continue to block her way, but instead he stepped aside and gave a mocking bow. She shoved him hard as she passed and he staggered, giving her the chance of escape she needed.

Tugging Helen behind her, she ran out of the house as if her life depended on it, fearful the dreadful man would come after them.

They ran all the way to the corner, Jane struggling to hold back tears.

What if we can't find anywhere to live? she asked herself over and over again. Helen was tiring, so when they passed a sweet shop, Jane got out the ration books and bought Helen some Fruit Pastilles.

As they came out, they bumped into Mrs Gregory with her daughter, Hetty. They recognised each other from the library.

'You all right, love?' Mrs Gregory asked. 'You look a bit down in the dumps.'

Jane was proud to see Helen offer Hetty a sweet.

'We need some rooms, but we've got nowhere so far and I don't even want to tell you about the last landlord...'

Mrs Gregory smiled. 'Well, it's lucky you ran into me then. My neighbour's got a couple of rooms free. The family what lived in there decided they'd 'ad enough and moved out of town. Only 'appened yesterday so they're still free. She's an old lady and needs a bit of 'elp sometimes, but she's a real sweetie. You'll love 'er.'

Jane's shoulders relaxed for the first time since they'd begun their search. 'Can you take me there now? I want to get it before anyone else.'

She couldn't believe her luck when she saw the place, two cosy rooms with furniture that was old but in good condition. They'd need to share the kitchen and toilet with the landlady, but Jane was used to worse. Mrs Spencer was tiny and round with her hair tied up in a scarf and a wrap-around pinny over her black dress. Her face radiated good East End kindness.

'Can me and Helen move in tomorrow?' Jane asked. 'And it'll be my husband when he's on leave from the army.'

Mrs Spencer sat down heavily on her kitchen chair and rubbed her aching knees. 'That's all right with me, girl. But can you 'elp me with a bit o' 'ousework and cook me a bit when you do your teas? I'll share my ration book with you. It's 'ard for me to get around these days.'

Jane smiled, feeling hopeful for the first time. 'Of course we will, Mrs Spencer.'

Mrs Spencer took hold of her hand and nodded. 'Well then, you can move in tomorrow! I think we'll get on like a house on fire.'

Jane beamed as she emerged from her new landlady's house. She thanked the woman profusely, hugging her tight, and waved goodbye with an effervescent joy she hadn't felt since before George was posted abroad. She got an instinctive feeing that Mrs Spencer would be a fantastic substitute grandmother to Helen, one who would always be ready with a smile and a kind word.

As they walked down the streets of the East End, she felt a warmth spreading through her. Everywhere she looked, she noticed signs of the wonderful community that was the East End – the neighbours chatting outside their front doors who said hello as she passed, the children playing in the streets and the market vendor who hollered out his wares with enthusiasm and even gave Helen a bruised apple.

18

THE WOMAN AGAIN

The day Robert would be coming in to do a surgery in the library seemed to take forever to come round, the week stretching like elastic that gets weaker each time. But the day finally came. Cordelia was aware that Mavis and Jane behaved differently towards her on 'his' days. She thought, she hoped, she hadn't given any signs of attraction to him. Not to them, not to him. But she'd learned that Mavis had sharp eyes and rarely missed a thing. So without anything said, they always managed to leave the desk to her when he was around. Even though she couldn't wait to see him, she hadn't been able to put seeing him dancing with another woman out of her mind. Rosalind was right to make her see it another way, but what if he was involved with someone else?

Even so, she kept looking at the clock, waiting for him to arrive, reminding herself of the saying about a watched kettle never boiling. But then there he was, smart as ever, looking tired but not too tired to give her a big smile.

'How is my favourite librarian today?' he asked, holding her gaze for a few seconds.

'I think Mavis and Jane might be a bit hurt to hear that!' she said with a laugh.

Before he could respond, one of the waiting patients came bustling over.

'You've already got a full house, doc,' she said. 'Better get a move on.'

Cordelia saw Robert turn round and realised all his patients were watching him, anxiously waiting their turn. He went over to a gaunt boy in the corner who was coughing ceaselessly. He gave Cordelia a grim look and she wondered if he thought that the boy had TB. She saw him change his demeanour to a more cheerful one as he looked at the queue of people waiting to see him.

'I won't keep you long,' he said. 'Just give me a minute to get myself sorted out.'

When he'd gone into his room, Cordelia approached the children's section of the building. She had never expected to find such a transformation there when she tasked Jane with looking after the area. Following her suggestion, Jane had breathed new life into the area, going far beyond Cordelia's expectations. The walls were brightly covered with pictures drawn by the children, along with letters of the alphabet, giving the area a feeling of warmth and joy that it had been missing. Even the bookshelves seemed to glow with the energy of new life.

Cordelia stood still, taking it all in, smiling.

Jane was still tidying, but stopped when she noticed Cordelia there. She smiled, and the two shared a silent moment, looking around at the changes Jane had made. Cordelia felt her heart swell with pride for the hard-working young woman, and gratitude for the gift she had given the children who visited the library.

'Look what I found at a jumble sale,' Jane said proudly. 'These cushions are just the ticket. They make the area seem friendlier somehow. I got the material to cover them there, too. From an old dress that was beyond saving.'

'You're a wonder, Jane,' Cordelia said, delighted at the way she was gaining confidence. 'And I like the way you've left some of the picture books on the table. I hear your mid-morning sessions with the little ones are going well. I'm sorry I haven't been able to get over to see them.'

Without a word, she stepped forward and gave Jane a brief hug, conveying her gratitude and appreciation for all the hard work she had done. Jane smiled brightly and brushed away a tear that had sprung to her eye.

'Thank you,' Cordelia said softly. 'You've done an amazing job.'

Unused to praise, Jane went pink and looked away. She put some books on the shelf, leaving the most attractive and colourful ones with their covers facing outward.

'We're getting more kids every day. It's only half an hour, but they seem to love it. And let's face it, now a lot of schools are closed, it might be the only regular thing in their life.'

'I'm glad you're doing something right!' a familiar voice boomed. Mrs Montague-Smythe had crept up on them. The relentless honking from the street outside did nothing to muffle her irritatingly authoritative steps. 'But I should have been consulted about this idea. It's a major change for the running of the library.'

Jane went pink, clearly not sure what to say, but Cordelia had no such hesitation.

'Mrs Montague-Smythe, I'm glad you like this, but perhaps you've forgotten I am not answerable to you. I run new ideas through the area librarian for approval.'

'Humph!' Mrs Montague-Smythe grunted. 'It's my responsibility to be aware of everything that goes on in my ward.' She took a deep breath. 'And while we're talking, I want a word about the type of books that are left for people to look at while they're waiting to see Dr Fernsby.'

As she spoke, Cordelia gradually walked her away from the children's area to somewhere more private.

'And what is your worry, councillor?'

'I looked at them and I have to say I was shocked. Shocked. Romantic trash. No literary value whatsoever, and there are more of them on the shelves. Books should be educational, worthy.'

'I can't agree.' A man's voice made them jump. Robert. 'I don't think we've met,' he said, turning to the councillor. 'I'm Dr Fernsby. You must be Councillor Montague-Smythe.'

She spluttered and blinked several times. 'You don't agree with me! Why ever not, may I ask?'

Robert smiled just a little. 'Every day I see people in my surgery and at the hospital who are struggling with life. You must see them in your work, too.' He paused as if waiting for an answer, but for once none was forthcoming. 'So I think anything that lifts their spirits or takes their minds off their difficulties is going to be good for their mental health. I'm sure with your knowledge of people, you'll agree that's important.'

'Yes, but—' Mrs Montague-Smythe began.

'I'm really sorry to interrupt you, but I need to speak to Miss Carmichael urgently about something.'

And with those words, he implied the conversation was over.

Cordelia walked beside him back towards his room.

'What is it you wanted to speak to me about?' she asked, hoping everything they'd prepared for him was in order.

His grin stretched wide. 'Nothing. I was being naughty, I'm afraid. I was on my way back from the WC and overheard your conversation. I thought you might like some support.' He suddenly stopped walking. 'Not that I think you need it. Please don't think I think that!'

She raised an eyebrow again. 'Of course not. I assume you have the highest regard for my abilities.'

He chuckled. 'I certainly do, Cordelia. May I call you that?' He looked at his watch. 'Now I must use my abilities and get back to my patients. Do keep encouraging them about the diphtheria vaccinations. There are a worrying number of cases at the moment.'

As they walked back towards the desk and his room, they could hear Mrs Montague-Smythe questioning Jane about the books she read to the children, and whether she thought they were receiving an appropriate literary education. Cordelia was tempted to go back to rescue her, but decided that Jane sounded as if she was coping.

'I'll have to go in a minute,' Robert said. 'But I meant to mention – I saw you in a nightclub recently when I was with my sister. I don't get time to go dancing often, but would you be interested one evening if we are both free?'

Cordelia's heart soared. So it was his sister! She'd jumped to conclusions and got upset over nothing. Rosalind had been right to tell her off.

'I'd love to,' she said. 'Let's fix up a date soon.'

19

EVACUATION

The sweet smell of freshly baked fairy cakes filled the small kitchen, but the aroma couldn't mask the sadness that hung in the room like a thick fog. Sadness because of Helen's imminent departure to her new home in the safe countryside. With a heavy heart, Jane turned away from the window and walked to the dresser, wishing she could keep Helen safe with her, but London was so dangerous with untold deaths and injuries every day that she had reluctantly become convinced evacuation was the best thing to do. She wrapped four of the cakes for her daughter to eat on the train and kissed the pack as if her love could follow her wherever she was going.

Helen stood silently by the door, watching her every move. She was young, but she seemed to understand that this was a serious moment. Jane moved around the room, her hands trembling slightly as she filled a small suitcase with a drawing Helen had done for her, a photo of her and Helen's dad, and some of her favourite things as well as her clothes and shoes. She wanted her to have something to comfort her when she arrived in the countryside. Then she paused, her arms still as she stared out of the window at the clouds scudding by. She tried to imagine her life without her daughter. It seemed impossible. Her shoulders drooped and silent tears ran down her face. Her chest ached, and she struggled to breathe.

'Mummy, can I take my teddy bear?' Helen asked, her voice small and hopeful, interrupting her reverie.

'Yes, of course you can,' Jane said, wiping a tear away. 'You can take your teddy. He'll be lonely if you leave him behind.'

Helen smiled, relieved, and Jane hugged her close, breathing in her small girl scent.

'Remember, Helen, everything's going to be all right,' she said, her voice full of love. 'I hope you'll soon be back here and we can be together again.'

'Will Daddy be here?' she asked, scratching her knee where she had a scab from falling over earlier.

'I don't know, love, but I hope so.' Jane kissed her forehead, and together, they made their way out of the door. Even though she had decided Helen should be evacuated from war-torn London, it broke her heart to think about her being away from her.

She gripped her hand tightly as they walked towards the Underground station. Everywhere they looked, people were rushing around, cars revving or beeping their horns, horses neighing as they clip-clopped along, all too hurried to give some space to a little girl and her mother.

But the two of them had to continue towards their destination, and so they pushed ahead, the noise and chaos of the city only growing louder as they approached the entrance to the station.

Finally, they reached the stairs and began to go down, step by cautious step, with Jane clutching the case in one hand and Helen in the other. As they descended further and further, the noise of the city faded away and was replaced by the sound of an Underground train approaching.

Even though she'd been on the Underground before, Helen was still a bit nervous of the trains and the station itself – the stale air smelling of cigarettes and sweat, the whooshing sound of the train arriving, the many people on all sides. Jane held Helen closer and hoped she would find the steam train more exciting. She'd never been on one before.

The train was packed, but a kind woman gave up her seat and Jane sat down with Helen on her knee.

'Will the people like me?' Helen asked, struggling to hold back a tear.

'Of course,' she replied, hoping this was true. 'You're a lovely girl. They are sure to like you.' Parents were never told in advance exactly where their child would be going, or what type of home they'd be going to. Even the thought of a caring person looking after her lovely daughter pulled at her heartstrings. But what if she was placed with someone who didn't care and was just doing it for the money? Or worse still, was downright cruel? A sob escaped her lips, and she got out her hankie and blew her nose so Helen wouldn't see her distress.

Eventually, they reached the mainline station. The wind carried the sounds of the trains before they were even in sight. Helen stopped in her tracks, her eyes widening with awe when she saw all the soldiers gathered there. They were preparing for departure, some saying goodbye to families and others alone, just waiting for their train to arrive.

'Is one of them my daddy?' Helen asked, eyes bright with excitement. She was tugging Jane's hand, pulling her towards the men. She could barely remember what her father looked like, but she saw his photo often and looked around hopefully.

Jane bent down to her level. 'None of them are your daddy, love, but he wears a uniform just like them and he's just as brave. You'll be that brave in your new home, won't you?'

They joined the huge crowd of children waiting at the station. They were of all ages, from toddlers clutching their mothers' hands to bigger boys pretending to be grown-up and trying to look unafraid. All wore their winter coats, had their gas masks over their shoulders and carried their belongings in a small case or a fabric bundle. Some, like Helen, were clutching their favourite soft toy. Every child had a cardboard card pinned to their chest with their details written on it.

Volunteers from the WVS were in charge of everything. In their practical clothes and sturdy shoes, they gave a sense of order even amongst the throng. They moved calmly amongst the children and parents, speaking kindly but with authority, telling them where to wait.

The platform was alive with a chaotic mix of emotions you could almost hear – fear, sadness, excitement and confusion. Despite their best efforts, it was impossible for the children or their mothers to keep their feelings completely in check. In amongst the hustle and bustle, there were tears, hugs and whispered reassurances.

As the train's engine started up and the driver blew the whistle, a wave of excitement swept through the crowd and boarding began. One of the WVS women was waiting at the top of the steps of the carriage designated for children Helen's age. She looked kind and welcoming, holding out her hand to help the little ones up the steps. Jane kissed Helen one last time, hugging her tight as if she'd never let her go, then, before she lost her nerve, gently pushed her forward. Helen was still holding her teddy and her case, ready to embark on an unknown journey.

Jane caught sight of her in the carriage and was immediately filled with a powerful wave of loss. She looked so small and vulnerable standing there at the window. She wanted to run to her and pick her up in her arms, to take her home again, but she knew she couldn't. She had to be brave and let her go where she would be safe from the awful daily bombings. All she could do was wave and blow kisses until the train finally pulled away.

As it left the station, Jane felt a deep emptiness settle in her chest. She wanted to cry, but didn't want the other mothers to see her sorrow. They had enough of their own. Instead, she turned and forced her feet to move, walking slowly away from the platform and back into the busy streets. What she saw convinced her even more that her decision to let her daughter go away was the right one. She was walking along roads where she had to step carefully around fallen bricks and other debris. On one street, men were working to clear the remains of a house, calling instructions to each other. On another, fires burned here and there, reminding her of the awful incendiary bombs that were dropped every night.

Walking slowly down the street, head down against the breeze, she was aimlessly searching for a distraction from her heartache, when she noticed a small café tucked away on a side street. The smell of frying bacon wafted out from the open door, drawing her inside.

The warmth of the café was a welcome respite from the brisk wind outside. She chose a seat near the window, watching the people going about their lives, oblivious to her plight. Logically, she knew each of them would have their own stories, their own happiness, fears and sorrows, but at that moment hers seemed greater than anyone else's.

The café was bustling with some vaguely familiar faces, people she had seen around town but never really stopped to talk to. Two were regular library users who waved as they spotted her and then went back to their conversation. She was glad they didn't call her over to join them. She'd have been poor company.

She ordered a cup of tea as if it might fill the void in her heart. As she held the warm mug in her hands, she looked out of the window and noticed a group of children playing off-ground-touch in the street. She was reminded of her Helen yet again and another wave of anguish washed over her. Tears welled up in her eyes, but she forced them down and took a sip of her drink. She knew that she had to stay strong, no matter how much she wanted to run back to the station to bring her girl back home.

She sat for over an hour, unable to shake herself from her low mood. But then the café door opened and an elderly man walked in. His right trouser leg was pinned up, and he walked with crutches. But his eyes sparkled, and he greeted the café owner with a cheery hello and chatted about the weather. Watching him, she felt a sudden shame at her self-pity, and a profound respect for this man who still enjoyed life despite his disability. She realised life is full of struggles and hardships, as transient as summer clouds that pass by quickly on a windy day, and we should be thankful every day for what we have. She resolved to shake herself and get up.

With a firmer step, she headed to the market, ready to queue for whatever vegetables were available. She would make herself and Mrs Spencer a Woolton pie, full of healthy vegetables and some Marmite for flavouring.

Suddenly, in a shop she often used, she felt a tap on her shoulder. It was the shopkeeper, an old lady with a lined face and a kindly expression. She handed Jane an unmarked bag and grinned, holding her finger to her lips in the universal symbol of 'say nothing'.

'You know why I'm giving you this,' she said, her voice full of understanding and compassion. 'Your girl'll be fine, just you wait and see.'

Jane nodded back, feeling deeply moved by the gesture.

'Thank you,' she said softly, taking the bag and leaving.

As she made her way back home, carrying the precious bag, she couldn't help but feel a mixture of emotions. This war had made so many people suffer, but it had also brought out such kindness in others.

20

TERROR

Mavis was on the front desk, inspecting books that had been returned. As usual, some were perfect, but others had writing in the margins that needed to be rubbed out, page corners turned over that needed to be straightened, or odd bookmarks. She smiled as she removed an old Christmas card with the message *With love from May and John* inside.

She heard brisk footsteps as someone entered, disturbing her concentration. She looked up from her work and froze, a chill running down her spine. At first, she couldn't understand why this tall, unremarkable-looking man approaching her had caused this feeling of foreboding.

He wore a suit that had once been smart. It was well cared for, but showed signs of wear. The same was true of his hat and shoes. The shadow from his hat at first hid the features of his face, but when he approached the desk, he removed it and then she saw who it was.

The chill down her spine became terror.

His face was familiar, but changed. That was to be expected after nineteen years. But one thing hadn't changed. The face was still cruel, even if he was putting on a polite face.

All those years ago, she had been walking home from visiting her friend. It wasn't late, but it was winter, so the days got dark early. Shivering, she took a shortcut down an alleyway to get home and into the warmth sooner.

Little did she know that that decision would change her life forever.

As she made her way down the alleyway, pulling her thin coat round her in an attempt to keep warm, she heard a noise behind her and turned to see what it was. Puzzled, she paused for a minute to listen, seeing nothing, but the noise had gone. Shrugging it off, she carried on her way, looking forward to getting home and warming her hands by the fire.

Suddenly, someone grabbed her from behind, pulling her backwards and almost knocking her off her feet. She struggled against the attacker, but his grip grew stronger. The more she struggled, the tighter that grip became. And when she tried to scream, he shoved something in her mouth, making her gag. It smelled of some sort of oil and sweat. She attempted to turn her head, but his grip was unrelenting. She felt his breath on the side of her face.

'Keep quiet,' he whispered in her ear, in the cruellest voice she'd ever heard, 'or I'll cut your pretty throat.'

Paralysed with fear, she could feel tears streaming down her face as he began ripping off her clothes. He violated her, taking away something that could never be replaced.

These memories flashed through her mind as she faced him now in the peace and quiet of the library, remembering the young, innocent woman she had been, just starting her life. He had taken away the future she should have had as he met his own evil desires.

She took a deep breath and struggled to keep her shaking hands under control. For a split second, she was surprised he didn't recognise her, but then she realised he wouldn't – he'd never really looked at her face. She was just a body to him. But she remembered him so clearly – the memory of his face in the dim light had haunted her dreams ever since.

Without really looking at her, he spoke.

'I want to join the library, sweetheart.' His voice was less threatening than it had been in that alleyway, but still recognisable. Again, a wave of fear arose within her, and for a moment, she forgot why she was standing behind the tall wooden counter, her fingers fiddling with the returned books.

The man seemed oblivious to her apprehension, his attitude casual and expectant as he waited for her to respond. She looked up at him, her face a mask of calm, though her heart was pounding so much she thought she would choke. She realised that dealing with him for the next few minutes, filling in the form and getting him his library card, was more than she could cope with.

'Excuse me,' she said, struggling to speak normally. 'I have to be somewhere. I'll get someone else to help you.'

Cordelia was nearby and Mavis went over to her.

'Can you give this... man a library card? I can't.'

Cordelia clearly saw Mavis's pale face, wide eyes and trembling bottom lip. 'What is it? What's happened?'

Mavis shook her head. 'I'll tell you later,' she said and walked towards the ladies' toilets, refusing to look back at her attacker.

She locked herself in one of the stalls and sobbed for ten minutes, barely able to breathe. Each breath caused waves of anguish as she remembered what had followed his attack. The shame, the rejections, the loss of the life she had wanted. Then, as she gradually got control of herself, she remembered that although she'd had years of hardship, she had survived and was proud of herself and her achievements.

If only Ken didn't look so much like his father.

It was fifteen minutes in all before she left the toilets, taking tentative steps towards the desk, looking round each stack of books in case he was still there. Her relief that he was gone almost made her cry again.

Cordelia was still on the desk as she approached.

'Sorry, Cordelia, that man was someone I came across in the past.'

Cordelia pulled her to one side, keeping an eye on the door.

'It's more than that,' she said, speaking quietly. 'Do you want to tell me about it?'

Mavis bit her lip. 'He... he... attacked me many years ago. Luckily, he didn't recognise me.' She shook her head. 'I don't want to discuss it any more.'

Running her fingers through her hair, she turned away and began to pile the returned books on the trolley. But then she turned back.

'What's his name, anyway? I never knew.'

Picking up his application form, Cordelia read, 'Noah James. And, oh dear, he lives a couple of streets away from you. He said he'd recently moved into the area.'

'Anyone working today or are you 'ere for the social life?' Bert said, pushing between them, his breath as bad as ever. 'I need some 'elp 'ere.'

'I'll help you,' Cordelia said. 'Mrs Kent needs to do something else.'

Gripping the library trolley as if it might keep her upright, Mavis walked between the library stacks, replacing books in the right place without really being aware of what she was doing.

He lives near me. The thought went round and round in her mind. *I might bump into him any time.*

Everywhere she looked, she would see his shadow lurking. Every corner turned might be the one where she encountered him. The thought filled her with dread. What if people who knew Ken saw him and commented that they looked alike? Would he put two and two together? Would her attacker even care that he had a son from his heinous act? Worse still, what if Ken saw him and realised they were like two peas in a pod?

As Ken grew into boyhood, his likeness to his father had become stronger and stronger, filling Mavis with dread. From the shape of his brows to the set of his mouth, he was the spitting image of the man she hoped never to see again. She would look at her son and wonder if he had inherited his father's personality, his violence. The thought made it hard to love him as she should. It was no fault of his that he was conceived in a cold alley by a brutal man. She reminded herself of that every time she felt impatient with him, realising she was interpreting his personality through the behaviour of the man who had done her so much harm.

Eventually, all the books were put away and Mavis was relieved when Cordelia told her to take a tea break.

As she sipped, she couldn't help wishing something horrible would happen to this Noah James.

She couldn't anticipate what part she would play in that.

21

THUGS

The pounding on the door made Cordelia's blood turn to ice. Her mind was sucked away from the book she was reading into a void of fear.

Before she could get up to answer, the hammering came again. Strident, heavy, insistent. She'd just got out of the bath and was dressed only in a nightdress and dressing gown, so she was reluctant to answer the door to anyone she didn't know. And no one she knew would knock like that.

'Who is it?' she called.

The only answer was more knocks, making the stout door shake and Cordelia tremble.

She looked through the peephole. On the other side stood two men, both wearing black suits and looking like criminals, scowls on their faces. Cordelia's heart sank. It wasn't hard to guess why they were there. It was obvious this was to do with Jasper. He'd got in trouble many times before, but this was the first time this had happened.

'He's not here!' she shouted.

The knocking started again and didn't stop. Terrified, she realised she'd have to speak to the thugs.

'Wait a minute!' she shouted and hastily went to her wardrobe and selected a coat that covered her up to her neck and almost down to her feet.

So scared she could hardly breathe, she opened the door a crack, intending to speak to them through it. But the tallest man, one with a scar that went the whole length of his left cheek, didn't wait to be invited in. He pushed hard against the door, almost knocking her over.

He and the other one looked around at the elegant room.

'Not short of a bob or two, then.' The man smirked.

Everything, all the furniture, carpets, curtains, even the ornaments, was cream and gold. The book she was reading, *Black Narcissus*, lay thrown on the sofa. She could see the place through their eyes. The whole room spoke of wealth.

'Who are you, anyway? 'Is lordship's bit o' stuff? 'Ow much does 'e pay ya?'

Cordelia struggled to keep her anger under control. How dare they think she was a paid woman?

'I presume you're looking for my brother, Jasper.'

'Yeah. Where is 'e? In the bedroom, 'iding in the wardrobe?'

Before she could answer, he strode confidently towards the internal door, threw it open and went into her bedroom.

'That's my room!' she shouted, but he ignored her and walked round, looking under her bed and in the wardrobe. She made to stop him, but the other man, a hulk who was at least six-foot-six-inches tall, blocked her way, his arms folded, his face impassive.

'I wouldn't if I was you,' he growled.

Shaking with fury, her fists clenched, she had no choice but to watch the first man as he went from room to room, searching everywhere where someone could hide.

When he got to Jasper's room, he was far more ruthless. Sauntering around, he overturned the mattress, emptied the contents of Jasper's drawers onto the bed and rummaged through it. She saw him pocket two small boxes which she was sure contained gold cufflinks.

'Hey, you can't take those!' she shouted.

The hulk simply muttered, 'Call it part payment!' then went back into silent mode.

The search in Jasper's room went on and on. The man flung open the wardrobe doors, throwing clothes anyhow onto the floor, even looking in Jasper's shoes and the brim of his hats.

When he'd finished, he walked back to where Cordelia stood.

'Right. Where is the bastard?' The glint in his eyes was merciless.

Anger was replaced by fear and Cordelia struggled to stop herself from shaking. She was determined not to let these two monsters get the better of her.

'Where's who?' she asked.

He gave a bitter laugh. 'Come on, doll. I ain't got time to play games. I'm a busy man. Where is 'e?'

She folded her arms and looked away, in a clear refusal to answer.

He walked over to her sideboard, picked up an expensive and beautiful Lalique vase.

'Pretty,' he said. 'Pity if it was to break.'

And, without warning, he flung it at the wall. The noise of it smashing made her jump and every nerve in her body jingle.

He walked towards her and stroked her face again in a parody of affection.

'So, doll, want to tell me where 'e is or shall I have some more fun?' He looked around. 'Plenty more damage I could do 'ere.' He looked at the hulk. 'And my friend 'ere likes posh girls like you. Says they know a few different tricks.'

At that, Cordelia's legs felt as if they would give way. His meaning was abundantly clear. The hulk looked more than capable of rape. She was so scared, she could barely put words together to reply. But there was no point in holding out. Telling the truth would not give away where her brother was, anyway.

Cordelia felt a tremor of terror run through her as the hulking figure took a step closer and looked her up and down as if mentally undressing her. Her heart pounded so powerfully she could feel it in the back of her throat and her limbs refused to obey her, no matter how hard she tried to make them move.

'So I'll ask you again. Where's your brother?' The voice was low and guttural, laced with a cruel edge that spoke of nothing but malice. It felt like a physical force, as if it had reached out and grabbed Cordelia's throat, squeezing it shut until she just about managed to whisper her reply.

'It's true. I don't know where he is,' she said, her voice shaking with fear. The hulk reached out and grabbed her arm, pulling her close to him with an iron grip. His face was close to hers now, only a few inches away, and his breath reeked of rum.

'Are you sure?' he snarled. 'You'd better not be lying or else I'll make sure you regret it.'

She tried to speak, but her throat was so tight, the words wouldn't form. The man leaned forward again, and this time stroked her hair.

'What's that, sweet'eart? I couldn't 'ear what you said.'

Desperation made her find her voice. 'I don't know where he is. I haven't seen him for three or four days. He comes and goes as he pleases.'

'That right?' he said with a sneer. 'I think you're just covering up for 'im. Don't know why. If I had a brother who didn't pay off 'is debts, I'd disown 'im double quick.' He checked his watch. 'I ain't got time to mess around now, so you have two choices. You pay 'is debt off 'ere and now. It's one thousand three hundred pounds. Or you tell me where 'e hangs out. If 'e's not there, we'll be back and you won't like the consequences.'

One thousand three hundred pounds! Cordelia could hardly believe her ears. It was a fortune. She knew he gambled, but had no idea he'd lost so much.

'I can't pay you,' she said. 'You surely don't think I have that sort of money here.' She thought quickly. 'I could give you a cheque.'

He laughed. 'We don't deal with cheques, do we, Fred? We want cash and we want it soon. Now, for the last time asking before I let Fred loose on you, where is the little scumbag?'

Although Cordelia didn't know exactly where Jasper was, she knew the type of places he liked to visit.

'Your best bet is to try the nightclubs. And I suppose gambling dens if what you've said is true. He's never told me where he goes and that's the truth.'

He stroked her face again. 'That's 'undreds of places. I need better info than that. I ain't got time to go round all of them.'

The truth was Cordelia had seen matchbooks from a couple of nightclubs and even seen her brother in one she'd been to, but she wasn't going to tell these thugs that.

She took a deep breath. 'I'm sure someone with your... contacts... will be able to find him.'

He stepped away from her and walked towards the door. On his way, he picked up a silver cigarette lighter and put it in his pocket.

'Remember. Either I see 'im, you pay 'is debt or you'll give Fred 'ere a right good time.'

* * *

The next day, Cordelia was late for work for the first time ever. She'd tossed and turned for hours after the visit from the thugs, jumping at every sound, sure she was going to be murdered in her bed. Because of that, and an hour spent in the air-raid shelter in the basement, she overslept. Calming her nerves with several whiskies during the night left her with a hangover and she groaned when she looked in her mirror. She did her best with extra make-up, but she knew her astute workers would know something was up.

Mavis and Jane had already opened up the library so, when she walked in, all was in order. That didn't stop them hurrying over to her when she arrived.

'Are you okay, Cordelia? You look like you 'ad a right rough night,' Mavis said. 'Not at all your usual self.'

Cordelia had never shared much about her private life with Mavis and Jane. Being a manager often made her hesitate do so, and she didn't want to bother them with her worries. She knew they had enough of their own.

'I just had a stomach upset and didn't sleep much,' she said. 'I'd better go and catch up on paperwork. Forgive me if I'm not very lively today.'

She could feel their eyes following her as she made her way to her office. She felt like a fraud; she had always prided herself on her punctuality and commitment to her job, and here she was, late and dishevelled. She was embarrassed, but also grateful for their concern. She hadn't been more than fifteen minutes in her office when Mavis knocked on her door and came in, closing the door behind her.

'Call me a nosy old bat, if you like, but what's really up? And don't tell me it's a stomach upset. I didn't come down with the last shower of rain.' She put her hand over her mouth. 'Oh dear. I suppose I shouldn't talk to me boss like that, should I? Don't sack me, will you? Want me to bugger off?'

Cordelia put her head in her hands. 'Sit down, Mavis,' she said, wondering how honest to be.

Mavis pulled a chair towards Cordelia's desk, and the screech the legs made on the wooden floor made Cordelia flinch.

'Give me a minute to think,' Cordelia said. She drank a glass of water then decided to tell at least part of the truth.

'My brother, Jasper, is in trouble. I can't tell you what sort, but I need to find him quickly.'

Mavis frowned. 'Don't ya know where 'e is then?'

'I don't and I must find him urgently. He'll probably hang out at night-clubs. I know two or three of the ones he likes. But I can't go in them on my own and my friend Rosalind is away for a few days. I don't know what to do.'

'That's easy,' Mavis said with her usual bluntness. 'I'll come with you. I've never bin to one in me life. It'll be an adventure.' She paused. 'No one's gonna kill us, are they?'

Cordelia didn't have the heart to say it was her brother who might end up dead. 'You'd come with me? Really?'

'I'd love to. You'll need to lend me a posh dress, though. Mind you, it'll 'ave to be one of them cocktail ones. Any of the long ones would be so long on me, I'd look like a kid in her mum's dress.' She ran her hands down her sides. 'Good job this rationing's made me lose some weight, but you'd better make it a loose one if you've got such a thing.'

'Come to my flat at seven and we'll get you all kitted out. And of course I'm paying because you're doing me a favour.'

* * *

Mavis got off the Underground at Notting Hill Gate and got the note from her bag to check the address: 52 Pembroke Villas. She'd never been to this part of London before and looked around her. She knew this was a more wealthy area than she was used to, but in this busy road it didn't seem much different. From where she stood, she could see a café, a butcher, a cobbler and a men's outfitters. She smiled when she walked past the greengrocer. It had a display of spring flowers for sale. She was tempted, but they were expensive and she knew they'd be drooping before she got back home. Buses and people going about their business made the scene every bit as busy as the East End. The sight made her feel more comfortable. She knew Cordelia was from a different class from herself, but this seemed very familiar. Before she left the library, she'd looked in a *London A–Z* and drawn a sketch of how to get from the station to Pembroke Villas. Now all street signs had been removed, it was essential if she wasn't going to have to ask people the whole time.

She walked along Pembroke Villas, which sounded like a building but was actually a small street. Three storeys high, the houses were in groups of four with an entrance hall between them. Number 52 was in the second set and she stood outside looking up. Unlike so many properties in Silvertown, these were well maintained, with no sign of broken windows, sagging roofs and, most importantly, no bomb damage.

Feeling suddenly nervous, she pressed the doorbell, unsure of herself. To her surprise, a moment later she heard Cordelia's voice coming out of a box beside the door. 'I'll open the door, come up, first floor.' There was a loud click and the heavy door swung open. She went up the carpeted stairs, thicker than any she'd ever owned.

Cordelia was standing by her open door. 'Come in and welcome!' She stood back and let Mavis walk through. Mavis struggled to stop her jaw dropping open as she looked around when she walked into the living room. 'Blimey O'Riley, girl, I knew you was posh but not this posh.'

Cordelia laughed. 'I'll let you into a secret. It's not my place, it's my parents'. They let me and Jasper stay here. They're not keen on coming to London now. But go on, take off your coat and I'll make some drinks.'

Mavis removed her coat, aware of her cheap shoes and dress in a way she'd never been before.

'What would you like to drink? Tea or something stronger?'

'Will we be drinking in these nightclubs?' Mavis asked.

'You bet. My favourite is a nice cocktail...'

Mavis's eyes grew wide. 'I've never 'ad one of them. Are they nice? Can you make me one?'

Cordelia turned towards a cabinet against the wall opposite the windows. When she opened it, Mavis saw it was full of bottles of alcohol, more than she'd ever seen outside of a pub.

'I'm no expert,' Cordelia said, reaching for a bottle of vodka. 'I can manage a Martini, though.' She got two cocktail glasses out of the cabinet along with the cocktail shaker. 'I've laid out a few dresses on the bed if you want to try some on while I do this. Through there,' she said, pointing. 'Bathroom is the next door on the right.'

'Thanks, sweet'eart,' Mavis said, looking forward to trying on clothes she would never normally wear. She went through to the bedroom and there on the bed were four wonderful dresses, one midnight blue, one black, one emerald green and one pale pink. She hardly dared touch them in case she made them dirty so she went through to the bathroom and washed her hands.

As she walked back towards the bedroom, she passed a small table against the wall. On it were two unopened letters. She glanced at them as she passed then stopped in her tracks when she saw who they were addressed to: Lady Cordelia Carmichael. She couldn't believe her eyes and picked up one of the letters to look at it more closely to see if she was imagining it. Then she turned to Cordelia. 'Is this right? Are you really a Lady?'

Cordelia nodded as she shook the Martinis. She looked embarrassed. 'I'm afraid I am. I didn't get a choice, I just inherited the title.'

Mavis grunted in disbelief. 'The only thing I ever inherited was an undertakers' bill. Should we be curtseying or something every time we see you, Lady Cordelia?'

Cordelia passed her the drink. 'Of course not, it doesn't mean anything and I certainly didn't do anything to earn it. I'd be glad if you forgot you ever knew about it.'

Mavis took a sip of her drink and licked her lips. 'Not bad. So I suppose you want me to keep your little secret then?'

'Yes, please, and in return I'll lend you the dress of your choice and buy the drinks all night.' She went to the kitchen and returned with a plate of dainty sandwiches. 'Better eat some of these or we'll be tiddly before we find my brother.'

Mavis spent fifteen happy minutes trying on the dresses and admiring herself from all angles in the wardrobe mirror. In the end she chose the black one because she decided it was the most flattering. She did her best to improve her unruly hair and returned to the living room. Cordelia took one look at her and wolf-whistled. 'Wow, Mavis, you look a million dollars. You'll have a lot of admirers in that.'

* * *

Cordelia and Mavis had no sooner taken the last step down into the Blue Moon nightclub when the air-raid siren blared, audible even from down there.

'I hope Jasper is here, otherwise if this raid goes on, we might be stuck here for hours,' Cordelia said.

'Won't worry me,' Mavis said. 'This is turning out to be the best night of me life.'

The club was packed with many men wearing uniforms. All the women were dressed to kill. The air was thick with the smell of perfume and cigarette smoke and the sound of chatter almost overwhelmed the band who were playing 'By the Sleepy Lagoon'. The nightclub pulsed with energy, the dance floor so packed they weren't sure how anyone could move.

They found a table at the back and Mavis sat down, trying not to gape at the people around her in their finery. 'So this place is deep enough to be an air-raid shelter?' she asked Cordelia. 'Bit bloody different from sleeping in a smelly Underground station.'

Cordelia left her there and walked around the dimly lit room. There was no sign of Jasper.

Frustrated and fearful, she sat down and sipped the Old Fashioned that she had ordered.

Mavis took a tentative sip of her drink and pulled a face. 'Not so keen on that one,' she said, putting it on the table and pushing it towards Cordelia. 'Any sign of your brother?'

'I've looked. He's not here, and there's a raid on, so we can't go anywhere else.' Her voice rose in panic and people at the next table turned to see what was going on. 'What if I can't find him?'

'Have you got a photo of him with you?'

Without looking up, Cordelia got one out of her handbag.

'Hand it over.' Without another word, Mavis went to the bar staff and, showing them the photo, asked if they'd seen Jasper. All but one shook their heads, but a pretty blonde waitress with bouncy curls nodded.

''E often comes in, but I ain't seen 'im for a few days. No idea where 'e'd be. Sorry.'

Mavis went from table to table, showing the photo and asking the patrons, many of whom were tipsy, if they'd seen Jasper. Most just shook their head, but when she'd almost been ready to give up, a tall man with black hair and an Errol Flynn moustache nodded.

'Yes, I know him, always good for a laugh. Can I buy you a drink? It's a pity for a pretty girl like you to be all alone.'

Mavis felt a warm glow at the compliment and thought that perhaps she should wear more flattering clothes every day if they got you noticed. If only she could afford them.

'I'm not alone. I'm with a friend, but I must find Jasper urgently. His father is ill and we have to go to see him.' It was a lie, but better than telling the truth. 'Have you seen him, or know where I could look?'

The man took a little notebook and gold pen out of his pocket.

'Pity you can't stop for a drink, but I do understand.' He scribbled some names on the paper. 'These are clubs I know he goes to, but I expect there are others.'

Mavis thanked him and sat back down, impatient for the chance to go to the clubs she'd just been told about.

'We'll go as soon as we hear the all-clear,' Cordelia said.

Mavis looked at her, at the dark rings under her eyes and the frown on her usually smooth forehead. Her fingers were tapping to the song the band were playing, 'Putting on the Ritz'.

'I know you're worried about him, sweetheart, but there's nothing we can do, so why don't we just relax and enjoy the music?'

But relaxing came hard to Cordelia, who had been tense since that first knock on her door. Her breathing was too fast, her body fidgety. But she didn't have to wait long to spring into action again. Two numbers later, the all-clear sounded and, downing the remainder of their drinks, they headed outside.

'We were lucky,' Mavis said, wrapping her coat around herself. 'Looks like only incendiary bombs this time, though that's bad enough.'

They stepped carefully around scattered debris as they headed down the street to the next club, Club Capital. On their way, they passed several ladies of the night who called out, 'Fancy going with a girl for a change?' and then leaned forward so that Mavis got a view of their ample bosoms. Another lady was leading a smartly dressed man in a bowler hat down a nearby alleyway, holding on to his hand as if to ensure he didn't change his mind. She must have come outside as soon as the all-clear sounded, and there she was – on the streets, just like any other worker.

'I 'eard they 'ave a bloke every fifteen minutes, and that includes getting them up to their room,' Mavis said when they were out of earshot. 'It makes me shudder to think about it.'

Club Capital wasn't very different from the last place.

'We're not stopping,' Cordelia said. 'Well, maybe one drink. We'll just look around and then go if Jasper isn't there.'

Cordelia paid the entrance fee again and was about to order more cocktails when Mavis stopped her. 'Just a lemonade for me, or I'll be useless tomorrow and me boss will fire me!' She grinned as she said it and Cordelia smiled back.

'I'll sit while you look for Jasper,' Mavis whispered when their drinks were in front of them. 'I'll look after your drink.'

Mavis watched Cordelia as she walked round, talking to people sitting at the small round tables or dancing. But she was aware people were looking at her askance.

She was almost back to Mavis when a man wearing a black suit with extravagantly wide shoulders stepped in her path. He was obviously a bouncer. He had dead eyes and looked as if he'd never smiled in his life.

'I ain't seen you 'ere before, but you need to know we don't 'ave girls like you in this club.' He looked Cordelia up and down as if she was someone to be despised. 'Not even expensive working girls like you in your posh dress. It lowers the tone. Go on, 'op it before I call the Old Bill.'

Mavis's mouth dropped open and she stared at him, astonished that he would think Cordelia was working the room and soliciting for business.

'She's not on the game, you silly man!' she said, louder than Cordelia wanted. 'This is Lady Cordelia Carmichael, and she's looking for her brother, not a trick!'

She took his photo from Cordelia and handed it to the bouncer. 'His name is Jasper. He's very good-looking and probably drunk. Have you seen him?'

His impassive face didn't change a jot while he looked at the photo, then he handed it back. 'Never seen 'im in me life. Now, are you two going to buy another drink or what?'

He waved a waitress over to serve them. She approached their table with a smile as they sat down again.

The waitress took their order, then bent towards Cordelia, lowering her voice.

'I know who you're looking for. He does come in here sometimes. I saw him a few nights ago.'

'Do you know where he might be?' Cordelia asked.

The waitress made a play of taking their orders before replying.

'You could try La Passion. I heard him saying he gambles there. They must have a back room. Worth a try.'

Cordelia held up her hand, telling the waitress to wait. Opening her bag, she took out a ten-shilling note. 'Please cancel our orders. This is for your kindness. Thank you.'

She picked up her coat and indicated for Mavis to follow her outside.

'Cheeky sod!' Mavis said, doubled over with laughter as they stood outside the nightclub. 'Fancy thinking you were on the game! Mind you, you'd be a high-class madam!'

Cordelia thumped her so hard she almost fell over but, as they walked the short distance to La Passion, they laughed at the absurdity of their encounter.

Until that night, Cordelia had always enjoyed going to nightclubs with her friends, but as they stood outside the door she sighed, thinking she'd rather be at home quietly reading her book.

Giving herself a shake, she put her arm through Mavis's. 'Come on, let's make this the last place. By the way, it's a casino, not nightclub. Don't be tempted if you want to hang on to your money.'

The doorman led them to a door at the far end of the bar. It had a black background with a drawing of the Moulin Rouge painted in red on it. He opened the door for them and waited until they'd gone in, then went back to his post at the entrance.

The sound of clinking glasses, clattering chips and boisterous laughter filled the room. The scent of cigarette smoke and whisky permeated the air. As they walked through the crowded area, they caught glimpses of men in flashy suits and women wearing revealing dresses. 'How the other 'alf lives,' Mavis thought, looking around at the opulence of the surroundings and the people there.

As they approached a roulette table, Mavis spotted Jasper there, and nudged Cordelia. 'Isn't that your brother?'

Cordelia nodded and approached him with purpose, but her steps faltered as she got closer. Mavis looked at her then looked at Jasper and the men with him. Something about the way he was laughing and joking with these men chilled her to the bone. Jasper's laughter looked false and his body language was more tense than a happy man would have.

Mavis made to walk towards him, but Cordelia held her back.

'Let's just look for a minute.'

As they watched, he put more chips on the table, bidding on number twenty-seven.

'My lucky number,' he cried out. 'Be lucky for me again!'

The croupier waited until everyone had placed their bets, then spun the roulette wheel. A woman dressed in a gold figure-hugging Celeste evening dress clung on to Jasper's arm and kissed his cheek.

'You know I bring you luck, darling,' she said, holding her black cigarette holder to one side.

The croupier spun the roulette wheel and the red and black numbers flashed around it in a blur. Everyone round the table held their breath as the wheel slowed, and finally settled on the number twenty-seven. A cheer erupted from the crowd and several people patted Jasper on the back in congratulations. The beautiful woman in the gold dress embraced him tightly, as if to confirm her charm was lucky.

He was about to place his entire winnings back on the table when he glanced up. When he caught Cordelia's eye, the laughter died, and was replaced by a look of confusion and recognition. The beautiful woman saw where he was looking and clung on to him tighter.

'I am more beautiful than her, darling,' she said in her husky voice.

Putting the chips back in his pocket, he pushed her to one side and stumbled towards Cordelia, his steps unsteady with alcohol. He stopped a few feet away, as if wary of her reaction.

Cordelia didn't speak.

'Cordelia,' he said, his eyes narrowing. 'What are you doing here? Come to do your big sister act and smack little brother's bottom?'

Dragging her eyes away from the woman, Cordelia took a step forward.

'I need to speak to you. Now. In private.'

He laughed. 'You're joking, aren't you? I'm on a winning streak here.'

'What do you think the odds are that you'll walk away with any winnings?'

He waved his chips at her. 'Doing all right so far, sis.' He looked at Mavis and gave one of his winning smiles. 'And who do we have here? I don't think I've seen you before.'

'Never mind that,' Mavis said. 'I think you'd better listen to what your sister has to say.'

They were interrupted by one of the staff.

'Will you be playing again, sir? Madam?' he asked in a calm voice, belying his need to get them on the gaming tables as quickly as possible.

Jasper took a step back towards the roulette table, but Cordelia grabbed hold of his sleeve.

She turned to the man. 'We need a private room for a few minutes. Do you have one we can use?'

He looked at Jasper. 'Are you in agreement with this, sir?'

Jasper sighed heavily, fiddling with the chips in his hands.

'I suppose so, but don't worry, I'll be back soon.'

The man bowed. 'Follow me, please.'

They followed the tall, silent man as he made his way through the hustle and bustle of the casino floor. As they passed the gamblers, some of them broke away from their games to follow them with their eyes, no doubt wondering what was so special about these two strangers that warranted the man's attention.

He led all three of them through the gambling tables, past the gamblers crowing when they won or groaning when they lost. Past the croupiers whose faces never showed their feelings. Past the waitresses in their short black dresses with cute white aprons tied round their waists.

As they walked, Mavis could feel the eyes of the other patrons on them. It was almost as if they were being watched, not just by the gamblers, but by the staff, too. It made her want to get out of there as quickly as possible. She hoped Jasper wasn't going to be difficult.

Finally, they reached the end of a long corridor, where the man paused and opened a door.

He stepped back and let them enter. It was a meeting room with eight chairs round a polished oak table. On a side table was a selection of drinks and glasses. Jasper immediately strode towards it, but Cordelia stepped in his path.

'No more drinks, Jasper. I need to speak to you and it may well be a matter of life and death.'

'Whose life?' he asked with a strained laugh.

'Let's sit down and I'll explain.' Mavis noticed that he sat as far away from his sister as he could and she shook her head at his childishness.

'Come on, then. What's this mysterious threat to life and limb?' he asked, steepling his fingers. 'It had better be good to pull me away from my winning streak.'

Cordelia glared at him. 'Be serious for a moment, Jasper, and listen to what I've got to say.'

He hiccoughed and went to make some silly remark, but then her words seemed to sink in.

'What's the problem, Cordelia? Did I leave my bedroom untidy?'

Mavis had to resist the urge to go and slap him like she would a naughty child.

'Yesterday evening, two thugs came to the flat,' Cordelia began. 'They forced their way in, looking for you.'

His face went white. 'Were they... did they...?'

'They didn't attack me, if that's what you're asking. But they did threaten me. They're looking for you, for the money you owe them. Over a thousand pounds! How can you be so irresponsible, Jasper? Father would disown you if he knew.'

'I... I... What...?' he began, but it seemed the shock of this news had stolen his tongue.

Cordelia sat back and folded her arms.

'I presume you can't pay this debt, or did you just win enough?' She watched his face contort in pain as he shook his head, eyes downcast. 'If you don't pay up, they will beat you up. They may even kill you. And if they can't find you, they'll come after me!'

Mavis, who was hearing the detail for the first time, glared at him. 'So what are you going to do about it?'

To her surprise, he let out a cry and leaned forward, putting his head on his arms. His shoulders shook as he began to sob.

'I can't do anything. I don't have the money. I don't know what to do.'

His misery was palpable, his desperation and helplessness so strong it could almost be touched. He was a pathetic sight, sitting there feeling sorry for himself.

'I've helped you again and again,' Cordelia said, her face steely. 'But this is different. Your life is at stake, and maybe mine too.'

Mavis turned to her. 'He's not even trying to find a solution.' She looked again at Jasper, his head still buried in his arms. 'Jasper, I've never met you before but I can see you're a pathetic excuse for a man. Your sister tells you thugs have threatened her and might kill her and all you can do is feel sorry for yourself. I'm ashamed of you!'

She clearly thought that being tough with him would bring him out of himself, but it didn't work. He continued to stay exactly as he was.

Cordelia stood up and went to stand next to him. For a moment, Mavis thought she would put her arms around him, but then saw her step back.

'Jasper,' she said, loud enough to be heard over his sobs. 'I will use my inheritance from Granny Gibson to pay off your debt on one condition.'

He looked up, his eyes red, his nose runny. She handed him a handkerchief and he wiped his face.

'You would? You'd help me?' His voice was shaky and tears looked about to spring again.

'Yes. But on one condition. Are you listening?'

She waited until she was sure she had his full attention.

'You have to join the army.'

His mouth opened as he gasped. 'But I—'

'Yes, I know you dodged being called up, but you can tell them that was a mistake. You will join up tomorrow. Tomorrow, do you hear me? As soon as you have, you come to the library and show me the papers.'

His face went pale and his lower lip trembled. 'But I...'

Cordelia folded her arms. 'I want no excuses from you. You've got yourself into this mess and dragged me into it as well. I was terrified when those thugs came to the flat and I won't tell you what one of them threatened to do to me if this isn't sorted out.'

He went paler still. 'I'm so sorry, Delia. I had no idea they'd come to the flat. I'll see if I can sort it out.'

Mavis grunted. 'Sort it out? Do you mean get into debt with moneylenders? Your kind-hearted sister is offering to use her own money to get you out of trouble. Take up her offer. I reckon being a soldier will teach you discipline. Goodness knows you need it.'

He shot her a look that was pure poison.

'It's nothing to do with—'

She cut across him. 'It's to do with me if you upset my friend. Not to mention me traipsing around nightclubs looking for you this evening. Trying to save your life, I might add.'

He seemed to crumble in his chair and ran his hands through his hair. 'Okay...'

Cordelia stood up.

'We're going now. We've got work tomorrow. Remember, I expect to see you at the library with your army papers.'

22

ILLNESS

''Ere, this newspaper is wet. 'Ow am I supposed to read it like this?' Bert waved the soggy page around as if it were a flag. It began to tear and Mavis snatched it off him before he could do any more damage. Before she could reply to Bert, the Captain intervened. He was wearing a purple uniform with gold epaulettes.

''Ay, mate, give 'er a break. It's raining out there, ain't it? Use your bonce and spread out the pages to dry.'

Bert glared at him, muttered a swear word under his breath and stormed off, dragging the paper behind him like a dead cat.

'Thanks, Captain,' Mavis said with a rare smile. 'What can we do for you today?'

He pointed to his neck. 'Got a bit of a sore throat. It ain't the doc's day so I thought I'd look it up in a book. Can't afford to go to the hospital, can I? Feel a bit 'ot an' all.' As he spoke, he undid the top button of his jacket and waved one hand in front of his face to cool himself down. His brows puckered and he sniffed loudly as he dug into his inner pocket for a spotless hankie to put up to his nose. Then he sneezed, loud enough to be heard all over the library.

'Medical books are over there on the right,' Mavis said, backing away and pointing.

He blew her a kiss and wandered off, avoiding the area where Bert was sitting, moaning to himself.

Two minutes later, Cordelia came out of the office and joined her. She kept her voice low as she spoke. 'I'm expecting my brother in sometime today as you know. If I'm in the office, will you send him straight up, please?' She paused and put her hand on Mavis's arm. 'Thank you again for last night. I don't know what I'd have done without you there. I don't know how I can ever repay you.'

Mavis wondered how she had ever thought Cordelia was too stuck up to be friendly with. 'Well, Cordelia, if you really want to repay me, you can lend me that dress again next time there's a dance at the 'all. I'll wow the lot of 'em, even if I am the oldest.'

Cordelia grinned. 'I can do better than that. I'll bring it in tomorrow. It's yours!'

Mavis's jaw dropped open. 'You can't do that! It must've cost a bomb!'

'I can and I will. It's yours.'

Mavis looked at her more closely. 'You look a bit flushed. You feeling okay?'

'Just a bit of a headache, that's all. I'll take it easy and catch up with paperwork, but give me a shout if you need me.'

* * *

Cordelia made them both some tea and took hers up to the office. It was time to do the monthly figures, but she had difficulty concentrating and sat back in her chair, sipping the tea. As she did so, she realised her throat was a little sore. With the number of children who came into the library, it seemed as if there was always some bug or other going round. She was sure she'd caught the cough and cold she'd had for a couple of days from them.

Her gaze kept flicking towards the clock as she tried to concentrate on her work. She was on tenterhooks, wondering if Jasper would come in.

Would he really sign on? It was difficult to imagine him in an army uniform, but the military training and discipline would teach him to control his impulses better, something the army would provide in spades.

Could he really follow orders? It seemed impossible that he could be a soldier, but it would also take him away from his usual haunts and friends who encouraged his bad behaviour.

She looked at the pile of work in front of her and remembered she had to fit in a visit to the bank to get out the money the thugs demanded. She wiped her damp forehead with her handkerchief and went to get herself a glass of water.

She was just sitting down again when there was a knock on the door and Jasper entered. One look at him and she sighed. She knew, before he even opened his mouth, that he hadn't signed on. Guilt was written all over his face. His cheeks were red, and he was looking everywhere but directly at her.

He stared down at his feet, then spoke quietly. 'I tried. I really tried. I went to the recruitment office, but I just couldn't do it.' He lifted his head and looked at her for the first time. 'I'd have to fight, Cordelia. You don't understand. I might get killed. You wouldn't want that, would you?'

He was shaking with fear as he spoke. Once she would have felt sorry for him and offered him some comfort, but the thought of what that thug might do to her wiped away any sympathy.

She felt anger flooding through her body like a wave, making her heart race. She couldn't believe it. After all she had said, all he had agreed to. Didn't he care that his actions could result in one or both of them being beaten up – or worse? He'd always been selfish, but to put her in danger like this was way beyond anything she'd ever known.

She stood up to face him, although his eyes had become downcast again. 'So does that mean you borrowed the money to pay off your debts?'

For a minute, he didn't move. Then she heard a sob, and he shook his head.

'I couldn't,' he whispered. 'No one would help me. What am I going to do?'

'Sit down!' she commanded, pointing to a chair opposite her desk. He shuffled over to it and sat on the edge as if he might bolt any minute.

Cordelia looked at him despairingly. Once again, he was looking to her to solve his problems, just as he had all their lives. She took a few deep breaths to calm herself, actually wanting to walk around the desk and hit him with something.

Unable to sleep the previous night, she had tossed and turned, trying to find an alternative solution. Two early-morning phone calls ensured that her idea was feasible.

'Right,' she started, and had to hold back all the names she wanted to call him. 'I have an alternative solution and you absolutely have to take it. If you don't, you will ruin both our lives.'

He looked up again, hope in his eyes. 'What's that?'

'You remember Great-Aunt Bess who lives in the north of Scotland? We used to have wonderful summer holidays there.'

His eyes narrowed as he tried to work out what she was going to say next.

'As you know, she has a farm. We used to enjoy playing in the fields and feeding the animals. Well, Bess's farm manager is in poor health and you are going to replace him.'

Jasper started and stood up. 'You're joking! Leave everything behind and go to Scotland? Leave all my friends and everything I know! I know nothing about farming.'

'You may be irresponsible, Jasper, but you're not actually stupid. You're capable of learning. The farm manager will stay on for a few weeks to show you the ropes, then he can retire and you can take over. Getting away from your friends and current lifestyle will be the best thing for you.'

He sat down heavily as if felled.

'Cordelia, do you realise how cold it gets in the north of Scotland in winter?'

'Yes, and you'll survive.' She looked at some notes she'd made earlier. 'Now. There is an overnight train this evening. That gives you time to pack and get to the station.' She paused. 'Are you going to do it or are you willing to gamble with your life and mine? If you agree, I will go to the bank in my break and get the money needed to get you out of trouble. If you don't, they will come after you and if they can't find you, they'll come after me.'

He sat, shell-shocked, silently absorbing the implications of everything she had said. His body was as still as a statue, no doubt his mind desperately trying to find an alternative to her solution.

Tapping her fingers on the desk, Cordelia waited for his response. As she did so, she became aware her throat was more sore than it had been first thing in the morning. She resolved that when she went out, she would go to the pharmacy to get some sort of throat medicine.

'Are we agreed? You'll go to work for Great-Aunt Bess?'

His bottom lip stuck out like a sulking child. 'Will I get paid?'

'I have no idea. You'll have to discuss that when you get there.'

There was a loud tap on her door and it opened without the person on the other side waiting for an answer.

Mavis leaned in, looking worried.

'The Captain has collapsed and he can hardly breathe. I've called an ambulance. You'd better come.'

Leaving Jasper where he was, Cordelia hurried after Mavis, but first she turned to him.

'You've got to do it, Jasper. There's no choice.'

The Captain was lying on the floor, conscious, but in great distress. His eyes were not as focused as usual. He had a high temperature and was gasping for breath.

'Will it help if you sit up?' Cordelia asked.

His response was to look from her to Mavis pleadingly.

'Let's try it,' Mavis said, bending towards him.

At that moment, the doors were thrust open with a bang and two ambulancemen rushed in, carrying a stretcher between them.

'We'll take over now, ladies,' they said. 'Please get everyone to stay well back.'

The two women moved readers who were watching the scene with some fascination.

'Please, everyone, move further away,' Cordelia tried to say, but her voice was somewhat hoarse.

The men took one look at the Captain and carefully put him onto the stretcher.

'I've seen this before,' one of them said. 'We need to act quickly. We'll take him to St George's.'

They were already walking towards the door when the man looked back.

'Does he come in regularly?' he asked over his shoulder. 'If he does, you should watch out for a sore throat and a temperature – see a doctor if that happens.'

Mavis looked at Cordelia.

'You're still looking flushed.' She held her hand to Cordelia's forehead. 'You've got a temperature. Have you got a sore throat?'

With a deep sense that something terrible was happening to her, Cordelia nodded.

'Right, then, get your stuff. You're going to see the doctor now.'

And with that, she pushed Cordelia towards her office. But when she got there, she felt as if she'd been punched in the stomach.

Jasper was nowhere to be seen.

She almost fell into her chair. Strength drained from her with the physical and emotional challenges of the day. She dragged herself upright and picked up her bag. Her next task was to go to the bank to get the money to bail him out, and then try to find a doctor who would see her.

23

THE HOSPITAL

Cordelia opened her eyes and looked around. Everything around her was white, and she briefly wondered if she had died and gone to heaven. But the pain in her throat and her throbbing head told her she was firmly on earth, but must be dreaming.

Robert was bending over her, his face etched with concern.

'Are you with us, Cordelia?'

She looked into his eyes, the eyes she'd come to love so much, but the effort of staying awake was too much. He held her hand, and she drifted back to unconsciousness.

She dreamt of books flying through the air like missiles exploding on roads and roofs, scattering thousands of pages of stories through the air, of dancing in nightclubs and horrible, threatening men in black suits attacking her. When that happened, she became restless, turning this way and that, whimpering. Someone, a nurse perhaps, would always speak soothingly to her. She didn't consciously hear them, but all the same was calmed by the voices. The gentle words seemed to weave themselves into the fabric of the dream, chasing away the fear and allowing her to drift off once more.

When she next half surfaced, she was sure she'd dreamt seeing him, Robert. The room she was in was empty, but outside she could hear voices and metal trolleys trundling past. She tried to call out, but the effort exhausted her and she slept again.

'Ah, you're awake,' a warm voice said the next time she was aware of her surroundings. 'We were worried about you. How are you now?'

Feeling as if her head were inside a foggy room, she tentatively turned her head towards the voice. A smiling nurse was leaning towards her, but something was wrong and it took a while for her mind to clear enough to work out what it was. The nurse was wearing a mask over her face. Her name badge said Nurse Simpkins.

'Where am I?' Cordelia croaked.

'You're in St George's, love,' the nurse said. 'Come on, let's get you sitting up.' She put her arm behind Cordelia's back and leaned her forward so she could put several pillows behind her. 'We put you in a private room. When we looked up your name, we saw you had insurance.'

She handed Cordelia a glass of water.

'It'll probably hurt to drink this, so just have tiny sips.'

Cordelia did as she was told, every sip like a knife cutting the inside of her throat, and then she asked, 'How long have I been here? What happened?'

'Don't you remember, dearie? Poor you. You've been here about...' She looked at her watch. 'About forty-eight hours. A couple of days. Do you remember coming in?'

Taking another sip of water and flinching with pain, Cordelia shook her head with care. 'No, the last thing I remember was walking towards my bank.'

As she said the words, she was filled with panic. Her mouth, already dry, felt like sandpaper and her heart beat so fast she could hardly breathe.

'My bag...' she gasped.

The nurse was tidying her sheets. 'You had rather a lot of money in your bag, dearie, so we put it in the safe. Do you want it?'

Relieved her money hadn't been taken, she shook her head again.

'What's wrong with me? My throat hurts a lot.'

'You've got tonsillitis. Not so bad when you're a kiddie, but at your age it can hit you hard. You've had it more seriously than most and it really knocked you out. But you'll be right as rain before you know it. Oh, and you've had some visitors. They'll be glad to know you're on the mend.'

She left the room and Cordelia leaned back into the pile of pillows, feeling uneasy, as if there was something she should do. In her muddled state, she couldn't work out what it was.

She dozed off again and when she awoke, the nurse was taking her pulse. Once again, Cordelia felt a sense of unexplained panic. She knew there was something urgent she needed to do and searched her mind for it, running through everything she could remember from before she became ill. Then she had it.

Jasper!

She'd told him to go to Scotland to get away from the thugs.

'Did my brother come to visit me?' she asked.

The nurse placed a thermometer under her tongue. 'I don't think so, dear. Two friends came in. They said they worked with you. They were very worried. Dr Fernsby has looked in several times. He has taken a particular interest in your case.' She paused as she removed the thermometer, read it, shook it and put it back in its holder. 'Between you and me, I think he might be rather fond of you, Lady Cordelia. But I might be speaking out of turn.'

Her words were the tonic Cordelia needed, and she felt her heart sing. But it lasted only a minute.

'Have two men in black suits been here? They look like bouncers,' she asked as the memory of her conversation with the thugs returned to her.

Nurse Simpkins shook her head. 'I'd remember them, for sure. They sound most unpleasant. Unless they came when I was off duty, they haven't been here.'

After tidying the sheets so they looked freshly starched and ironed, she left the room.

Two days! Panic crawled under Cordelia's skin. She'd been unconscious for two days! The thought made panic rise in her. She had to get out of there. The thugs had given her that long to pay them and it was already nearer three. She tried to move, but her body felt heavy and hot, as if her legs wouldn't support her weight.

She forced herself to swing her legs to the side of the bed, ignoring the dizzying pain that made her feel sick. The cool floor was a balm on her feet and she took a deep breath, ready to attempt to stand.

But she got no further.

The door opened and Robert came in.

'What on earth are you doing, Cordelia? You're not well enough to leave. Get back into bed immediately.' He walked over to her, lifted her legs and swivelled her round. Then he covered her again. 'Now, what's so urgent that you need to put your health at risk?'

As he spoke, he put his hand on her forehead.

'You've still got a temperature. This is the best place for you. Now, what's this all about?'

Her mind was a whirl. Should she tell him? She sensed there was a special connection between them, but nothing had been said. Would it be ethical to tell someone who didn't know Jasper about what had happened?

'It's something I should have done yesterday. If I don't do it, something terrible will happen.'

He frowned and sat on the chair next to her. 'I can't imagine what that might possibly be. Do you want to talk about it?'

She looked into his kind eyes and knew that she could trust him. But it didn't feel right to darken her brother's name or to let Robert know the danger she was in.

'It's something I've got to do for my brother,' she said. 'I'm afraid I can't tell you what.'

He tried to persuade her to confide in him, and she understood he wanted to help her, but she couldn't own up to having such a feckless brother. Reluctantly, he left her to continue with his rounds, and she sat back, wondering what had been happening about Jasper while she had been in hospital.

During visiting time that evening, Jane came into her room, looking tired and sad. She took off her coat and put down her bag.

'I'm so glad to see you in the land of the living,' she said. 'Me and Mavis were really worried about you.' She was carrying a tiny box of chocolates. 'Sorry they're not bigger,' she said as she sat down. 'You know what rationing is like.'

Cordelia immediately grabbed her wrist. 'I don't suppose you've heard anything about my brother, have you? I'm really worried about him.' As she spoke, she remembered that Jane didn't know what had been happening to Jasper.

Jane smiled. 'We have. We had a phone call at the library. He had been trying to call you at home and when you didn't answer he decided to try work. He sent you his best wishes and said not to worry. Everything is sorted out and he is a farm manager now.'

It was something, but there were still the thugs to worry about. Panic struck Cordelia again, but she didn't feel she could burden Jane with her problems. She just hoped that when they couldn't find her in, they would keep coming round. Eventually, she would be able to pay them, unless Jasper's message meant that somehow he had managed to do so.

* * *

Cordelia was kept in hospital one more day then allowed home on the understanding she took it easy for at least another week. Afraid of what she might find, she inserted her key into her front door, scared to see what might be behind it. Hardly daring to breathe, she walked around, but everything was just as she left it when she became ill. At least the thugs hadn't broken the door down and ransacked her home.

She was about to go to her next-door neighbour's flat to ask if they had been back again when she saw a letter on the doormat. She immediately recognised Jasper's handwriting and sat down on the sofa to read it.

Dearest Sis,

Sorry I've caused you so much trouble. Quick note to let you know that Great-Auntie has loaned me the money to pay off my debt. I won't get paid here until I've worked off my debt, but it's the best solution all round. If you can pay them, I'll get the money to you in a few days.

I'll phone you soon.

Love, your errant brother x

Relieved, she got out her phone and address book and dialled Great-Aunt Bess's number. The phone rang many times before it was answered, then a shaking older voice said, 'Hello, who is this?'

'It's Cordelia,' she shouted, knowing she needed to in order to be heard. 'I'm phoning to see if my brother is still with you, Auntie.'

'Your brother? You mean Jasper? Yes, he's still here. Do you want to speak to him? I can fetch him. He's outside closing the gate to make sure the cows don't escape.'

Cordelia put her hands over her mouth to stop herself from laughing too loudly when she heard that. Jasper. Cows! It was impossible to imagine. The expensively dressed man about town with his coiffured hair, tailored suits and handmade shoes would be wearing old clothes and wellington boots. Instead of the West End streets he was used to sauntering through, he'd be walking through fields, trying to dodge cowpats. It was too delicious for words.

24

THE SON

Mavis returned home to an eerie silence. Although Jane and her little girl had left several days earlier, the house still felt empty, as though the laughter and joy of having them around had been absorbed by the walls. As Mavis walked through the silent rooms, memories of happier times with her own son came flooding back.

When she had first arrived in the house with Ken, life was hard. She juggled three cleaning jobs where she could take him with her, and just managed to keep a roof over their heads and food on the table. There'd never been any money for extras, but everyone around her was in the same boat, so Ken had no reason to feel deprived. She had moved to the area to start a new life and had pretended she was a widow, though that was really nobody's business. All she wanted was to ensure that her son wouldn't be judged or labelled a bastard.

Despite the struggles, there had been happy days when Ken was a little lad, playing with the other kids in the street, and chasing the coal-man's horse and cart. Sometimes she'd stand on her doorstep watching him, tears of happiness in her eyes. But she knew she hadn't been a perfect mother. She was so young and there was so much she didn't know. How to calm a baby who cried all night, how to calm herself when he irritated her beyond belief with his constant questions or demands. How to keep being a kind and loving mum when she was worried about how to find the money to pay the rent man. She'd given him the occasional clout, but nothing compared to what she saw other mothers do.

She still had his first shoes upstairs, in an old shoebox, as well as a picture he'd drawn her at school and some fading photos of him as a lad. Those were happy times. Now, things couldn't be more different.

Mavis looked around her cosy room, feeling a pang of sadness that pierced her heart. What had she done wrong to cause him to become the man he was now? She had done the best she could. The only thing now was to make the best of what she had. But that didn't stop her from dreading his imminent visit.

Sighing, she looked at the clock, got up, and went to the kitchen to make him a meal. With rationing, it was difficult to give him what he wanted, but she determined to do her best. He was still her son, after all.

She was stirring the stew when the door opened and he walked in, bringing the clamour and smells from the streets with him. Without him even saying a word, the atmosphere in the house changed like a spreading virus, tense and strained.

'Hello, love,' she said, trying to smile. 'You're early. That's good. Your tea'll be ready soon. 'Ow was your journey?'

Ken grunted and took off his coat and scarf.

'Trains are bloody terrible, as usual.'

He dug in his rucksack and rummaged round for what he was looking for.

'There,' he said without looking at her. 'Thought you could use this.'

He put a tin of corned beef on the kitchen table, then went and sat on the settee, where he lit up a cigarette and opened a newspaper. He held it so she couldn't see his face. Mavis knew better than to interrupt him, but glanced over anyway. She hadn't had time to read the paper, but saw the headline was 'Rise in deaths from diphtheria'. She shook her head. Dr Fernsby had talked about that several times when he'd been in the library. She shivered at the thought of those poor children who were affected.

She turned to get out the bowls to dish up the stew.

'Tea's ready,' she called, placing the bowls of stew and plates of bread and marge on the little table. He took his time folding up the newspaper, as if eating the meal she'd spent so long preparing was something that was too much trouble. Sometimes she wanted to ask him why he visited at all. It wasn't as if he ever seemed to enjoy her company, but somehow she couldn't get the words past her lips.

They ate in almost complete silence, but she was pleased that he seemed to enjoy the stew. When he'd finished, he put down his knife and fork and looked at her. She knew that look, and her stomach clenched.

'Right,' he said. 'You've fobbed me off enough times. Time you told me who my father is.' He looked over at the photo of a soldier on the windowsill. 'Is that really 'im? I've never seen your marriage certificate, nor any other photos. Were you even married to 'im? I've got a right to know.'

His voice got harsher with every word and she could see the tension in his face and neck. That was a danger signal.

Mavis tried to stay calm, but her stomach was in knots and her mouth was dry as a desert. She had never wanted to lie to her son, but the truth was so complicated that she was not sure where to start. She had no way to explain the circumstances of his conception without hurting him further.

She swallowed hard, a million thoughts rushing through her mind, wanting at all costs to avoid telling him her dreadful secret. He might not believe what had really happened, or worse, might call her all sorts of names – a slut, a whore, a tramp. In any case, she wanted to protect him from the implications of the knowledge. She'd rehearsed her story a hundred times in her mind, even said it out loud in front of a mirror.

The words she spoke were as delicate as glass, and she hoped she sounded convincing.

''Is name is 'Enry. He was someone I knew when I was younger, too young, someone I thought I loved. We got married quick when you was on the way, but it didn't last long. 'E upped and vanished one day and I never knew where 'e'd gone. I'm sorry, but that's all I can tell you. I don't know where 'e is. 'E could be dead for all I know.'

Ken wouldn't want to know the truth. He wouldn't want to know the horror of how he had been conceived. That part of him was the work of a dangerous, brutal man. Better that he never knew.

Ken narrowed his eyes, searching her face for any hint of falsehood. His expression hardened, and she struggled to hide a feeling of panic. He could be violent if he considered he'd been crossed. Had something in her face given away that she was lying?

He spoke again, his voice even harsher.

'How old was 'e? Where was 'e from? Are my grandparents living round 'ere?'

She guessed he'd been hoarding up hundreds of questions that had gone through his mind since he had first asked 'Where's my dad?' when he was a little kid. He used to ask why all the other boys had dads and not him.

She knew he blamed her, thought it was all her fault. She saw in his eyes that he despised her.

Mavis had had years and years to invent the background to the fictitious father. But now, with all her son's questions, she wished she'd just said that his father was dead.

'He came from somewhere up north,' she said. 'I can't remember where. 'E was 'ere for work, some sort of engineer. I never did understand it. So I never met 'is family.'

She was searching his face, needing to know if he believed her falsehoods.

'But I can tell you one thing. You 'ave 'is lovely eyes and that dimple on your chin comes from 'im too.'

He sneered at that. 'Sez you. I don't believe a word of it. You're a lying bitch.'

He raised an arm to swipe her round the head, but changed his mind at the last minute and stormed out of the house, slamming the front door so hard the whole place rattled.

25

PROTESTERS

'Did you ever see that man you met at the dance again? Joe, was it?' Jane asked Mavis during a quiet moment in the library. 'You've had a bit of a spring in your step since you met him. He seemed nice.'

Mavis knew Jane was trying to cheer her up. She hadn't told Jane about the set-to with Ken, but struggled to be cheerful the next day. Hearing Joe's name gave her a lift as it always did.

'Joe? Well, yes. I didn't want to say in case it came to nothing, but 'e 'ad a few days' leave and we met every one of them when I wasn't working. We spent one of them working with a rescue team, too depressing to talk about. But we went skating at Forest Gate. I 'aven't done that for years and years, fell on my bum more times than I could count. We went to the pictures and all sorts. We 'ad a good time. 'E is nice. Trustworthy, I think.'

Jane's jaw dropped open. In all the time she'd known Mavis, she'd never shown any interest in having a boyfriend.

'Well, I never. What a dark horse you are! I'm so happy for you. So, are you keeping in touch?'

Mavis looked away and put a book on the returns trolley. 'Well, 'e's not been gone long, but we're going to write. You 'eard from your George lately?'

Before Jane could answer, they heard it – the faint sound of chanting coming from outside. The noise was getting louder, nearer, a swelling chorus of voices growing in strength and intensity. The two women glanced at each other, wondering what it was all about.

Curious, Mavis moved nearer to the door, trying to catch the words, and suddenly it burst open, causing her to jump back to avoid being knocked over.

'What...?' she began, but never finished her sentence.

A group of people, some with children in their arms, pushed their way into the library. They were holding placards that read 'No diphtheria vaccines' and 'Leave our children alone'. One held up a poster of a little girl with blonde curls wearing a flowery dress. That poster said: 'Do you want to kill children like this?'

Mavis moved closer to Jane, and they looked at each other in alarm. They had heard about the anti-vaccination campaigns, but never expected it would affect them in the library.

One man walked towards the poster on the wall, tore it down and ripped it into pieces, scattering them on the floor like confetti.

Mavis stepped forward. 'Could you leave, please? You're disturbing our readers.'

Ignoring her, a woman turned towards her followers. She had a little boy on her hip, a dummy in his mouth. The woman was wearing a long black dress, her hair curly and wild and her face determined. She faced the protesters, held up her hand, cleared her throat and began to address them and everyone in the library.

'My fellow citizens,' she began, her voice strong and clear. 'We, and all parents, must take a stand against the government's plans to mandate vaccinations for our children. We must have the right to choose what is best for them ourselves!'

The crowd erupted in a chorus of cheers, and the woman continued, her voice full of conviction.

'We can no longer sit idly by and let our children suffer, or worse, die because of this government's policies. We must fight for their right to live healthy, safe lives!' She paused and waited for the cheers to subside. 'Now, follow me!'

She pushed through the throng and led them up and down the

library aisles, waving their banners all the while. As they marched, they chanted.

'What do we want?'

'No vaccine!'

'When do we want it?'

'Never!'

Once or twice, someone would pick up a book and fling it across the room. There weren't many readers in the library, but none could miss what was going on. Some looked scared and hurried to get out of their way, some ignored them, and one or two cheered them on.

The noise had brought some passers-by to the door. They looked at what was happening, unsure how to react.

When the protesters returned to the desk, Mavis tried to reason with them, beginning to explain the benefits of vaccination. But then, without warning, one of the men lunged towards her, pushing her to the ground. A bystander screamed and Jane, seeing her friend was unharmed, reached for the police whistle they kept behind the desk in case of trouble. There had never been a need for it before.

She blew it as hard as she could without pausing. The sharp, piercing sound made the angry mob still.

'Go on!' she shouted. 'Get out of here. The police will be here in a minute and they'll arrest the lot of you!'

As if her words had called them, a police siren sounded in the distance and the protesters scattered, pushing their way through the bystanders and knocking over two chairs on their way out.

'Bastards!' someone shouted after them. Then one of the bystanders turned to Mavis and Jane. 'Are you two okay? I was too afraid to do anything.'

In truth, the two women were shaking, desperately wanting to sit down and rest.

'We're fine, thank you,' Jane said to the woman. 'Mavis here can take it easy while I check the library. Thank you for your concern.'

She put the kettle on, made sure Mavis was settled in a chair and walked around the library. She picked up the books that had been thrown, putting aside two that would need to be repaired. Then she spoke to all the readers to make sure they were okay. Most of them wanted to speak about what happened.

Keeping an eye on the desk in case anyone else came in, she listened to them attentively. When she'd spoken to them all, she went back to Mavis.

'Are you okay, love? You took a good tumble there.'

Mavis rubbed her elbow. 'Sore elbow, but that's about it. My pride was hurt more than my body. But how on earth do they expect people to support them when they act like mobsters?'

Keeping an eye on the desk in case they were needed, they made some tea and sat down to try to relax after their frightening experience.

'I'd wish one of their kids got diphtheria, but that'd be mean. It's not the kiddies' fault their parents are barking mad.' Mavis shook her head as she spoke, stirring half a spoon of sugar in her tea. 'But at least we can relax for a minute.'

But the day hadn't finished with Mavis yet.

26

THE PUSH

When they'd locked up the library for the day, Mavis decided to treat herself to something to eat in Jim's café just round the corner. After all the fuss in the library, she didn't fancy cooking and Ken had said he'd be out all night. It was a pity she couldn't get a half of stout at Jim's, but she could always stop off at Cundy's Tavern on the way home if the rotten siren didn't sound.

The café was busy with a mixture of people, some like herself just finishing work, others about to start and yet more on their breaks still wearing their uniforms. It was a warm and inviting place, with worn wooden flooring and round tables close together. The smell of fried food and toast lingered in the air, and the steady buzz of conversations was somehow comforting.

Mavis walked to the counter, reading the menu chalked up on the wall behind it. It was hard to choose, but while she waited in the queue she decided on shepherd's pie, mushy peas and a cup of tea. Good comfort food.

She chose an empty table towards the back of the café and got out the *Evening Standard* she'd just bought. The headline was 'Herbert Robinson becomes Home Secretary!' She read as she waited for her meal, absorbed in the latest war news. Even though the news was worrying, after the problems with the protesters, she felt herself relaxing. It was a relief not to have any responsibility for a while.

The waitress bustled over with her meal a short while later and Mavis gave her a small tip. She never thought anyone's shepherd's pie was as good as her own, but she enjoyed it nonetheless. When she was done, she pushed her plate away and got out her newspaper again.

As she reached the centre pages, she became aware of a voice that seemed to leap out at her amongst all the other voices around her. It made her insides turn to ice.

It was *him*. Noah James. The man who had taken away her innocence. She'd have recognised that voice anywhere.

Her hands shook uncontrollably as she held her newspaper gingerly and peeked around the edge. He was seated mere feet away, nearer the door than her, hunched smugly in a chair as if he didn't have a care in the world. She could feel every muscle in her body coiled tightly like a spring, ready to explode with rage, but she dared not move for fear of him seeing her. She watched intently as his gaze slid from one woman to another, settling on the pretty young blonde woman alone at a nearby table reading a book. His intense focus on the woman seemed almost palpable, as if an invisible thread connected him and her.

Mavis felt like a helpless prisoner at her table. She couldn't leave the café without walking past him and she wasn't prepared to do that. Also, she was certain the way he looked at the pretty girl was dangerous. He was like some kind of predator, looking for his next victim, and the young woman was his unsuspecting prey.

All around Mavis normal life went on, people chatting, eating, drinking, laughing, reading. But inside, everything had changed. It was as if she was seeing through a glass wall into an alternative reality.

It was several more minutes before she saw the young woman close her book, put on her coat, and pick up her bag. He did the same, following closely behind her as she left the café.

Hastily, Mavis left too, walking a short distance behind him. It had become dark outside and no moon or stars showed through the clouds. All the shops and cafés had their blackout blinds down for the night. But streaks of light appeared every time someone opened a door, and there were dim lights from the shielded vehicle headlights.

The pavements and streets were busy with people hurrying to get home before the next air-raid siren.

Feeling breathless with tension, Mavis followed her attacker, watching him match the young woman's footsteps but keeping far enough back that he wouldn't see her. She knew there was an alleyway not far ahead and wondered if that would be where he would strike, dragging the poor woman to a terrible fate.

But perhaps she was wrong. He could be innocently taking the same route as the woman. Was she letting her imagination run away with her?

As she walked, the air seemed to thicken, pressing down on her chest. Taking a deep breath, she forced herself to calm down, to keep focused on the couple ahead. He had to be stopped before they got to the alleyway. But how? She looked around, but there were no policemen in sight. That option was closed to her and, in any case, he had so far done nothing illegal. She could shout, but that might scare him away to strike another day.

Thinking she must be crazy, she closed the gap between herself and the man. There were too many people about for him to notice her footsteps amongst all the others. Her heart pounded so strongly in her chest, it was as if it could be heard by anyone around.

But then she recognised it, the distant sound of planes, hundreds and hundreds of planes. A man near her looked up at the sky and shook his fist.

'Bugger off, you Nasties, leave us alone!' As he shouted, tears poured down his cheeks.

Then the air-raid siren began.

Its deafening wax and wane seemed to control the people nearby, who all started hurrying towards safely. As always, there was no uniformity to their movements. They went this way or that, depending on the safe place they were headed towards. Traffic continued to flow and Mavis saw two buses coming along her side of the road, one after the other, close.

Appealingly close.

Her attacker was walking near the edge of the pavement, dodging other people who were not looking where they were going. He was still following the young woman he'd spotted earlier.

Without hesitation or even thinking about what she was doing, Mavis hurried next to him.

He glanced at her briefly, without recognition.

She seized the chance and, without hesitation, shoved him with all her strength towards the speeding bus. At the last second, as he was toppling, he glanced at her and his eyes opened wide with recognition.

People around paid no attention to what she had done, too focused on finding safety from the imminent bombing. Her attacker's body careened under the wheels with a sickening thud. That and his agonised scream were muted by the sound of the sirens and the footsteps of people running in terror. The bus screeched to a halt, dragging his body along with it for a short distance.

But Mavis didn't stop to watch what happened next. Instead, she hurried on, blending in with the crowd as everyone scurried to the nearest shelters. She was just another faceless middle-aged woman in search of safety. Easily ignored, overlooked, forgotten.

She followed the crowd underground as if in a trance. With each step, she felt lighter, as if the tension of what she had just done was flowing away from her with every footstep she took.

At last, she arrived at the platform, which was already crowded with sheltering people. She found a space to sit down and, almost as if she was in someone else's body, assessed how she felt. She knew she should feel guilty. He was probably dead. Certainly, he would be badly injured. She searched her mind as if she was prodding a hole in a tooth, but no matter how hard she tried, she could find no trace of guilt, only a strange kind of peace. A letting go of anger and hatred she had felt ever since he raped her in that grimy alleyway all those years before.

She felt relief. She had almost certainly saved that young woman from a dreadful ordeal and other women he would have attacked in the future, too.

She found a free space, sat down, and leaned back against the platform wall. The station was plagued by mosquitos again, their harsh buzz ringing in her ears, so she placed her hankie over her face, closed her eyes and tried to focus on her breathing, as if it could help her find some answer within herself. The minutes passed and gradually her thoughts drifted away, replaced by the soothing sensation of drifting off to sleep.

The raid was thankfully a short one, and Mavis was able to go home before her bedtime. She usually dreaded trying to sleep. Every night since the attack, for year after weary year, she had relived it in her mind. She felt again, over and over, the rough brick alley wall scraping against her cheek, smelled her attacker's beer-soaked breath against her face, the sound and feel of him ripping off her underwear, the pain of him violating her and the terrible sound of her own sobbing and cries for mercy.

But this night was different. As she lay in bed waiting for the dreaded images to appear, they did arrive, but were somehow changed. Where before they had been in full technicolour, bright and vivid with loud sound, they were blurred, unclear. As she watched in her mind's eye, the picture altered. It softened like butter on a sunny day, losing its shape and definition. It became harder to make out what she was looking at. And the terrible sensations faded too – the feel of the alley wall against her cheek simply vanished and the feel of his violation along with it. His voice, strident and threatening as it had been, became quieter and quieter until it vanished altogether. As all this happened, she felt a great weight lift from her as if she had been crushed all these years and now was freed.

Mavis observed all this in wonder. It was like a miracle. Finally, she could let go of that terrible night. It no longer needed to invade her thoughts every day and night. And with it went the fear. The fear of trusting another man, even someone as lovely as Joe. The memories that had made her heart hard, and her voice harsh all this time.

But now, with this transformation, she felt a difference. She could let go of the painful memories. She could finally take a step forward and move on with her life.

* * *

'Hey,' Jane said the next day. 'Have you seen this in the *Evening Standard*? I think this man they're talking about is one of our readers.'

She passed the newspaper to Mavis.

TRAGIC DEATH AS MAN CRUSHED BY BUS

Noah James, 48, of Percy Road, Canning Town, met a tragic end yesterday when he stumbled and fell in front of a bus on Barking Road. He was taken to St Mary's hospital where he was pronounced dead on arrival. The air-raid siren had just sounded when the accident happened and the bus driver, Mr Alan Smith, said he believed Mr James was running towards a shelter and tripped. No bus passengers were harmed.

His landlady told this newspaper that she believes he has no living relatives. If you have any further information about Mr James, please contact Canning Town Police Station.

'Sounds like him,' Mavis said when she'd read it.

She walked over to their card system, found his card, tore it into tiny pieces and threw it into the bin.

27

HISTORY

It was Cordelia's day off, and she was glad to be away from the East End for a while. She loved that the library helped the locals, but with daily bombings, it could be difficult to keep positive all the time. Lunch with Robert was what she was looking forward to the most, and just thinking about it brought a smile to her face.

She started the day with a luxuriously long soak in the bath, scented with her favourite perfume. As she lay there, the wireless playing quietly in the background, she almost nodded off, but was rudely awoken by her doorbell ringing.

She recognised that ring. Only Rosalind rang it like that.

'Hang on!' she shouted and, wrapping herself with her soft white towelling dressing gown, went to open the door.

'Well, this is a surprise!' she said, standing back so Rosalind could enter with her usual flourish.

Rosalind threw her fur coat on the sofa. 'Well, sweetie, you mentioned today is your day off, so I wangled it to get the day off too. I thought I'd treat you to morning coffee at a little café I found. They still have real coffee and their cakes are out of this world. It's still standing, as far as I know. From what I hear at the bus depot, the same can't be said for much of Silvertown. Apparently, you could see it burning from all over London. Dreadful.'

'Coffee is a great idea, Rosalind. Help yourself to a drink while I get dressed.'

As she donned simple black trousers and a red sweater, Cordelia thought about how much both their lives had changed. Before the war started, she would never have believed that Rosalind would do a job like driving a bus, much less that she would enjoy it. And she'd learned so much about life, she could write a book.

She loved all the people she met, their energy despite hardships, their pride in their courage, the way they enjoyed a good laugh even when their world was collapsing around them. She loved the mixture of people, of cultures, of food, and the way that, despite occasional clashes, they lived together harmoniously. Most of the people had nothing, but they shared what they had generously.

As the two women walked down the street, their heels clicking against the pavement, Cordelia felt a buzz of excitement. It was a cold day, but she enjoyed the walk and looked forward to having one of the cakes Rosalind promised. Their destination was aptly named the Home Front Café, and Cordelia stopped in with a feeling of pleasant anticipation. She inhaled the almost forgotten warm, comforting scent of freshly brewed coffee that greeted her. The walls were painted a soft yellow and were covered with old photographs, each telling a story. As well as a few small, round tables, each with four chairs, there were also a few well-worn and much-loved armchairs in the corner that looked inviting.

Cordelia gazed around, captivated by the homely atmosphere. It was like being in a grandmother's front room. They took their seats at one of the small tables and looked through the window on to the street at the front.

Soon, the waitress came over to take their order. Cordelia ordered a cup of coffee and a slice of chocolate cake, and Rosalind ordered coffee and carrot cake.

'We're so lucky,' Rosalind said. 'We can sit in luxury and forget the bleakness of war. So many people don't have that opportunity.'

'I've had some good news from work,' Cordelia said. 'We've achieved our goals for getting new readers to sign on. It's so wonderful to see so many new faces as well as the regulars.'

Rosalind laughed. 'Like the bad-tempered bloke who reads the papers? He sounds dreadful.'

Cordelia smiled. 'They're not all like him, and Jane and Mavis are amazing with the way they deal with him and everyone else. It's a real skill. Sometimes I look at them handling a situation and realise I couldn't do it half as well. I'm really lucky to have them.'

They were interrupted by the waitress carrying a tray with their coffee and cakes. And Rosalind soon lit another cigarette and began to tell funny tales about her work as a bus driver. But all too soon she was looking at her watch and declaring she had to rush off. 'So sorry, sweetie, but I've got another appointment and a handsome one at that!'

They paid their bill, stepped outside and went their separate ways with promises to meet again soon. With a lightness in her step, Cordelia wrapped her coat tightly around herself and began walking to the restaurant where she was due to meet Robert.

28

THE FUTURE BECKONS

'Come in, come in,' Luigi said as Cordelia opened the inner door to the restaurant. It was warm and cosy after the cold outside, chilly even for midday. The waiter bowed with a flourish, then stroked his fine black moustache. 'Let me take your coat. Are you waiting for someone?'

But before she could answer, Robert was there beside her, smiling and kissing her cheek.

'I'm so glad you could make it.'

As Luigi showed them to their table, she took in the surroundings. She'd never been to this restaurant before, and immediately loved its relaxed atmosphere. Loved the smell of garlic, the red and white checked tablecloths with a lit candle on each, the black-and-white photos of Italy on the walls and the long wooden bar along one side. It was laden with glasses, bottles of wine and limoncello.

The waiter held out a chair for her.

'This is the perfect spot for a beautiful lady,' he said, a gleam in his eye. 'I will return in one moment and give you my full attention.'

When he'd gone, Robert grinned.

'I'll have to watch my step or you may be leaving with a lusty Italian!' He took Cordelia's hand and looked deep into her eyes. 'You look lovely today, Cordelia.'

Her cheeks flushed with pleasure and she returned his smile, feeling light with happiness.

'Why, thank you, Robert. You look particularly handsome, too.'

The waiter approached again and, with another bow, offered them the menu. It was an extravagantly large piece of white card, decorated with colourful images of wine glasses and grapes, a stylish logo and the list of dishes.

'Take your time. Would you like me to bring you some wine while you wait? I'm afraid our choice is limited at the moment.' He handed Robert the drinks menu and, after asking Cordelia's opinion, Robert ordered a bottle of Merlot.

'I hope you didn't mind me suggesting lunch instead of dinner,' he said. 'We're less likely to be interrupted by the air-raid siren. And once the bombing starts, the hospital is so busy with the injured. I go in even on my day off.'

She was glad to have something familiar to talk about, easing them into their time together. The nearest to a date they had ever had was a quick visit to Jim's café near the library. 'How on earth do you cope with the huge number of patients? There must be dozens, if not hundreds, each day.'

Robert nodded. 'We have our systems, but to be honest, we're often so overwhelmed it feels like chaos. The walking wounded are treated in one area and sent home if they still have one, or to a reception place if they don't. Others are given immediate treatment and then they're sent to hospitals further out of London until they are completely recovered. But enough of work. I'm hoping this meal can be all about us instead.'

Luigi returned with the wine, poured them both a glass, and put the bottle on the table between them.

They picked up their glasses, and Robert looked at her over the top of his, his eyes telling her things he had yet to say.

'Here's to our first date!' he said. 'May we have many more.'

She sipped the wine and sat back in her chair, feeling the tension of the past weeks beginning to fade away.

'Mmm, that's so smooth.' She put her hand to her throat as she relaxed and smiled at him.

They had barely had time to glance at the menus when a man approached their table. He was elderly with a permanently brown lined face that spoke of decades in the sun. With a smile, he tucked his violin under his chin and began playing 'O Sole Mio', swaying to the music as he played. The romantic song was haunting and evocative, fitting the occasion perfectly, and Cordelia's heart swelled with happiness.

Despite the number of other diners in the restaurant, the music seemed to create a bubble around them, isolating them from the rest of the world. As she listened, Cordelia momentarily felt lost in the enchanting music and the intensity of Robert's gaze.

As the violinist finished his song, he bowed before moving on to the next table.

'That was so beautiful,' Cordelia said. 'In the future, if I ever hear that song, I'll remember this moment.'

Luigi returned with his notebook at the ready, and asked if they were ready to order their food.

'Mushroom risotto for me, please,' Robert said, then looked at Cordelia. 'What will you have?'

She looked at Luigi. 'Spaghetti and meatballs, for me, please,' she said, then regretted it. When he'd gone, she laughed. 'Promise not to laugh at me when I get spaghetti sauce all over my face.'

He raised an eyebrow. 'I might laugh *with* you, Cordelia, but I'd never laugh *at* you, and your face is beautiful with or without spaghetti sauce!'

They picked up their glasses and raised a toast, their eyes locked together.

'Here's to more peaceful times. May we both live to enjoy them.'

Cordelia took a sip of the deep ruby-red wine, and felt its warmth and smoothness as it moved down her throat. She set the glass down and looked into Robert's eyes – they really were an intense deep blue, and she could feel herself falling into them.

Robert leaned towards her, his eyes never leaving hers.

'Cordelia,' he murmured, his voice low and deep. 'I've been looking forward to getting to know you better since we first met.' He moved his wine glass aside, reached out and took her hand, and began to trace light circles on her skin with his thumb.

She responded to his touch, her skin tingling with desire, but she pulled her hand away.

'Robert, you are the most attractive and interesting man I've met for a very long time, but I've been hurt in the past and…'

'I understand,' he said quietly. 'I hope you know I would never do anything to hurt you.'

She smiled at him, her face showing warmth and appreciation.

'I do,' she replied. 'Thank you for understanding.'

He picked up her hand again. 'You don't want to be hurt. You certainly don't deserve to. You need someone you can trust who will always put you first. I've been hurt in the past, too. That's why I've avoided getting involved with anyone for a long time and concentrated on helping others. But when I met you, something changed, and I began to feel hope again.'

'When we know each other better, perhaps we'll feel confident enough to share our stories.'

He smiled and gave her hand a gentle squeeze. At that moment, she knew they were both taking a leap into the unknown, but somehow, she was certain it was the right thing to do.

They paused as the waiter brought their meals, and Cordelia reached out for the glass of water. And knocked over the wine glass. The deep red liquid spread across the starched white cloth like blood and they both instantly began dabbing at it with their napkins. As they did so, they bumped heads and started to laugh, first Robert and then Cordelia, the sound of their laughter echoing off the walls of the restaurant.

In that moment, a new connection grew between them, as if the spilled wine had cast a spell of closeness around them. The waiter appeared with a fresh cloth and more napkins, but the spell was already in place, and as he moved away again, they looked into each other's eyes, drinking in the feeling of comfort that had come over them.

'I've never told you I can be clumsy,' she said, checking there was no wine on her dress or his shirt.

'That's nothing to my clumsiness when I'm exhausted after twenty-four hours on duty,' he said and took her hand again. 'I hope we can meet again, Cordelia. It's hard for me to get away and I'm often exhausted, but—'

It was her turn to interrupt him. She smiled as she picked up her cutlery.

'I hope that too,' she said. 'In fact, I can't think of anything I'd like more.'

They leaned across the table and exchanged a brief kiss. Then as they ate, they talked about everything and nothing. They talked about their work, their families, their childhoods and their dreams. They laughed at each other's jokes and listened intently to each other's stories. The connection between them grew stronger with each passing moment, and they both recognised that this was something special.

After they'd finished, Robert walked her back to her flat, holding her hand the entire way. As they stood in front of the entrance, he turned to her and took her hand between his. 'This has been, without doubt, the best meal of my life.'

She laughed. 'The pasta must have been special!'

He pulled her towards him. 'You know I mean you, your company!' He paused. 'It's difficult for me to know when I'm free, but I should know by my next stint at the library. Can we arrange something then?'

'You don't even have to ask,' she said with a smile. Then she kissed him again and walked towards her flat. When she turned the key, she looked back at him. He was still there and blew her a kiss before walking on.

29

CONGRATULATIONS

'Your boss is coming in? That Mr Wood you talk about sometimes? What've you done wrong?' Jane had a smile as she spoke.

Cordelia grinned. 'Less of your cheek. No, he phoned to say he was coming on a visit because he's neglected us ever since I started.'

'Can't argue with that,' Mavis said, raising her eyes to the heavens. 'Never even met the man. I was beginning to think he was a figment of your imagination.'

A rattling on the front door distracted them, letting them know that Bert was impatient to come in and it was opening time. Cordelia stepped outside the library, blinking against the bright morning sun, and looked around. Silvertown had been bombed heavily, but their street had escaped so far. It was as busy as ever – petrol rationing meant that fewer and fewer cars were on the road, but the traffic was still heavy and noisy.

But what Cordelia noticed most of all was the people. Everywhere she looked, there was life. Men and women were heading to work, children to school, and mothers were wheeling prams up and down the street. A group of elderly men were deep in conversation on the corner, smoking their pipes and nodding in agreement.

Cordelia smiled to herself, feeling a sense of comfort and safety that she hadn't experienced in weeks. Then, a group of children came running down the street, a flurry of giggles and bright eyes. They passed close to Cordelia as they ran, their laughter ringing out like a chorus of birds on a summer's day.

As she watched them disappear around the corner, Cordelia felt an unfamiliar emotion swell in her chest; a feeling of hope, determination and courage despite all the misery the war brought everyone. She glanced around the street one last time, and knew that no matter what happened, the people of Silvertown would continue to find strength and resilience in each other.

At long last the winter had said goodbye and, despite the inevitable fine dust from the damage done by bombings, the air felt fresher. Weeds clung to gaps in the pavement, and although Cordelia had no idea what they were called, some had little white flowers that made her smile. Jane came out and linked her arm through Cordelia's. 'Think we can hope those rotten Nazis will stop bombing us now the weather's cheering up?' She paused. 'It's been over two hundred days now. I don't know about you, but I've forgotten what it's like to have a good night's sleep.'

Before Cordelia could reply, three people walked past them into the library and they hurried in to take up their posts. Cordelia strolled around the library, feeling the familiar comfort of the place wrap around her like a hug. With Mr Wood due to arrive mid-morning, she wanted to make sure everything was in place.

She walked up and down the stacks of the main room, straightening a chair here, putting a book in the correct place there, picking up a piece of paper the cleaner had missed and dusting off an occasional shelf. She felt a little like she was tidying her own home, except this was so much bigger and filled with so much knowledge.

As she approached the back of the library, Cordelia noticed a light coming from one of the smaller reading rooms. She stopped, curious, and peered in. To her surprise, a woman was sitting in one of the old armchairs they had rescued from the basement. It was almost threadbare and faded with age, but still good enough to use. Cordelia hadn't seen the woman before and was happy to see her looking so relaxed with her book. The woman looked up. 'I just love it here,' she said, taking her glasses off and cleaning them. 'I can get a bit of peace away from everything.'

They chatted for a couple of minutes, then Cordelia continued on her way. She was tempted to ask the woman to tell Mr Wood how much she loved the library, but felt that would be too cheeky.

She went to the front desk and looked back over the way she'd just come. The reality was, the library was old and shabby in places, but it had a wonderful comfortable feel to it. Its oak tables shouldn't have been sanded down so many times, and some of the bookshelves needed a good going-over with linseed oil. Yet throughout the day she knew it brought pleasure and escape to many people, from students doing their homework, to mums finding a book for their child, to elderly people just passing the time. And, of course, Bert, keeping up with the latest newspapers. Then, when the air-raid sirens blared, it brought safety to many more people.

Noticing the time, she hurried to her office to make sure it was tidy before her boss arrived. She was just putting away the last papers when there was a knock on her door and Mr Wood entered. Although she'd only seen him a few weeks earlier, he looked older, and more careworn. She smiled and moved towards him, holding out her hand to shake his.

'Come and sit down,' she said, taking his coat and hanging it on the coat stand. 'Would you like some tea?'

He sat down heavily as if too tired to stay upright. 'I'd love some if it's not too much trouble.'

Cordelia opened the door and caught Mavis's eye. She made a T sign and Mavis nodded her understanding. While she waited, Cordelia got out a packet of fig biscuits she'd been keeping for this visit, and put four on a plate she kept in her desk drawer. He immediately took one and ate it almost in one mouthful. 'No breakfast!' he muttered, spluttering crumbs over his jacket.

Mavis knocked on the door and walked in with a tray with two cups and saucers and the library's only pretty teapot, one they'd found in the basement, thick with dust. She looked over Mr Wood's head at Cordelia and gave her a look that said, 'Everything okay?' Cordelia merely smiled in response.

Cordelia poured the tea and handed Mr Wood his. He looked at the empty plate in surprise. 'Oh dear,' he said, looking shamefaced. 'I seem to have eaten all the biscuits and I do like one to dunk in my tea.'

With a rueful smile, Cordelia took the packet of biscuits out of her drawer and handed it to him. 'It's lovely to see you at the library,' she said. 'Is this a routine visit or is there some news?'

He gulped down a mouthful of too-hot tea and shook his head. 'No news. But I wanted to come to see you and your staff so you would know we haven't forgotten you. Just this morning I checked the number of loans the library has made in the last three months. I have to congratulate you. You have exceeded your targets. And you've managed to keep within budget, too.' He took a biscuit and dunked it in his tea. Half fell off and he attempted to rescue it with his spoon.

'I'm almost wondering if you could give some training to other libraries on what you have done to increase loans.'

Cordelia was flattered, but thought more experienced librarians would hardly appreciate a newcomer like her telling them what to do. She decided to change the subject.

'My staff, Mavis and Jane, are as responsible as me for our success. I would very much like it if you would take a few minutes to speak to them and congratulate them.'

Mr Wood finished his tea with another big gulp. 'Of course, of course. Let's do that now, and perhaps one of them could show me round the library as we speak.'

* * *

'Well, I was a bit nervous meeting him, but he was quite kind,' Jane said when Mr Wood had gone.

'So 'e should be,' Mavis retorted. 'We've knocked our blooming socks off to get this place this good.'

'If you two are free after work, why don't we go out and celebrate? My treat. The ARP wardens will look after the basement.'

An elderly woman came towards the desk to have her books stamped. 'You lot look cheerful,' she said.

'We are,' Mavis replied. 'The boss 'ere is going to buy me and Jane a meal after work.'

The woman smiled. 'Well, don't fall down any of the potholes!'

At closing time, Tim, one of the regular ARP men, came to relieve them. His Woodbine cigarette was almost finished and the smoke was making his eyes water. 'You lot doing anything nice this evening?' he asked, straightening his tin hat.

Cordelia looked at the other two. 'What do you fancy, girls? Lyons Corner House? Jim's café? Cundy's pub?'

'The Corner House,' the other two said simultaneously.

'And we expect some afters, too,' Mavis said. 'No going cheap on us.'

Linking arms, they walked down the street, splitting up only when they were blocking the pavement. 'Please, please, God, don't let them start bombing until after I've had my jam roly-poly and custard!' Jane said.

Lyons Corner House was as busy as usual, with queues at the self-service counter. A myriad of smells greeted them – frying food, cigarette smoke, coffee and the perfume of the woman immediately in front of them. They were so busy talking they didn't notice the time going by as they queued. 'Have whatever you want,' Cordelia said. 'I'm having pudding as well.' She rubbed her flat stomach as she spoke.

They stopped speaking to study the menu.

'I'm having meat pie, mash and carrots, followed by ginger pudding and sauce,' Cordelia said.

'I'm going for smoked haddock, mash and peas. Then apple turnover and custard. Oh, and at least one cup of tea. What about you, Jane?'

Jane bit her bottom lip, a gesture she was using less and less as she gained confidence. 'Sausages, mash and beans, then jam roly-poly and custard for me. That'll be more than I've eaten for ages.'

Somehow they made themselves heard over the sounds of the food being served and the many customers in the huge dining room. They took their laden trays and looked for an empty table, spotting one across the other side of the room. They made their way through, dodging the Nippies who were busy clearing tables. Despite the heat, they always looked bandbox fresh.

Like all the other tables, theirs was covered in a spotless white tablecloth. With little sighs, they put down their trays, took off their coats and sat down.

'That's better. Me plates of meat need a good rest,' Mavis said, taking off her shoes and rubbing her feet.

They spoke little as they ate, but when they'd finished, Cordelia raised her glass of squash. 'Here's to you two. The library wouldn't be half of what it is without your hard work. And luckily Mr Wood recognises that. So I want to thank you for being so kind to a newcomer like me and making a success of what we've done.'

'Well, we've done a lot, that's for sure,' Mavis said. 'We cleared out the basement – and found out our boss is scared of spiders. We got a load more readers too, even if 'alf of 'em want romances.'

'Nothing wrong with romances,' Jane said, and Cordelia thought that when she had taken the job, Jane would never have contradicted her co-worker.

They all lifted the remains of their drinks and clinked them together.

'To think,' Mavis said, looking at Cordelia. 'I thought you was too posh to fit in with us East Enders when you came. Took me ages to get used to your snooty voice!'

Jane laughed and almost splattered the remains of her water across the table. 'Don't hold back, will you, Mavis.'

'Never 'ave, never will! Don't do no good, does it!'

'She's right, Jane,' Cordelia said. 'I'm so proud of all you've done for the library. Encouraging readers, building up the children's areas, and gaining confidence to have your say.'

Jane blushed. 'There's something I haven't told you about that. The vicar noticed I'm better at talking to people. He's asked me to be a reader in the church! Imagine! I'll be reading bits from the Bible! I'm terrified, but I'm damn well going to do it!' Her eyes widened and she put her hand over her mouth. 'Oh, no! I swore and I was talking about the Bible.'

Cordelia and Mavis broke into spontaneous applause, then patted her on the back. 'That's marvellous, Jane,' Mavis said. 'And I'm sure God will forgive your dirty mouth. I suppose we've all 'ad changes. I've got meself a bloke for the first time in centuries. And he writes to me regular as clockwork. Not that I always get them when I should but still...' She stopped and her eyes gleamed as she spoke. 'There's something else I 'aven't told you. Didn't want to in case it didn't work out.'

She paused and the other two looked at her expectantly. 'What's that then? You're not in the pudding club, are you?' Jane said with a grin.

'Better, 'cos I don't 'ave to go through all that agony. Do you remember Joyce, that little girl I found on the bomb site? Her mum had just died and she had no family.'

'You took her to the Red Cross people, didn't you?' Cordelia said. 'Has something happened to her?'

Mavis straightened her shoulders before she spoke again. 'I've seen 'er several times and... well... if everything goes to plan, I'm going to foster her! She's a smashing little thing. She misses her mum and I hope I can be a second mum for her. Not that I'll expect her to forget her first one. What do you think of that, then?'

She looked at Cordelia and Jane. Both hesitated to reply. 'But what about Ken?' Cordelia eventually said.

''E'll 'ave to like it or lump it. Any trouble from 'im and 'e's out on 'is ear. If it all goes well, I'll be adopting 'er. I'll 'ave a little girl of me own.'

'Then that's wonderful news,' Jane said. 'She'll be lucky to have a mother like you.'

'Thank you!' Mavis said, then looked at Cordelia. 'So I'm going to be a mum again, Jane is going to be a reader in church and you, you've got yourself a bloke. Ain't we all doing well!'

Cordelia smiled and felt deep happiness being with these two wonderful women. Her life before she met them seemed pale and dull by comparison. The two women were as different as night and day, but they were united by their deep compassion for the others in their community. They had welcomed Cordelia into their fold with enormous generosity that she would never forget.

Looking around to check no one was looking, she topped up their water, got a hip flask out of her bag and poured some whisky into their glasses.

'Let's drink a toast!' she said. 'Here's to the wonderful East End library girls!'

ACKNOWLEDGMENTS

For my husband Rick who has great plot ideas, my writing buddy and friend, Fran Johnson and my proofreader friend Maggie Scott. Thanks also to my wonderful editor Emily Yau at Boldwood.

ABOUT THE AUTHOR

Patricia McBride is the author of the very popular Lily Baker historical saga series. She is now writing a new WW2 series for Boldwood, based in the East End of London during the Blitz, the first title of which, *The Library Girls of the East End,* will be published in November 2023.

Sign up to Patricia McBride's mailing list for news, competitions and updates on future books.

Visit Patricia's website: www.patriciamcbrideauthor.com

Follow Patricia on social media here:

facebook.com/patriciamcbrideauthor
instagram.com/tricia.mcbride.writer

Milton Keynes UK
Ingram Content Group UK Ltd.
UKHW041024131123
432469UK00002B/21

9 781785 139864